For Kathy —
Who keeps the
home fires burning
at OJ Forest!
Joyce

Night Light
—an anthology

—an anthology—
the 2014 Collection

Blank Slate Writers Group
www.blank-slate-writers.com

Other works by
Blank Slate Writers Group

Midnight Oil, **an anthology (2013)**

Works by our authors

Stefan Barkow — *In Sickness and in Hell*

Timothy Cole — *The Selected Poetry of Frederick Hayes Cole*

Rich Elliott —
The Competitive Edge: Mental Preparation for Distance Running
Runners on Running: The Best Non-fiction of Distance Running

Gail Galvan —
Sneezing Seasons: The Inside Story about Allergies and Immunology
On the Literary Road with a Writer

Joyce Hicks — *Escape From Assisted Living*

Marilyn Kozmatka — *Time Spike*

Bob Moulesong, contrib. — *Fiction Break Favorites* (2014)

Tom Saine — *The Conrad Kidnapping* (spring 2015)

Carla Lee Suson — *Independence Day Plague*

This book is a work of fiction. Names, characters, places, and incidents are the product of each author's imagination or are used fictitiously. Any resemblance to actual events or locales or actual persons, living or dead, is entirely coincidental.

No part of this book may be used or reproduced in any manner whatsoever without the written permission of the respective author or Blank Slate Writers Group.

Copyright © 2014 Blank Slate Writers Group

Unless specifically noted otherwise, copyrights of all works contained herein, the stories, memoirs, poetry, etc., are held by the respective writers, and all rights are reserved by them.

Cover design and layout: Tom Saine
Interior design and layout: Timothy Cole
Cover photo: ©Alessandra Caronna–Getty Images.

ISBN-13:978-1502827685
ISBN-10:1502827689

DEDICATION

Under a blanket, flashlight in hand,
the words painted pictures forbidden.
It was well past lights out, the house wrapped in sleep,
our clandestine reading well hidden:
Plots fraught with danger, secrets, and lies,
love stories to make the heart race;
sex cloaked in words that we later looked up;
creatures attacking from space.
Swashbuckling pirates, gunfights, and ghouls,
werewolves that howled at the moon,
spirits who haunted the realms of the soul
heroes to make our hearts swoon.
Those books shined a light on a bright world of dreams,
on lands rife with unexplored glory,
inspirations that mined writers' deeply felt themes
and more than one Blank Slater's story.

2014
Olga M. Zulich

CONTENTS

Contents i

Acknowledgments iii

About Blank Slate v

Fiddle Away—*Mike Ripley* 1

Local Talent—*Joyce Hicks* 3

White Picket Fence—*Bob Moulesong* 17

Last Night—*Barbara Funke* 23

The Neighbor—*Olga M. Zulich* 25

Posted—*Mel Braun* 41

Aviophobia—*Stefan Barkow* 43

Legal and Binding Agreement—*Carla Lee Suson* 45

Hard to Kill—*Olga M. Zulich* 55

In My Head, Things Go Differently—*Christina O. Phillips*.. 63

's No Contest—*Olga M. Zulich* 65

Ode to the Eraser—*Barbara Funke* 67

Twice the Fun—*Olga M. Zulich* 69

The Fantasy Lottery—*Christina Ortega Phillips* 75

It's Just Her Nature—*Mel Braun* 85

Traveling Companions—*Joyce Hicks* 87

The Ballad of Don Alphonzo—*Olga M. Zulich* 91

Prion—*Marilyn Kosmatka* 95

A Shady Grove Welcome—*Mike Ripley* 97

Absence—*Bob Moulesong* 101

Half Breed—*Mel Braun* 103

A Dark and Stormy Night—*Bob Moulesong* 105

Class of 1980—*Rich Elliott* 107

Resistance $R=V/I$—*John Schaub* 113

Jocelyn Dreams—*Mel Braun* 115

Adventure Roll Call—*Gail Galvan* 121

Flies of the Lord—*Peggy Westergard* 123

IoT—*Bob Moulesong* 127

Cont'd. next page

Contents, *cont'd.*

Katfish Karma—*Gail Galvan* 143

A Flight of Fancy—*Timothy Cole* 145

Ode to Hermione Granger—*Christina Ortega Phillips* 151

The Hen that Lays the Eggs—*Timothy Cole* 153

Open, Sesame—*Barbara Funke* 159

In Passing—*Bob Moulesong* 161

¡Paleta!—*Christina Ortega Phillips* 165

Spotlight News—*Mike Ripley* 167

Nightwalk—*Barbara Funke* 191

Waiting for Santa—*Joyce Hicks* 193

Desolation Angel—*Bob Moulesong* 201

Home at Last—*Joyce Hicks* 203

Stuck in Time—*Timothy Cole* 211

A Love Villanelle—*Christina Ortega Phillips* 219

My Chinese Relatives—*Rich Elliott* 221

Monster—*Gail Galvan* 227

For Whom the Belle Trolls—*Timothy Cole* 229

On Finding Inspiration—*Christina Ortega Phillips* 243

Desert Escapade—*Tom Saine* 245

Fishing Expedition—*Barbara Funke* 259

Three Rail Christmas—*Robert Thomas* 261

Hostage Situation—*Barbara Funke* 265

Static and Silence—*John Schaub* 267

The Waiting Room—*Christina Ortega Phillips* 269

Hard Boiled—*Joyce Hicks* 283

Seth Donald Saves the Day—*Stefan Barkow* 287

Mi Familia—*Bob Moulesong* 295

The Passengers in Cabin 6742—*Robert Thomas* 297

About the Authors 301

Acknowledgments

We would like to thank the Wanatah Public Library and Uptown Café in Valparaiso, Indiana, for welcoming Blank Slate, month after month. Without tables pulled together, drinks, and sandwiches, we wouldn't have had the setting for sharing these stories and their revision. Special thanks go to Tom Saine, leader, newsletter writer, and tech editor for working with Create Space for publication. To group members, we owe much appreciation for their hours of editing and proofreading. Also, thanks go to members not represented in the anthology but who helped shape these pieces. Lastly, we thank Darlene Cohn who organized Blank Slate at its first home at Barnes and Noble.

2014
Blank Slate Writers

iv

About Blank Slate

If you're familiar with the first Blank Slate anthology—*Midnight Oil* (2013)—you know that the group started meeting in Valparaiso, Indiana more than ten years ago. Today, we're going stronger than ever, with writers from many different backgrounds: Merchant Marines, area universities, the medical fields, journalism and more. Since the introduction of *Midnight Oil*, the members of the group have spread out to attend special sessions and monthly meetings of other assemblies of writers in the area, and invited others to join Blank Slate as well.

You'll see new names in this second volume of stories—*Night Light*—which reflects the growth of our group. Of course, you'll also be able to enjoy stories from the original cast of characters.

Still under the able leadership of Tom Saine, Blank Slate continues to meet twice a month, bringing the stories we're working on at the time, or a new story based on the writing prompt that Tom provides prior to each meeting. The continued productivity of the group has led to the publication of *Night Light*. We sincerely hope you enjoy the stories and messages shared in this book, as Blank Slate once again celebrates enjoyment and friendship in the way that writers do—with the printed page.

Thank you for reading.
Mike Ripley

vi

Blank Slate Writers Group

Poem

Fiddle Away
Mike Ripley

While the world spins backward, they fiddle.
Ignoring ill stricken minds, having forgotten their lives,
amidst malignant growths,
they fiddle along.
As ice caps melt, as penguins die, as soldiers do,
they fiddle on.
Where hot winds blow on fields of fuel,
they fiddle tunes spun on greed,
and lure us to sleep with rhetorical words
of threatening hands in faraway lands we don't understand.
While tall trees fall and waters rise,
they hide within sight,
keeping fiddles in hand, their bows always in motion.
While we debate,
they fiddle; content to keep us busy,
they fiddle away.

Night Light

Blank Slate Writers Group

Short Story

Local Talent
Joyce Hicks

Still single at 33, the ever-impressionable Nate felt that a significant relationship might never be his. Sure, he dated occasionally, but like seedlings planted too late in the spring, the relationships flourished only briefly.

Neither had his job of activity aide at a skilled care facility, nor his status as homeowner, nor his victories in regional bridge tournaments made his life feel complete, though he had many admirers in the senior set. His *ladies*, as he called the residents at his employment, saw an energetic, boyish man, whose chatty kindness invited their coddling. The most coherent lamented his bachelorhood: "Nathan, why haven't you found anyone yet?"

They offered their nieces or nominated staff members: "Nathan, have you met that nice girl Sherrie who does hair on Wednesdays?" Often he could interrupt their match-making during Memory Hour only by breaking into a pre-war tune, and then even the shyest residents would tap their palms along with his gestures.

At home one evening, an ad in the paper in caught his attention: "Auditions for *South Pacific*. Newcomers welcome!"

He hummed a few bars of "Some Enchanted Evening" while he made a fried egg sandwich. Stacking the dishwasher, he found himself singing aloud, "I will find my true love across a crowded room, da, da, da, di-dum—"

Night Light
Joyce Hicks

Funny, romantic, and tragic, *South Pacific* was a terrific musical. After watching the 1958 film again, he felt confident enough for the tryouts.

On the first night, among two-dozen other townspeople he recognized Marie Devereux, entertainment critic and columnist for the regional paper.

"I'm here to audition!" she announced, moving among the thespians, shaking hands or turning up her cheek for a kiss.

Nate knew her Victorian house was down the block from his little ranch, but he was not part of her social circle.

"We live on the same street," he said when she introduced herself. She was taller than he would have guessed and wore a silk shirt over a black leotard, strappy sandals, and a glittery silver necklace.

"However is it we haven't become acquainted?" she cried, pressing his hand. "We must make up for lost time." Whether it was his gelled and parted hair, his blue eyes, or sensible slacks and pressed shirt that spoke to her, she proposed they sit together to await their turns to read.

"Now, don't be nervous and speak up!" she advised when it was his turn with the script. "Remember the balcony!"

No matter the outcome of the tryouts, for Nate it was ACT I: BOY MEETS GIRL. By the end of the evening, he was sharing coffee from Marie's Thermos as she compared each hopeful Nurse Nellie to her own reading for the young Navy nurse.

"Those gestures! Her hands are like bats flying. . . Too wooden . . . W-a-ay off key . . . That one is a terror."

Nate's own reading and a song verse he chose for his audition were "first rate," Marie declared. He nodded and smiled.

"Have you trod the boards before?" she asked, her necklace sliding into an intriguing cleavage, as she leaned toward him.

4

Blank Slate Writers Group
Local Talent

"Pardon me?" He glanced at the pile of lumber on his left.

"The *boards* refers to the stage, my man!" She patted his arm. "Have you been in a play before?"

"I act for my ladies, you could say." He explained about his employment. She listened with acute attention, nodding when he expressed doubts about carrying off a role in front of a less captive audience.

"Think of me as your mentor. If you get a part, I shall be Henry Higgins to your Eliza Doolittle."

He looked apprehensive.

"Genders reversed, of course," she added with a smirk.

"Oh, yes, I see what you mean, like *My Fair Lady*. I appreciate so much your interest in me." He pictured intimate instruction on language (and perhaps other things) and resolved to read all the theater lore he could get his hands.

As it turned out, the years he had spent singing hit lines like "When the red, red robin, comes bob, bob, bobbin' along" paid off. His appealing tenor and flair for unselfconscious antics got him a part as a sailor, not a lead role but one that would require many rehearsals and even tap lessons. In short, guaranteed camaraderie.

"I'm going on the stage," he told his cat at home and did a sailor's hornpipe around his coffee table. The *joie de vivre* he coveted was within reach.

Together again at the first rehearsal, Marie confided, "I only accepted Bloody Mary for laughs," wiggling her fingers seductively toward the sailor extras. She was regretful of no offer to play Nellie—only four seasons ago she had enchanted locals in *Oklahoma*. However, she promised the director to carry out with élan the role of the betel nut-chewing Tonkinese who connives to marry her daughter to the male lead.

Night Light
Joyce Hicks

Later, on their way out, Marie offered to help with the lyrics for "There's Nothin' Like a Dame," though she suggested Nate also apply himself to more serious drama.

"You should learn the master first, Shakespeare, of course!" she said as he helped her with a velvet cape.

"Guess what! I already started! I stayed up until 2 o'clock last night reading *A Midsummer Night's Dream*."

"Very good, Nathan, but there's nothing like a tragic hero for cutting one's chops—say, Hamlet or Macbeth. Or perhaps a romantic tragic hero. You'd do a fine Romeo." She smiled lifting an eyebrow. He resolved to read and study late every night, even after the strenuous tap lessons.

By the second week of rehearsals he and Marie had entered, what he knew from trolling the Internet for theater jargon, was ACT II, RISING ACTION. More than mentor, she had become a confidant and playmate—well, in many senses, but not all, he regretted. In one post-rehearsal chat on a park bench, he learned she was considering divorcing her husband who preferred to be away on business most of the time. Weeping, Marie told him about the late phone calls from a woman and mysterious items on their credit cards. Nate patted her hair as she rested her head on his chest.

He felt the man was a brute to treat a talented, lovely woman so badly. "You do deserve much better than that, Marie."

She admitted that Nate's allowing her to guide his theatrical education was helping her immensely to ward off a terrible depression that affected her periodically.

"It's a dark cloud that hovers above me. Without you, I'd be lost, Natie. You're my savior." Holding his lapels, she gazed at him for long moments.

Nate knew his life had been much simpler before Marie entered center stage, but so much less exhilarating. Now, he lived in a maelstrom of activities and emotions. Marie's house down the block was like a sensitive tooth; he couldn't keep from probing it with his binoculars. If an

Blank Slate Writers Group
Local Talent

unfamiliar car lingered in her driveway, his pain was nearly unbearable, but his chest tingled delightfully when an email summoned him for instruction, perhaps at a park or the theater, and once very late at her house.

And Nate's free time was gone. He was reading plays or memorizing scenes, taking acting lessons with Marie, or rehearsing *South Pacific*. Each run through of "Bali Ha'i" tantalized him, how his special island—Marie done up in a rather large tapa cloth and grass skirt—beckoned him. He longed to be where "sky meets the sea," but intimacy with her stayed just over the horizon. Frustrated, he searched for ACT III: THE TURNING POINT and pondered what more he could do to orchestrate it.

Marie said her tutelage was incomplete until he had mastered a heroic death scene, though for weeks he had been pressing for the touching balcony scene where Romeo declares his love for Juliet. Marie, however, insisted on the lovers' death scene.

Finally giving in, he suggested her backyard as a locale: "How about we try that in your yard? When the gardeners aren't there, of course." Though only a city lot, her yard required daily care by strange women in dark skirts who bent over like peasants as they weeded, watered, and dead-headed.

"Oh, the sisters. You pay too much attention to them," she said.

To his consternation, the three chattered in guttural syllables and gestured at him, even if he was only walking by. "I feel like they're talking about me."

"Maybe they are!" Marie grinned lasciviously. "Natie, you know my yard wouldn't be right for a death scene. You're doing Method acting and we're going to stick with it."

She reiterated that setting was key in staying in character, and thus they should meet at the city cemetery near a particular mausoleum.

Night Light
Joyce Hicks

"Bring a bottle of poison and a sheathed knife. We'll begin the scene right when Romeo mistakes Juliet as dead. It will be wonderfully creepy there."

"But you will be unconscious," he said still lobbying for the balcony scene. His objections were overruled as usual, and they agreed Marie would arrive first to arrange herself on a stone outside the mausoleum.

On the appropriate night, Nate arrived at the cemetery eager to show his worth. The moonlight on the graves and Marie's convincing stupor made his lines easy to deliver. Assuming his Juliet was dead, Romeo became determined to die too.

O, here
Will I set up my everlasting rest,
And shake the yoke of inauspicious stars
From this world-wearied flesh.

The various difficulties surrounding their real romantic relationship—longing, secrecy, anxiety, let alone her husband—put Nate truly in the zone. Finally, he let the knife fall near Juliet, drew the bottle of poison from his pocket, and chugged it back.

O true apothecary!
Thy drugs are quick. Thus with a kiss I die.

He collapsed manfully, with an arm flung over his face, sure his performance had won him an invitation to the bedroom.

A strong hand gripped his shoulder before he saw the two cops. "Are you all right, bud?"

Then they saw Marie, lying with her white neck exposed. Nate expected her to sit up, but she didn't.

"What's going on here?" Nate felt cold steel snap on to on his wrist.

Blank Slate Writers Group
Local Talent

"We're only play-acting. Marie?" Her head lolled to the side as one of the cops tried to sit her up after finding her pulse.

"I'm Romeo and she's Juliet. And it's the end of the play where she going to stab herself. Already she has taken sleeping potions, so she's dead, then Romeo takes poison, and well, uh, do you know *West Side Story*? Shakespeare didn't use a gun. Juliet stabs herself." Nate's exposition petered out as the cops manipulated Marie who still had not corroborated anything, lying with her bosom nearly exposed. The handcuffs hurt at his slightest movement.

"Get a grip, gentlemen," Marie suddenly addressed the officers. "Nobody is poisoned or stabbed. We're rehearsing *Romeo and Juliet*."

Disgusted, the cops made them get in the squad car while they made scrupulous identity checks, pondering over details that turned up. Finally, after tickets were issued for loitering and cars were towed, the cops dropped the pair off on Marie's lawn.

"We'll be watching you," the driver said, particularly regarding Marie, before they drove off.

"Why didn't you say something to the cops right away?"

"I didn't need to. You were wonderful!" Marie cupped his chin. "You see how well the Method works?"

"How about now, Marie, let's do the balcony scene? I'm really in the mood." His zinging adrenalin was calling for more action.

Ten minutes later, she appeared on her upper deck in a filmy peignoir. He began:

> *But, soft! What light through yonder window breaks?*
> *It is the east, and Juliet is the sun.*

With no misstep, they continued the scene until she leaned down, their fingers nearly touching, and spoke the famous lines.

Night Light
Joyce Hicks

Good night, good night! parting is such sweet sorrow,
That I shall say good night till it be morrow.

After this perfect performance, Nate knew he deserved an invitation upstairs, and he waited for Marie to come down to open the side door. However, sticking to the script, his Juliet did not reappear that night.

He pondered his state as he limped home—still unfulfilled, even though he had read, studied, acted, and been nearly arrested. Enough preliminaries! He himself must bring things to a head and move on to ACT IV.

Nate had awoken early Saturday with a plan for getting things straight with Marie, once and for all. He would show her the man he could be. Finishing off his showering with a splash of after-shave, he jogged down the street and cut into her back yard.

"Something unscripted," he whispered, judging the distance to the deck off her second floor bedroom.

Thanks to a rose trellis, he was able to get to the deck edge and haul himself over the rail. Marie's garden was displayed to a perfect effect below. Gargantuan leaves waved helter-skelter among urns and sculptures in the shade. A birdbath sheltered Maidenhair ferns, each whorl of fronds creating such a seductive cavity, he licked his lips. On the sunny side, the purple dahlias next to red canna lilies intensified their color to a bloody hue. Nate shivered.

Flattening himself against the clapboards, he sidled up to the bedroom's sliding door and peeked in. The door was open slightly, with the curtains closed behind it. Should he knock lightly? After all, he didn't want to embarrass Marie—she might be snoring or on her way to the bathroom. On the other hand, knocking suggested timidity, not his present state of mind at all. Nate opted to squeeze quietly through the opening and was enraptured with the vision before him—Marie, looking naughty,

10

Blank Slate Writers Group
Local Talent

willing, and a bit like Mae West, he thought fleetingly—lying on a chaise, as if she expected him.

"At last you've come," she purred.

"I couldn't wait another hour." He pulled the door closed and sat beside her.

"This calls for a wardrobe change." She headed toward the closet before he could pin her down with a kiss.

"Oh, never mind any costume." Sometimes, Marie got carried away. The Method called for unusual props on occasion.

"No, if you won't do it right, then—" Her pitch began to escalate.

"Sure, OK." Nate folded arms in what he hoped she would interpret as agreement, not submission. "Give me some duds."

Marie pointed to a knee-length linen garment already on the foot of the bed. She disappeared into her closet while he took off his clothes, hastily restaging his climactic ACT IV and muttering under his breath, "I wonder who we'll be today."

Finally, Marie swept out of the closet in a red velvet robe with a gold medallion nestled between her breasts. Her hair was caught up in an elaborate wrap and clip, accentuating her height and the creamy skin of her bosom.

Nate paged through the roles he knew—a brain-freeze could muff his chances for intimacy. Then inspiration struck.

"*Now, fair Hippolyta, our nuptial hour draws on apace.*" He took a princely pose, touched that she had chosen *A Mid Summer Night's Dream*, his favorite play.

Marie strode up to him, dark eyes snapping. She took his chin in her hand. "*Your face, my thane, is as a book where men may read strange matters.*"

Nate paused. *Thane? Who or what was that? Thane?* His brain whirred through the Shakespearian lore he had sopped up. *Oh, God, a thane was a Scottish nobleman. She was*

Night Light
Joyce Hicks

the horrid Lady Macbeth! Perhaps he could steer her to his original choice with a graceful bow. He took her hand, but she ripped it away.

"Marie! You promised! Only the comedies from now on." After the cemetery and a later embarrassing incident involving swordplay, he had extracted an agreement.

"Look how perfect the porch will be for the enchanted wood scene. It'll be the Method. Please? If you don't like my Theseus, I'll do Oberon wooing Titania!" As King of the Fairies, Nate executed a dangerous leap across the room.

"*I know a bank where the wild thyme blows. . .um, where, ah, ah, ox lips and the redding violet—*" But it was no use going on.

Rooted in her defiant pose, Marie was Lady Macbeth. That made him, ah, Mr. Macbeth, her husband, the Thane of Glamis, an impressionable dupe taken in by women— witches and his wife.

As he fiddled with his costume to buy time, he thought of a remark whispered by one of the gardeners. "You could be top dog here, instead of those other men, if you dared." A prophesy he could fulfill this very day!

A few lines from *Macbeth* would show his gumption and get Marie into the sack. Unfortunately, he could only remember the line, "*Is this a dagger I see before me?*" which he bellowed. Then sure that someone must get killed in the plot, he scanned the room. *A dagger, I need a dagger*—his thoughts raced. Grasping the nail file on Marie's bedside table, he strode manfully over and stabbed at the curtains.

"What are you doing?"

"It's Polonius!" he said, sotto voiced. "Remember, he was eavesdropping behind the curtain?"

She glared at him. "We're in *Macbeth*, you idiot, not that scene from *Hamlet*."

Overlooking the bit of foam that flew from her lower lip, he cried, "Come, my lady!" tearing open her red robe. With the gold medallion denting his chest, he made his

Blank Slate Writers Group
Local Talent

move by reaching to the back of her neck to bend her head to meet his kiss with one hand and sliding the other under her robe to a moist breast. He was breathing hard.

"For God's sake," she hissed against his mouth, "put down the nail file!"

They heard the sound of garage door, then the front door and footsteps.

"Harold! He has perfect timing this once!" She snatched off the headgear and robe.

"Your husband?" Nate scrabbled around for his clothes. Coolly, Marie withdrew a carving knife from under her dresser doily.

"What are you doing? It's not a burglar," Nate whispered, hopping on one foot to get into his pants. Sounds of breakfast being made drifted up from the kitchen.

"My love! Defend me from this intruder." Marie flung Nate the knife, which he grabbed to prevent it from clattering to the floor, then set on the edge of the bed.

He backed toward the porch door. "Just let me get out and everything will be fine!" In his haste Nate turned the locking mechanism on the door, not the handle.

"You wanted to be my king. You said so a million times, Natie," she said, accusation and whine mixing. She gestured grandly: "*Was the hope drunk, wherein you dress'd yourself?*" Then added coldly, "*Macbeth.*"

"No. I mean, of course, yes, I want you, but—"

"You don't have as much valor as desire, huh?" She looked meaningfully at his trousers.

"There's nothing wrong with my, my valor. I'm just not in the mood for killing anyone, that's all." He flipped the slender door latch again, unlocking and relocking it. Being trapped was making him slap-happy.

"Don't you want to have what you called '*the ornament of life*'?" she wiggled a hip. "Or are you going to let '*I dare not*' wait upon, '*I would!*'"

13

Night Light
Joyce Hicks

"How about a divorce?" Nate said, as if suggesting something from the appetizer menu. He tried to look over his shoulder at the uncooperative latch.

"A divorce!" she barked. "I'd lose my house! This is a much cleaner way, and let me tell you, you poor excuse for a Thane-of-Glamis, when *I* make a promise, I keep it." He thought about her promise about no more tragedies, while watching her snatch the knife from the bed.

Then, addressing the light fixture above her, she grabbed her bosom and howled, *"Come you spirits . . . unsex me here/ And fill me from the crown to the toe top-ful/ Of direst cruelty!"*

From below a voice: "What's that you said, dear? I'll be right up!" Marie moved to stand knife-in-hand just inside the bedroom door.

As steps sounded, dithering among options—Marie, whom he was beginning to see as possibly unhinged, the hapless husband, and the scent of freedom via the sliding door, Nate jumped behind the patio curtains. Then he heard Marie make a quick move. He held his breath during the eternity of Harold's ascension.

"Ah. So nice to be home." Nate heard Harold cross the room, willing him not to turn his back on his wife. Then Harold said, "Why are you holding the boning knife? Oh, you're already at it. Nice costume."

So, she hadn't made a plunge quite yet with the knife, Nate thought.

"Here, let me catch up. ...h'arhhump, ah, ah, h'arhhump." *Was this his death rattle?* "It's my turn to start, you know," Harold said amiably in a clear bass.

Facing the patio door now, Nate could see the lock, and he slowly moved his hand toward it.

"By the way, how's it going with that new fellow in *South Pacific?*" Harold continued.

Nate's hand froze.

Blank Slate Writers Group
Local Talent

"He's trying really hard, but his Romeo wouldn't make a sponge weep. He's too conventional for us, anyway. He wants to marry me."

"H'umm, a loser then. OK baby, see if you can get this one: *'Now, mother what's the matter?'*"

"Really, Harold."

"You love being a queen."

"But not Queen Gertrude, Hamlet's mother."

"Come on, sweetheart. We'll play it naughty—Hamlet loves his mommy. Let your hair down, Marie. Here, let me help." His surety in reaching for the hair she had kept off-limits infuriated Nate.

"You're so awful, Harold." Marie giggled. "But you didn't stump me. I know the next line. *'Why how now, Hamlet! Have you forgot me?'*" It sounded like her Bloody Mary with an education.

Harold answered by doing something that made clothes rustle and Marie titter.

Nate slumped against the door. So this would be his ACT V: THE DéNOUEMONT. Except instead of being a player, his role was audience. As Harold's voice rose, he seemed to be dragging a protesting Marie across the room to the bed.

All the Shakespeare Nate knew got jumbled together, as he tried to recall the plot line.

"Come, come, and sit you down; you shall not budge." There was a thump and Marie cried, "Oh!" Nate tensed.

Harold snarled, *"You go not till I set you up a glass/Where you may see the inmost part of you."* Nate could tell Harold was pawing over the dresser top to find Marie's silver-handled mirror.

Nate tried to remember the scene. Did Hamlet pound his mother with the mirror, or with his—?

"What wilt thou do thou wilt not murder me? Help, help, ho!" Marie's voice rose to operatic pitch.

Nate couldn't help himself and called out, "Marie! Let me help you."

15

Night Light
Joyce Hicks

Then time slowed down as he saw the rest of the scene as if printed in his Shakespeare book

LORD POLONIUS [Shouting behind the curtain] *What, ho! help, help, help!*

HAMLET [Drawing his sword and plunging] *How now! a rat? Dead, for a ducat, dead!*

It was not the kind of curtain call Nate was so looking forward to in *South Pacific*.

Blank Slate Writers Group

Short Story

White Picket Fence
Bob Moulesong

Josh looked through the tattered screen out to the backyard. He saw Cassie leaning on the rickety fence, fingering a splintered white picket. "Honey? Cass? The realtor wants to show us the bedrooms."

She joined him in the kitchen. "Sorry. Lost in thought for a minute."

"No problem," Josh said. "Let's see the rest of this place."

It was the fourth home they had toured in a whirlwind week. All of the houses were in foreclosure and belonged to the fixer-upper category.

They were on their way home when Cassie told him of her decision. "Josh, I really want this house."

"It's the biggest of the bunch," he said. "Four bedrooms. And one day that alcove off of the kitchen could be some kind of room. It's also the house that needs the most money and work."

"I really think it's the right one for us."

"Well, let's sleep on it and call the realtor tomorrow - if we are sure," Josh said.

"I think we should call her when we get home, Josh. We're sure."

Six weeks never went by so fast. Josh was amazed at all the steps it took to get a mortgage on a foreclosed house. But finally, the family stood on the front sidewalk, staring at the peeling clapboard Cape Cod structure.

"Well, we're home," Josh said.

Night Light
Bob Moulesong

Their four kids exchanged apprehensive glances.

Mom took on the reassuring role. "It's going to be great. Wait until you see how it looks after we fix this place up."

The oldest child, Aubrey, spoke for the tribe, "If you say so, Mom."

They spent the day moving furniture into bedrooms and getting the kids settled in before dark. Jack and Carter, only a year apart, begged to share a room. Henry was barely two, and Cassie decided he would be in a separate nursery. Aubrey lobbied hard for the master bedroom, but Cassie cut that dream short.

After three extra rounds of goodnight kisses and fist bumps, Josh and Cassie stepped into the backyard.

She handed him a beer and held hers up in salute. "To a good first day."

Josh took a long pull and wiped his lips with the back of his hand. "I know I'm pretty handy with tools, and I don't mind doing all of the work, but it's going to take a while."

Cassie smiled. "We have time. I'm not worried."

He followed her when she walked over to the fence.

"I know this fence will have to come down," he said as he surveyed the leaning border. "But I have a lot of higher priorities inside, starting with that leaky kitchen faucet."

Cassie fingered a cracked picket. "I really want you to fix this fence. I want to put it at the top of the list. Please don't tear any of it down."

"You can't be serious, Cass. The fence is a shambles. Some posts are rotted. There is so much work inside…"

"The inside isn't going anywhere." She was animated now. "It's June 7th. You've got all summer to work outside on the fence. I can work on the inside now, and we can continue together when the kids go back to school."

Josh tried to be reasonable.

"Cass, honey, listen. We don't have much money. Bedrooms need painting. The kitchen needs a faucet. I've

18

Blank Slate Writers Group
White Picket Fence

got to check out the furnace while it's summer. This fence is the last thing that we should be fixing."

"When I was a little girl, my Grandpa had a white picket fence in his backyard." Cassie's voice was almost hypnotic. "Every summer, I helped him whitewash it."

Josh sighed. He knew his wife, knew the tone, and knew the look. The battle was already over. "Ok. But don't blame me when this goes south."

A sunny Saturday morning, seven o'clock. Josh decided to start in the northwest corner and work south. He hoped she caught the irony. Aubrey stood at his side, looking at the fence with one eyebrow raised.

"We're gonna fix this?" The eight-year-old was as blunt as she was smart.

"That's what Mom wants," her dad said with a wry smile. "You want to talk her out of it?"

Aubrey raised her pink hammer. "I wanna whack a picket."

Josh laughed and pointed to the corner post. "Start with that one."

The braces that ran from post-to-post were solid. Josh gave silent thanks. Replacing pickets and posts wasn't bad if he could still use the braces. Josh taught his daughter how to pull off a picket with the hammer claw. She scraped her arm twice but gritted it out.

Tough girl, Josh thought. A lot like her mama.

Josh struggled to make small talk with his helper. "Glad to be out of school for the summer?"

She broke into a big smile. "Oh, yeah. I like school, but I LOVE summer. And now we have a house to work on."

"I didn't realize you were so excited about the new house," he said. "Guess I've been busy working a lot."

Aubrey shrugged. "Is that picket a keeper?"

The boys burst out the back door, determined to be involved. Too small to wield hammers, they kept busy piling scrap lumber in one corner of the yard.

19

Night Light
Bob Moulesong

Carter figured out how to use Josh's pliers to remove loose nails from the old pickets.

"Pretty smart," Josh said. "We can reuse those nails. Good work."

The boy gave his dad a thumbs-up and a smile.

It took all day to complete just one eight-foot section. Covered in sweat and dust, the team stood back and admired their work.

"Looks better," Aubrey said.

"You're a hard worker," her dad said. "I'm impressed."

Her eyes sparkled at the compliment.

A full day of hard work and fresh air had taken its toll on the kids. They were in bed before the sun sank behind the backyard horizon.

Cassie and Josh sat on the steps, beer in hand, staring at the fence. She stroked his arm. "I really appreciate that you're letting the kids help with the fence."

"Thanks," he said. "I realized today that working overtime made me miss a lot of their growing up."

Cassie nodded. "It's going to be a long, hot summer. Maybe you'll find some ways to spend time with them."

By July, Josh realized Cassie was partially right. The summer was hot, but the time was flying. Every weekend, the crew tackled the herculean task. Josh spent as much time keeping the kids on track as he did working. He was making steady progress, but the pace was agonizing.

He expressed his concern on a steamy Sunday night. "It's halfway through the summer now, and we're only halfway done with the fence."

"Sounds like the timeline is working fine," Cassie said. "What's the problem?"

He sighed. "Let's face it; the kids' rooms look kind of shabby. I wanted to paint them so they if they have new school friends over they wouldn't feel funny about it."

That next Wednesday, Josh came home to find several of his wife's girl friends painting in Jack and Carter's room.

Blank Slate Writers Group
White Picket Fence

"Tomorrow we do Henry's nursery," Cassie said. "Aubrey is still choosing colors. Didn't want you to think you were getting out of the fence work. I'll pick up the next load of pickets Friday."

Towards the end of July, the family began to have Saturday night campfires, using the old pickets as tinder. Josh taught the kids how to make hot dogs and S'mores.

Jack was six, the perfect age to be fascinated by the flames. "I didn't know you could make such cool fires."

"I was a Boy Scout," Josh said. "One of the things we learned on campouts was how to safely build fires."

"Maybe I can try Scouts," Jack said. "Camping and fires sound kinda cool."

"I wanna scout," Henry said.

Josh smiled and rubbed the toddler's head. "When school starts we can check around for local scout troops," he told Jack.

The dog days of August were upon them. Heat and humidity sapped their energy as much as the work. But Josh noted that the kids hung right with him. They took ownership, he mused. It's their project now.

Finally, when Josh felt he couldn't drive another nail, they were done.

"Amazing," he said as the family reviewed their work. "I didn't think we'd ever finish. Now all we have to do is whitewash it."

They painted all Labor Day weekend. Henry stepped in Aubrey's paint tray and made footprints throughout the yard. Cassie brought out leftover colors from their bedrooms. She helped each child dip their hands and personalize a picket.

"Never saw that before," Josh said. "Looks pretty cool."

School started the next morning. Cassie got the tribe bathed and settled in while Josh cleaned up the last of the project. Later, the couple sat out back by a small fire.

"Nice job," Cassie said.

21

Night Light
Bob Moulesong

"Thanks. Actually it worked out pretty good. I got to spend a lot of time with the kids. I learned how tough Aubrey is. Jack wants to be a Scout. Carter wants a toolbox for his birthday. Henry wants all of it."

Cassie listened and fingered the long neck on her untouched beer.

"You did this on purpose," he said. "You used the fence as a way to get me to spend the summer with the kids."

Cassie looked into the flames for a few moments before she spoke.

"The first year I had to help my Grandpa paint the fence, I was pissed. I was twelve, and it was not how I wanted to spend two precious weeks of my summer.

"While we worked, he explained that a fence was a lot like a family. Kept the bad out, kept the good in. Provided boundaries. But it had to be a strong fence to do any good. And that meant maintenance. You had to work to keep it strong.

"Those two weeks turned out to be pretty cool. Grandpa taught me how to check for weak pickets and replace them. Grandma taught me at night how to bake cookies.

"That next winter two of my uncles——two of their boys—died in a car wreck. At the funeral, Grandpa asked me when I would be out to paint the fence. He said we had to make sure it stayed strong. It mattered to him that I helped. And I realized that it mattered to me that it mattered to him."

The couple sat silent, each lost in their thoughts.

Josh finished his beer. "Not thirsty tonight?"

"Might be a while before I have a beer," Cassie said as she rubbed her belly.

It took a moment for the meaning of her words to sink in. Josh tossed a picket on the glowing embers.

"Guess I'll start on that alcove next."

Blank Slate Writers Group

Poem

Last Night
Barbara Funke

The primary function of negative dreams is
rehearsal for similar real events.
                    --Finnish researcher Revonsuo

I dreamed my after-dark departure
to a furnished garden apartment,
its flowered patios lantern-lit,
inviting, exotic.

Inside, new chairs opened
strange arms,
fine hardwood chests of drawers
stood stoically,
cheerless incandescence
closed in.
You set down cartons,
shrugged when I claimed the small TV
you said you'd throw away.
Instantly, I missed what we'd amassed
in years of careful choosing,
my address book and calendar went blank,
photographs faded.

Night Light
Barbara Funke

Your pale face turned from me
with downcast eyes of Greek coins.
The door clicked and rattled its chain.
A rift widened,
the room split in two.

I wake to you, your tender smile,
a joke, your kiss when you go out.
I listen to the door bump
and garage door grind,
smile to see garden weeds
and breakfast dishes beckon,
feel sunlight on my day.

Blank Slate Writers Group

Short Story

The Neighbor
Olga Zulich

A commercial had just come on when Elsie DeFlorio's doorbell rang. Annoyed, Elsie put down her Diet Coke and tried to decide whether or not to answer it. It could be a package—Elsie often sent for merchandise from catalogs—or it could be the Jehovah's Witnesses, or the Mormons—either way it would just be a minute before she could get back to her "story."

As Elsie opened the door her heart sank.

"Elsie, dear, how are you?" the sweetly chipper voice of Patricia Cartwright bubbled through Elsie's screened outer door.

"Oh, Mrs. Cartwright, I'm fine, thanks. And how are you?" Elsie's voice was not the least bit friendly, but her visitor took no notice. Elsie involuntarily took a step backward as, Patricia Cartwright stepped into Elsie's living room and placed a basket on her coffee table.

"What...," Elsie stammered, "What's this?"

"Oh, it's nothing much. Just some poppy seed muffins I whipped up this morning. A little gift from one neighbor to another."

"Well, thank you, Mrs. Cartwright. That's really very nice of you." They were both still standing and Elsie took a tentative step toward the door to suggest to her neighbor the direction in which she should be headed.

"Elsie, please call me Trish. Honestly, we have been neighbors for so long and I feel I have really neglected you. I know we're going to be great friends!" If asked,

25

Night Light
Olga M. Zulich

Elsie would have used "chirped" to describe "Trish's" tone of voice.

Elsie took two more steps toward the door. Could this woman not take a hint? She could hear her story proceeding without her and Elsie longed to sit in her recliner and finish her Coke alone, immersed in the lurid trials of others.

"What a lovely home you have," critiqued Trish and to Elsie's horror sat primly on the sofa, picked up the remote and snapped off Elsie's TV midway through an intense and significant conversation between an adulterous wife and her embezzling husband. Elsie's eyes narrowed. The nerve!

Completely oblivious, Trish rambled on.

"You know, with Ashleigh and Stan both gone, I find I am having such a wonderful time doing whatever I darn well please. I'm sure you know that feeling, being alone and all. Ashleigh is doing so well at UCLA. She absolutely adores it. Her classes are fascinating, so inspiring and the social life there is positively frantic. She's thinking of pledging a sorority, one of the top ones, of course. She calls every Sunday and tells me everything. We have always been so close, like sisters, really. No secrets, you know…of course she's close to Stan, too, but he's gone so much of the time. With his career on the upswing, the company is always sending him all over the country, and out of it, for conferences and top level meetings. So we girls have always stuck together…"

"Ashleigh…" Elsie vaguely recalled that Ashleigh was Trish's eighteen-year-old overachieving daughter; Stan her constantly traveling executive husband. Trish went on.

"She's always come to me with her problems. We've made all her big decisions together. We gals just seem to agree on everything. Well, almost everything. UCLA was totally Ashleigh's idea. A good one, of course. It all had to do with classes she needs for her major and how good the specific programs are, you know."

Blank Slate Writers Group
The Neighbor

"What is her major?" Elsie feigned interest. Obviously Trish would tell her anyway.

"Oh, well, it's one of those technical fields—ecology of some kind, and then she's always been interested in marine biology. So, of course, she had to go where she could be taught by the best. That's my girl! Always wanting to be on top. I just wish it could have been closer to home. I miss her so much."

"Oh, I'm sure you must. I'm sure she misses you, too. Well, Mrs. Cartwright, Trish, I want to thank you again for the muffins. So nice of you." Again, Elsie ventured a few steps toward the door. She was missing one of her favorite stories. A crucial and much anticipated revelation would be made in today's episode of "The Seeds of Destiny" about the paternity of one of the main characters. A truth so shocking that the look of alarm on the faces of other cast members had already been shown on numerous previews. Elsie had her own suspicions about this long hidden secret, and could not wait to see if, indeed, she had ferreted out the guilty party. But here she stood, awkwardly sidling toward the door while her loquacious neighbor sat ensconced on her couch.

"A mother can't help but worry about her child being so far away from home no matter how well she has prepared her for the big world out there. The bonds between mother and child are so strong. Of course, dear, you wouldn't have experienced that visceral connection between a mother and daughter, having no children of your own, but believe me it can be very painful at times."

A bright flash of rage exploded in Elsie's head. Long years of caring for her own mother through ever more dire health issues and her death in Elsie's arms would probably mean nothing to Trish Cartwright. Elsie's eyes narrowed and her lips drew back in a rather frightening smile. Had Trish noticed, she might have stopped her sentimental replay of motherhood's joys and sorrows. She did not, however, and Elsie quickly regained her composure.

Night Light
Olga M. Zulich

"I'm sure that's so, Mrs. Cartwright." The return to the formal address sent no signal to Trish, now caught up in a dramatic recounting of Ashleigh's birth, which to Elsie sounded much like a normal hospital delivery. Trish, of course, was the heroine of the piece, enduring singular agony. Oddly, there was no mention of Stan in this story. Had he been there or on one of his business trips? Elsie suspected the former, since his absence would have been yet another element of heroism on Trish's part. Perhaps, Elsie thought, Trish had just forgotten to mention him? Elsie looked pointedly at her watch and then at her neighbor. At some point in Trish's narrative Elsie had sat in the blue velvet recliner, propelled there somehow by Trish. This had to stop! As soon as Trish paused to take a breath, Elsie asserted herself. "Thanks so much for coming over and bringing the muffins. Mrs. Cartwright, and I have certainly enjoyed hearing about your family, but I have some things I must take care of now. I'm sure you have a lot of responsibilities also."

"Now, Elsie, don't you worry one minute about that. I am so enjoying our conversation, and I have plenty of time to spend with you. We only live one block away from each other. You are very important to me. I am positive we are going to be friends. I have already mentioned your name to Pastor Raymond at my church and he is expecting to see you at our next 'Golden Ager' dance. There's no need for you to spend so much time by yourself when there is a world of activity and fellowship just waiting for you. I'm going to make it my special task to bring you into the real world."

Elsie had a sudden and surprisingly clear vision of pushing Trish through large window facing the street, glass shattering and falling to the floor with a satisfying tinkling sound around the finally silent form of her new "great friend."

"The truth is, Trish, I have a bad headache and it's getting worse. I need to take some aspirin and then lie

28

Blank Slate Writers Group
The Neighbor

down for a while, so, as I said, thanks for coming over and for the lovely muffins." Elsie put her hand to her head and closed her eyes.

"Oh, dear, and here I am running on. Well, let me make you some herbal tea. There are a several kinds in the basket with the muffins. Would you prefer strawberry or peppermint or some ginger peach, or perhaps just some lemon Constant Comment? Oh, I know just the thing-chamomile! It can do wonders for a headache, so soothing!"

Elsie threw good manners to the wind and took hold firmly of Trish's left elbow. "Thanks, but I would just like to lie down." Trish was somewhat surprised at Elsie's strength as she was steered to the front door, through it, and found herself out on to the front stoop. "Good afternoon, Mrs. Cartwright." Elsie shut the door decisively.

Elsie's Coke was warm and tasted cloyingly sweet when she sipped it from the haven of the blue recliner. She felt vaguely discombobulated. The visit from Trish Carmichael had cost her most of the afternoon and the rest of her stories. She could catch up on Monday with most of them, of course, but that wasn't the point! The excitement was in being there when secrets were revealed....

The phone rang. It would be Ida Corelli, Elsie's closest friend and fellow soap opera addict. After some particularly shocking revelation, Ida would call Elsie to gossip about what it all meant. Today, however, Elsie didn't want to talk to Ida. She would spoil the surprise, and Elsie would have to admit that she had missed the actual moment of revelation. Ida would launch into a detailed description of how and why and when and where. Elsie would rather see for herself on Monday.

She decided to let the machine take the call while she downed two aspirin. Trish's visit had, in fact, given her a headache.

Night Light
Olga M. Zulich

"You have reached 555-0876. Please leave a message." Elsie heard her brother-in-law Patrick's voice. It was her sister Verna's idea to have a man's voice speak the message for "protection."

"Elsie, where are you? Wanted to hear what you thought about the big secret! Can you believe..." Elsie rushed vainly to cut Ida off. "...that Pastor Martin is Tracy's father!? What a shocker!! Give me a call. We have to talk."

"Dammit!" Elsie swore to the empty kitchen. She had missed it! Pastor Martin, the nebbishy do-gooder who spearheaded bucolic Oak Vale Junior and Senior High's celibacy programs had been revealed as the father of reformed exotic dancer Monique La Fleur's child, Tracy. Elsie had suspected there was something hinky about that guy!

Resigned, Elsie poured herself a glass of milk. She put one of Trish's poppy seed muffins on a plate and sat glumly at the kitchen table. She might as well talk to Ida. She would appreciate Elsie's irritation with Trish Cartwright. Like Elsie, Ida lived alone and guarded her privacy zealously. Though she and Elsie were good friends, they seldom visited each other's homes. Their weekly routine had been worked out years ago and seldom varied. On Sunday one or the other drove to 10:30 mass at St. Monica's Parish. Afterward, the driver chose a restaurant where they would enjoy a leisurely brunch and dissect the week's events, mostly those on their favorite "stories." The afternoon would be spent shopping at the mall, seeing a movie, or enjoying an event at Kempton College. It was a pleasant highlight to the week and for both as much socialization as they required.

"Hi, Elsie," Ida's voice had a touch of excitement in it. "So what did you think? Did you see the stunned look on that stuck-up Cynthia Freely's face! Priceless, wasn't it!"

Elsie sighed regretfully, "Sad to say, I missed the whole thing."

Blank Slate Writers Group
The Neighbor

"Oh, no!" Ida was truly upset. "But why? You never miss *The Seeds of Destiny*."

"Two words…," Elsie paused for effect. "Patricia Cartwright."

"Oh, Lord! Don't tell me she called right in the middle of…"

"Called? Oh, no! I had the pleasure of a neighborly visit complete with muffins.

"How awful!" Ida shared Elsie's dislike of unexpected visitors. "The nerve!"

"Exactly."

"So you missed it all—even Pastor Martin throwing his cup of coffee at that antique mirror and. . ."

"Ida, stop, OK? I'd kind of like to wait and see the scene when they re-run it on Monday. Besides, I've got a bit of a headache, so I'll see you tomorrow—9:45, OK?"

Elsie hung up. She finished her muffin and headed for the living room. Maybe the mopes on Dr. Phil could cheer her up.

The 5:30 news barely registered as Elsie nibbled another of Trish's poppy seed muffins, which actually were quite good. Still hungry, she microwaved a South Beach dinner and made a salad. No sense letting Trish's visit throw her completely off her schedule. There was never anything on TV on Friday night, so as a special treat Elsie set up the DVD of "Rear Window" Verna and Patrick had given her for her last birthday. They knew she was fond of Hitchcock movies, where seemingly ordinary people harbored secrets and were given to surprising acts of passion and violence—just like the people in her afternoon stories, though in the Hitchcock movies the bad guys usually got caught. In some, though, there were deliciously disturbing elements like in "The Birds" and "Psycho". She liked those because they demonstrated clearly her personal belief that the universe and the people in it could be wildly and unexpectedly dysfunctional.

Night Light
Olga M. Zulich

Verna and Patrick had also brought her a bottle of Chenin Blanc for her birthday which she had opened while they were visiting. None of them were enthusiastic wine drinkers, and after they had toasted Elsie's birthday and sipped a bit as they reminisced, Elsie had put the rest of the bottle in the fridge. Now was the perfect time for a nightcap. She deserved it. After all, she had survived a visit from the formidable Trish Cartwright and managed to get rid of her, if somewhat more forcefully than was proper. At least Trish would have gotten the message loud and clear: *"Leave me alone."* Elsie sipped the last of the wine as the ending credits rolled. Pleased with herself, she turned off the TV and got ready for bed. She fell asleep, easily, assisted by the soothing effects of the Chenin Blanc.

Awake at 6:20, considerably earlier than usual, Elsie mulled over a fast-fading dream about her mother. In the dream Sarafina was contentedly watching her favorite afternoon soap operas. They were her mother's greatest pleasure as she grew older and weaker. Elsie had had another television hooked up in her mother's room, so that even as she lay dying Sarafina could observe and comment on the exciting lives of soap opera characters. It was a comforting thought to Elsie that her mother enjoyed this small pleasure at the end of her life, and another reason for Elsie's devotion to those same "stories."

For breakfast Elsie had another of the muffins— wasting good food was a sin, after all, and sat at the kitchen table making out the grocery list for her customary Saturday morning trip to Kline's Food Mart. This task done, she fetched the newspaper from the front porch and sipped a second cup of tea while she read of the crimes and accomplishments of the denizens of Parson's Corners and the more momentous events of the wider world. Since it was still so early, Elsie did the crossword puzzle and then headed for the shower to get ready to go marketing. The sun was shining on the promise of a crisp fall day.

Blank Slate Writers Group
The Neighbor

By 10:15 Elsie had donned a navy blue pin-striped pantsuit, one of her favorites, over a peach and navy flowered blouse and was about to leave the house when the phone rang.

It could be Verna, Elsie thought, though Verna almost always called on Sunday evening. And she had talked to Ida just yesterday. Probably someone wanting a donation to the Navajo reservation or the Sheriff's Police.

The machine can get it, Elsie decided as she picked up her purse and fished for her car keys.

The phone message finished and a familiar voice trilled happily, "Elsie, dear. Hi! It's Trish. I was worried about that headache of yours. It seemed to come on so suddenly. I'm in my car headed your way and thought I'd stop in to make sure everything is ship-shape. See you in a few minutes."

As a woman of seventy-seven Elsie DeFlorio moved with care in the world, but she also knew how to act in an emergency. Clutching her purse and keys she strode briskly to the front door, speed-walked to her car, leapt in, and before even fastening her seat belt, tore down Peony Drive at forty miles an hour, ten miles over the speed limit. At the first intersection Elsie took a left, then a right at the next. This was not the way to the Food Mart, but Elsie had only one thought—*escape*.

At the downtown branch of the public library Elsie browsed the fiction and non-fiction new acquisitions and then meandered to periodicals where she flipped through *People*, *Time* and *Ladies Home Journal*. In the middle of an article on the health benefits of beets, Elsie slammed down the magazine and gritted her teeth—she was actually hiding out at the library afraid of a visit from Trish Cartwright! This was unacceptable! Today was Saturday and she was, by God, going shopping!

There were four messages on her phone when she returned from Kline's, all from Trish. Elsie deleted them immediately. The phone rang as she put away her

33

Night Light
Olga M. Zulich

groceries, and Elsie listened as Trish speculated that Elsie must be feeling better since she had apparently been out of the house all day. Trish had stopped by and noticed that Elsie's car was gone, so she was relieved that Elsie hadn't just been too ill to pick up. Groaning, Elsie turned down the ringer on the phone and resolved to ignore it for the rest of the day. Tomorrow was Sunday and she could cry on Ida's shoulder about her stalker.

After mass Elsie and Ida sat across from each other at Gilroy's Diner, blueberry waffles and mugs of coffee from the excellent Sunday buffet before them. Elsie sipped her coffee and nibbled at a forkful of waffle before launching into a condensed version of her recent troubles. Ida was suitably horrified. At least someone understood, Elsie thought, grateful for her old friend.

"You know, I wish Trish's daughter hadn't gone off to school in California. I think with her away Trish just has too much time on her hands. And, of course, her husband travels all the time, too."

"Yeah, I've heard he's always gone. Carmen says that she has seen him lots of times at Big Cloud, just last week, even. His company must have some kind of deal where they hold meetings and invite big shots there. Probably cheaper rates for repeat business. I'm surprised Trish doesn't make Stan take her along."

"Big Cloud? Really? Seems like Trish mentioned that he travels all over the country—different states, even other countries. Didn't think he had meetings so close to home."

Big Cloud was the Indian casino eighty-five miles northwest of Parson's Corners, only twenty miles from Ida's daughter and son-in-law's home in Sandy Hills. Its success had triggered the construction of a sprawling shopping mall, and the combination had become a Mecca for tourists and gamblers alike. Elsie had gone with Ida twice and that was plenty.

Blank Slate Writers Group
The Neighbor

"Maybe she's been there enough times. She doesn't strike me as much of a gambler. Odd that Trish doesn't know he goes there, though."

"You're probably right. And I suppose the mall isn't posh enough for the likes of Trish Cartwright. Carmen did say Stan seemed to be with someone from his office. Tall redhead. Maybe she was his assistant or something. Carm said he was really rude when she tried to say hi—just totally brushed her off. Acted like it was a case of mistaken identity."

"But Carmen was sure it wasn't?"

"Positive. Maybe Stan is just a jerk."

"Could be." Elsie smiled. "What do you say to seeing *Strangers on a Train* at the university? It starts in half an hour."

"Great!" Elsie was in the mood for another Hitchcock thriller.

On the ride home Elsie and Ida discussed possible holes in the movie's plot, but decided it didn't make much difference. With Hitchcock it was more the crazy suspenseful ride than strict logic. Hitch knew that horrible things happened when people kept secrets. Wasn't that the basis of their beloved daytime stories?

"Liars and blackmail and snares, oh my!" Elsie sang—cleverly, she thought—and waited for Ida's appreciation." She was not disappointed.

"Ha! That's pretty good! You are so smart, Elsie, though I think your voice could use some improvement. You sure are in a better mood."

"I've been thinking that Father Branigan's sermon about small kindnesses today could apply to me. I guess I could be a little nicer to Trish Cartwright. Short of going to those church 'happy-agers' dances or whatever they're called, of course. I can take Trish in small doses, but I sure don't need to be fixed up with some old geezer!"

"Wow, Elsie! I think you are getting soft on me. You really are going to try to be friends with her?"

Night Light
Olga M. Zulich

"Not friends! God, No! I just think that the next time she calls, maybe I should pick up the phone. Chatting a little bit can't hurt, and I can't avoid her forever. I don't want to be rude. And she did bring me muffins."

"Better you than me." Ida stepped out of the car in front of her neat two-story and waved good-bye. "Keep me in the loop!"

As expected there were messages from Trish, the last of them promising a visit on Monday afternoon. Elsie hummed as she set her DVD to record her stories after one o'clock. This visit would be as painless as possible.

At 2:05 on Monday, just as Elsie was getting into *Love's Questing Heart* Trish Cartwright arrived. No muffins this time, but a cheery smile and a Corning Ware casserole covered with aluminum foil. "Elsie, dear, you look wonderful. Over that awful headache, I guess. I brought you my famous ham and bean casserole. I thought it might save you having to cook for a couple of meals."

"So nice of you." Elsie took the dish and put it in the fridge. She turned on the heat under the tea kettle.

"Have a seat, Mrs. Cartwright. Would you like some tea?"

"That would be lovely, Elsie. Jasmine would be wonderful."

"Jas…, oh, certainly." Trish had brought an assortment of teas when she had first "popped in." Elsie fished in the tea jar for jasmine tea bags. *Might as well make a whole pot.* Two of her mother's best china cups and saucers, a creamer and sugar bowl, and some raspberry Milano cookies from Kline's completed her fancy "company" tray.

"Oh, how lovely!" Trish was pleased with Elsie's hospitality. "You didn't need to go to all that trouble."

"No trouble at all. We really didn't get to chat much last time you were here—my headache and all."

"Oh, I remember. I was really quite concerned about you, but you seemed to have recovered quickly. I couldn't

Blank Slate Writers Group
The Neighbor

even reach you the next day. I thought you might have been a little annoyed with me."

"I guess I was somewhat abrupt. I don't like to be around people when I'm not feeling well. Please have a cookie."

"You know friends can be a great help when you are under the weather. You need to let those who care about you TAKE care of you. I think you would really benefit from a wider circle of friends. You are still planning to come to our Golden Ager dance, aren't you? That would be a great place to meet folks with similar interests, and there are men there who would be thrilled to get acquainted with someone like you. I'd be happy to give you a ride there and introduce you around."

"I'll have to check my schedule. But Trish, what about you? With your daughter away at school and your husband traveling, you must have a lot of time on your hands. Are you taking up any new hobbies—painting water colors or wine-tasting or knitting or something?"

"Wine tasting? Elsie, you do have a wicked sense of humor. I don't think Stan would care for that too much. He's pretty straight-laced. We aren't drinkers."

"Stan? Oh, come now, Trish. With all that traveling and entertaining of company big shots, I'll bet he has a great time on the road. I would imagine it's hard to be at a casino all evening without partaking of all that dining and drinking and gambling. I'm surprised you don't go with him. Especially now that Ashleigh is gone. I'll bet Stan would love the company."

"Well, Stan isn't big on casinos. He hasn't been to one for quite a long time. We went together once just to see what it was like. When he travels he takes his clients out to really high class restaurants. Casinos can be pretty tacky, those buffet dinners and all." Trish sipped at her tea, her brow slightly furrowed.

Night Light
Olga M. Zulich

"What about Big Cloud? I know his company must have an arrangement with Stan's people for meetings and such?"

"Why would you think that, Elsie? Stan doesn't go to Big Cloud to do business. He travels all over the world. He has been in four states in the last month, and Toronto. He called me just last night from a fancy steak restaurant in Omaha. He's flying home this afternoon."

"Hmmm. He doesn't go there at all? My friend Ida's daughter and her husband said they had seen him several times at Big Cloud. Carmen and Tony live near the casino and probably go there more than they should. They've met Stan here in Parson's Corners several times so they would recognize him. Of course, I guess they could be mistaken."

Trish pursed her lips, "Well, yes, of course. You know what they say—everyone has a double. I guess Stan's must hang out at Big Cloud." Trish smiled brightly, but briefly.

"I guess that would explain how he acted — this guy at the casino. Carmen said that he would just give them a get-out-of-my-face look, wouldn't even say hi, and practically ran in the other direction. Kind of rude, they thought. They did look around for you and, of course, you weren't there. This guy seemed to be with a tall redhead. They thought maybe she was some kind of executive herself. Had that smart, severe look—very classy and with a great figure."

"Well, there you are—mistaken identity. I guess it happens all the time." Trish sipped her tea and nibbled at the raspberry Milano tentatively. The slightest frown played across her face.

"Do you like the cookies? I know homemade are better, but I just haven't had the time to do much baking. And if I make a pan of brownies or a batch of cookies, I'm too tempted to eat them all. By the way, Trish, those poppy-seed muffins were just delicious. I don't think I thanked you enough for them."

Blank Slate Writers Group
The Neighbor

"Oh, I'm happy you enjoyed them." Trish stared distractedly into her teacup, apparently deep in thought, then abruptly stood up. Glancing at her watch, she shook her head, "I am so sorry, Elsie, but I have just remembered that Ashleigh said she would call me at 2:30 today with some important news, so I have to get home. It just totally slipped my mind. Thank you for the tea and cookies. I'll…I'll call you soon so we can get together…and talk about the Golden Agers…so sorry." Not even waiting for Elsie to walk her to the door, Trish was outside and into her car. Gone.

"Well," murmured Elsie to herself, "that was a quick exit." A small smile settled on her lips as she sat back in the blue recliner and picked up the remote. "Love's Questing Heart" was barely half over, and Trish had left so quickly Elsie could use the DVR and get completely caught up.

Elsie was folding laundry when she heard the sirens and looked out her front door to see two police cars streaking past her house, followed by an ambulance. Intrigued, she stepped out her front door and watched as the vehicles sped about one block west and slammed to a halt. A small group of onlookers began to gather. Elsie contemplated going to see what was happening, but decided against it. She would find out soon enough. News traveled fast in Parson's Corners.

* * *

This winter in Parson's Corners was cold but oddly snowless, so Elsie really didn't mind the drive to Carroll Hills Correctional Facility each Saturday. Carroll Hills was a maximum security prison for women. *Huh! Maximum security, indeed! As though Trish Cartwright was a danger to anyone! Ridiculous!* Trish's one moment of violence had occurred, quite righteously it seemed to Elsie, when she discovered that her model husband had been cheating on

Night Light
Olga M. Zulich

her with a senior vice president of his company, an ambitious and passionate redhead, for years and lying about his business trips. It was too much for Trish. She had her pride, after all, and she was in love with Stan. Her fool of a husband should have recognized these facts and acted accordingly — namely by not cheating, or at the very least not leaving incriminating e-mails on his home "private" computer. Of course, like so many of the characters in Elsie's television stories, Stan Cartwright was convinced he would never get caught. And like them, he was wrong—fatally so. How could he know that a slight woman like his Trish could wield a carving knife with such force? Even Elsie was surprised at the violence of Trish's reaction. She had pictured a frantic Trish pounding her tiny well-manicured fists on Stan's chest and screeching hysterically. The very worst scenario Elsie envisioned was a surprise attack with one of Trish's designer frying pans.

Elsie glanced at the passenger's seat which contained a basket filled with brownies and a loaf of pumpkin bread and smiled contentedly. Trish always made a fuss when Elsie brought her some goodies. "You are such an angel, Elsie. You don't have to do this. You're the only one of my friends who comes to see me every week. What would I do without your visits to look forward to?" Trish had seemed near tears last Saturday.

The truth was Elsie was happy to do it, really. It meant so much to Trish and it was the least Elsie could do. Life had such unexpected twists and turns sometimes. But you had to adjust, to roll with the punches. And happily, for Elsie it had been easy to rearrange her schedule to fit shopping in on Sunday evening, so the trips to Carroll Hills didn't interfere with her reclaimed life a bit. Elsie smiled contentedly, ...*not one little bit.*

Blank Slate Writers Group

Poem

Posted
Mel Braun

"Please stay on the designated trail"
A lone sign declares above
the wild growth, daring me to stray,
luring my rebel feet to step
onto undiscovered lands. I am urged
to remove my shoes and wade
into forbidden water, to cool my toes
in a rippling stream, looming over
grey stones and lazy crawfish.

"Take nothing but pictures"
Immediately my hand reaches to capture
seed pods of spent wild flowers,
snatch up fallen pinecones
and unusual rocks. I pocket
a twisted twig that catches
my fancy, remorseless.

"Leave nothing but footprints"
Beneath a bush, in the loose peat,
I write a message, in squirrelfish.
I arrange pebbles in the shape of a cross
at the foot of a mighty burr tree
and bless the beaver dammed stream.

I have tread, taken and left
more than allowed.
I will not repent.
The cricket and nuthatch
do not judge me.

Blank Slate Writers Group

Poem

Aviophobia
Stefan Barkow

I live in other men's dreams
Afraid to reach for my own for fear
I—*I*—will prove as fleeting as sunlight in winter.

I live in other men's dreams
Aware that should I wake myself to reach for my own
I could—*could*—hold them.

But I don't. Instead,
I live in other men's dreams.

Short Story

Legal and Binding Agreement
Carla Lee Suson

Jerry's fingers brushed against gritty stones as he turned yet another dim corner. Gray-skinned zombies stood at the end of the hallway, groaning and shambling forward. Eyeless holes in human faces pointed his direction. Killing the walking bits of skin, gore, and bones was easy with his trusty Colt .45. The bullets ripped through the skulls with a great deal of brain and blood splatter. The nauseating smell of dust and rot almost overwhelmed him, but it did nothing to dampen the excitement of the kill shot. If the splatter effect was this good with a revolver, he could not wait to upgrade to the shotgun.

The *Gates of Hell* computer game was arguably the best on the market. His buddy Steve had raved about the Comp2024 virtual reality system last week, and now Jerry saw that every word was true. No other VR technology featured such concentrated olfactory senses, and the scenario looked so realistic that the adventure left him panting as if he had run a mile. Searching for lost treasure while killing bad guys was a dull old-school formula, but the intense VR presentation was worth every penny of the expensive system. True, as predicted on the box, the effects made his stomach churn at the first few zombie deaths, but after the fifth one blew apart in techno-red and gray across the wall, the game ceased to make him queasy.

When the package had arrived in the afternoon mail, Jerry wasted no time in setting it up. Skipping his afternoon

Night Light
Carla Lee Suson

history class, he stayed in the dorm to install the specialized board and programs that quadrupled his weak computer's performance. The Comp2024 system integrated high-speed VR technology and computer functionality with crystal clear graphics. The goggles, throat mic, and gloves made working with the computer a matter of hand waving and talking. Gone were keyboards, mice, and stylus pens. Home computer systems had suddenly taken a giant leap forward.

The first step involved cracking the computer case open in order to add the VR integrated hardware. He normally would never dare to mess with the insides of the computer, but the instructions were clear about how to install the hardware. The company also made sure to ship the exact package needed to match each user computer's design. The board was unremarkable in its tiny size and needle-like pins. Pushing it into the slot on the motherboard resulted in a bleeding thumb and a string of curses.

Installation was another aggravating delay of multiple registration windows. For ten minutes, Jerry sighed and clicked "Next" and "Accept" repeatedly without bothering to read any of the legal info on the screen. Finally the monitor announced the system was ready and he could don the VR equipment.

With barely suppressed eagerness, he slipped on the head and hand gear for the first time. The metal sensors felt cold as he entered the game mode. The sensors reacted by displaying a blinding dance of brilliant reds, yellows, and greens. Crashing guitar riffs blasted his ears before he could find the volume control on the headset. From the drop down menu on the center screen, he chose the *Gates of Hell* game because it had ranked highest in all the reviews. Flames danced across the screen as feedback sensors generated an increasingly hot sensation against his hands and face. Smoke tinged with a faint sulfur smell

Blank Slate Writers Group
Legal and Binding Agreement

lingered in the air. Deep, mocking laughter started low then rose to a crescendo from the speakers.

Hours later, exhaustion and hunger broke through the gaming euphoria. Jerry took off the goggles and headphones, running his fingers through his dark hair.

The game was huge. It would take days, even weeks to explore just the first level. He looked at the clock, which showed past midnight, and grimaced. With Literature of the Twentieth Century class starting at 8:00 in the morning, he knew he needed the sleep. He had time for a quick sandwich and then off to bed. He leaned forward, reaching out to touch the glowing power button on the console.

"I wouldn't do that if I were you."

Jerry jolted up, knocking the chair over. Eyes wide, he jerked around see a tall man, leaning against the wall. "God, you scared me!" He looked behind the stranger to the closed dorm room door. The deadbolt looked locked in place, undisturbed from when he first came home.

"Who are you? How did you get in here?" he demanded.

The tanned stranger bared a dazzling mouth of white, capped teeth in an attempt to smile that ended up looking more like a snarl. "You're forbidden from turning off your system now that you're one of the Comp2024 family."

"What do you mean?" Jerry sniffed a little, noticing a taint of burning in the air. He looked to his computer first, then around the room, finally realizing the smell came from a light cloud of smoke rising off the visitor's shoulders. As Jerry stared, the man straightened the jacket of his well-tailored black suit.

"Let me introduce myself." The visitor reached out and shook Jerry's limp hand. The student noticed the man's touch felt feverishly hot. Two large gold rings flashed with embedded diamonds and a matching Rolex peaked out from under the brilliant red shirtsleeve. "The name's Braxis, associate marketing agent for Natas, Inc.

47

Night Light
Carla Lee Suson

I'm here to outline the rules of ownership before you make any, shall we say, painful mistakes."

"What are you talking about?"

Braxis clicked his tongue while he circled the room, examining the bikini-clad girl posters. "Pretty much C grade material, aren't you? Did you read your registration agreement?"

"No, but it's the standard software contract, right? Just a bunch of legal details."

A deep tone echoed in the tall man's chuckle. "You stupid fool. Didn't you ever learn about fine print? Most people don't, of course, but you're supposed to be a college student. That used to imply some level of intelligence." He picked up a silver-framed picture. One long manicured finger tapped against the photo of a middle-aged woman. "Good looking woman in her day, your mom. Didn't she used to say 'The devil's in the details?' You should have listened to her more."

Jerry wrenched the frame out of Braxis's hands. He straightened his five-foot, seven-inch slouch upright, attempting to match the stranger's imposing six-foot plus stature. "I don't know who you are, but don't let the door hit you on the way out."

Braxis leaned against the entrance, arms folded over his chest. "The rules of ownership are simple. *One*: You will not mention a word about irregularities in the registration agreement. *Two*: You will do whatever we require of you, any time and any place."

With growing confusion, Jerry stared for a moment before replying. "What?"

"Hmm, yep, not quick on the uptake. By installing our product, you indentured yourself to the corporation, forever."

"Are you crazy? You think you can order me around just because I own your package? Forget it! Here, just take it back." Jerry slammed the disks and instructions back

Blank Slate Writers Group
Legal and Binding Agreement

into the ripped box. "Give me a second and I'll dig out the board."

"You're not listening. This isn't about you owning our product." His friendly smile twisted into a sneer. As he spoke, he punctuated each word with a finger jab at Jerry's chest. "We—Own—You."

"What?"

"Hmm. Maybe that C grade was a bit of an overestimate." He murmured before replying louder. "Technically, only your soul." He flicked his fingers upward. "You really should have read the registration agreement. In corporeal form, you still have free choice in accordance with the CEO's contract with, you know." Braxis's eyes rolled upward as if regarding some spot on the ceiling. "However, your soul is now officially and eternally ours. If you don't follow our orders, we will make life," he paused, picking invisible lint off Jerry's T-shirt, "and afterlife," he smiled slightly "a living hell for you."

"You're the devil?" Jerry snorted in disbelief.

"No. He's the CEO and sole-owner of Natas." Braxis smiled. "We used to call him Master but everyone is modernizing these days. I'm just one of his humble servants." The tall man bowed slightly.

"Yeah, right." The derision was clear. "If what you said was true, I'm safe. I go to church. I've always been a good person. Besides, don't I have to ask for something or make a deal?"

"You did." One sharpened fingernail tapped the Comp2024 box still clutched in Jerry's hands. "You got the finest computing system that will ever exist in the short lived history of man. The moment you put in your name and registration number, you signed our contract. If you want to review it, simply hit the 'about C2024' icon or look at the hardcopy in the box. There are no loopholes or clauses. Trust me on that. Armies of damned lawyers made that agreement completely legal and binding."

Night Light
Carla Lee Suson

Jerry paused but the visitor seemed serious. Braxis watched as he tried to think things through. All the horror movies he watched in high school reeled as reference in his mind. "Yeah... but...," he stuttered, "but it was suppose to be sealed in blood, wasn't it?"

"Oh yes, we can't buck Hollywood, can we?" Braxis's voice rang with sarcasm. "The agreement between the CEO and Other party simply states that blood is provided for identification purposes only. Nowadays, we use social security numbers and IRS records. We've been into their system for years. The blood seal is considered a mere formality."

"Well you're not going to get it."

"Get what?"

"The blood! I'm not signing anything in blood."

"You really are an idiot." The demon smirked as he brushed his nails against his designer suit lapels. "You already gave it to us. Remember the VR board? You bled all over the computer's guts. Why do you think we shape them that way?" His laugh came out long and hollow. "Face it boy, you're ours."

Feeling dizzy, Jerry slumped back onto the small bed. His voice cracked when he spoke. "S... s... suppose I refuse?"

"Do you remember Steve Paulis?"

Jerry nodded dumbly. Steve got his program weeks ago when they first came out. He had bragged all over the dorms about the games but refused to let anyone try the new system on his computer.

"Steve hasn't been around much has he?"

The boy's eyes widened. Now that he thought about it, Steve had missed classes the last few days.

"Put on the equipment."

Jerry slowly placed the goggles back on his head and adjusted the throat mic. He then sat, unwilling to open up the program. The demon's voice echoed through the speakers, this time tinged with anger.

Blank Slate Writers Group
Legal and Binding Agreement

"Go on. I'm giving you a freebie. After all, you're already damned if you do and damned if you don't."

The *Gates of Hell* game blazed again in front of Jerry's eyes. The putrid smell that seemed irritating before now overwhelmed and choked him. Gunless, Jerry looked down at his arms, wriggling his fingers. Three gray nails slid off his right hand and his skin broke open across his palm without leaking any blood. The sound of scratching caught his attention and he rounded the corner, huddling against the cold stones.

One zombie rose out of the tangle of bones on the floor. The torn white t-shirt and remnants of a university jacket hung on the thin frame of what was left of Steve Paulis. Bits of bone poked through one of his sleeves and one shoulder looked completely blown away. Steve's black-ringed eyes looked into Jerry's face as his bloody fingers closed on Jerry's shirt. The whisper started out as "help me…, please…," then rose to a heart-stopping moan as the boy began to twitch. The sound of a shotgun being cocked came from behind them. Jerry spun around to see the barrels looking as big as cannon opening rising towards his head.

He tore off the headset and threw it onto the bed. Panting hard, he grabbed the nearby garbage can just in time for his stomach to clench in rebellion. Afterwards, he gasped, wiping his mouth with the back of his hand.

"Those that don't obey become players in the games. That specific death hurts like," Braxis grinned, "like hell. Being undead, you've got to keep coming back for more and every level gets a little bit worse. And that's only one game. Consider *Prison Breakout* with truly accurate character interaction scenes in the showers, if you know what I mean. Or perhaps you would prefer *Speed Demons*. The goal of that game is to see how many mangled or burnt bodies a player leaves behind as he drives down a busy freeway."

Night Light
Carla Lee Suson

Jerry's head ached as tears rolled down his face. "What do you want me to do?"

The man's voice now came out gentle, almost fatherly. "For now, it's simple. You'll change your major to Marketing instead of English. We have enough tortured novelists for now. You'll rave about this truly excellent product, encouraging everyone to buy it. However, no one but you touches your system and you will not tell anyone about this conversation. Ever. Break those last two rules and there won't be enough screams in the world to handle the pain you'll feel. Do you agree or do you want another first-hand experience?" Braxis straightened his tie and waited with arms folded across his chest.

Jerry ground his palms into his wet eyes. "I need time."

"You don't have any of that particular commodity. Agree now or suffer the consequences."

Panic filled Jerry. "I..., I...,"

Braxis raised his hand, leaning forward to touch the student's head. "Now or never, boy."

"I agree!" The words came out with a sob as Jerry fought to control his breathing.

Braxis disappeared and silence hung in the air along with the hint of smoke. As the clock ticked away the moments of the night, Jerry held his head in his hands and shook. Tears flowed as he clung to one desperate thought. He had to find a way out.

The door knock was so loud that Jerry yelped in surprise. Wiping the tears from his face, he opened the door only a crack. Pete Sims, his friend from down the hall, peeked through.

"Hey man, sorry to knock so late but I saw your light was still on. Are you OK?"

Jerry took a deep, shaky breath, "Yeah, what's up?"

"I just got my copy of Comp2024 in the mail today. Looks way cool. Heard you got yours too. I'm not real great at installing these things and thought you could help

52

Blank Slate Writers Group
Legal and Binding Agreement

me out." Pete hesitated, face creased with worry. "Hey man, are you sure you're OK? You look white as a sheet."

The demon's warnings swam through his head. Jerry shuddered in fear but looked at the open, honest face of the kid that was a year behind him in college. He pictured the boy's face melting off as he died screaming in the zombie program. Jerry's eyes slid down to the open program box in Pete's hands. The hardcopy agreement hung half out. He rubbed his face as the glimmering of an idea blossomed in his mind. Maybe he could find a loophole.

"Listen to me. Before you install anything, board, VR tools, or the program, pull out the registration agreement and read all of it, every word. There is a hardcopy in the box."

"Oh but that's just legal stuff about ownership and stuff. No one ever reads that crap. If you don't want to help me, then just say so."

"I'm serious, Pete. I promise I'll help you install it tomorrow if you still want it but you must read the agreement first." Jerry left the door ajar as he fetched his copy off the computer desk. He thumbed through the cheap booklet, searching the pages for key words. "Here, read page seventeen, that small paragraph."

Pete reached for Jerry's copy, but the pale man jerked it away, "No, look at your copy."

His friend snorted in irritation and dug out the registration agreement, "Got to go to a lot of trouble just to get some help," he mumbled. His eyes widened as he read the small words. He looked up, mouth open in astonishment. "They're joking, right?" Then he examined the page again.

Jerry grasped Pete's arm. "Just trust me. You gotta read the entire contract, even the small print. I won't help you until you do." Jerry made a sigh that was half sob. As he closed the door on Pete's pale face, he whispered. "Remember Pete, the devil's in the details."

53

54

Blank Slate Writers Group

Short Story

Hard to Kill

Olga M. Zulich

At long last Stella had killed her! Chloe "the Cat" Devereaux, reknowned beauty, crack shot, martial arts expert, top dollar PI and love-em-and-leave-em ball breaker was dead. DEAD! Her formerly lithe five foot nine inch smooth-as-alabaster carcass was on view for all to see. The deep emerald green eyes that had broken so many hearts and stared down swindlers, mobsters, and murderers were closed in peaceful repose. The bullet that had felled her had struck her heart leaving the perfectly oval face, the lush lashes, the model's cheekbones and the cascading chestnut hair intact. No questions about identity—No sirree!

No cremation—Oh no. No chance of a "mistake" or an elaborate ruse wherein the Cat still lived and would return to save the day in some clichéd nick-of-time scenario. Weeping mourners filled the mortuary, stunned to hear of the end of one who had seemed invincible. This was real. They were all witnesses. The Cat had used up her last life. Visitation at Ellison's Mortuary, 1412 Del Lago Drive, 1 pm until 8 p.m. , Thursday; burial Friday, St. Augustine Cemetery, 3 p.m., remarks by the Vice President of the United States, no less, befitting a national hero. Various grateful beneficiaries of the Cat's heroics would give short tearful speeches. And, then it would all be over. Finito. Thank God.

Stella had been generous, though. Cat Devereaux had died saving the kidnapped four-year-old daughter of a United States Senator. She would be remembered as a great fictional hero. A great way to go out.

Night Light
Olga M. Zulich

Stella had tried to end it before: Her previous book had even been titled The Cat's Last Case. In it, a disillusioned and suddenly rich (she had been remembered in the will of an elderly ex-client to the tune of $800,000) Cat had sold her jewelry and other gifts from clients and paramours, all but the stunning emerald earrings and necklace, the exact color of her eyes, and left Manhattan for a remote Pacific island. She left with tears in those eyes, not regret at leaving, but tears of relief.

"Good-bye, New York," Cat had whispered resolutely on the final page of *The Cat's Last Case*. "Never again."

But Stella Raines nee Esther Ransberger should have known to never say never. The Internet buzzed with hand-wringing over Cat's untimely departure. Not just sad, fans were irate. More, more, they needed more. Their heroine could not just desert them. No crook, no mob, no matter how badass, had been able to fell their idol. Certainly disgust, depression, angst could not do it. Superman had returned from his fortress of solitude. Cat would return from Santa Palma stronger than ever. They knew it. They demanded it.

Stella resisted stoutly. She was done cranking out "pulp fiction". She longed to write important stories of imperfect, complex people who muddled through life uncertain, unlucky, real. She could feel in her soul that she had it in her to create serious literature, maybe even the great American novel.

As clamor for Cat's return grew to a fever pitch, however, Stella understood that she had left things unfinished. Chloe Devereaux deserved a proper end, a decent burial, before Stella could move on to better things.

And so she had begun *Finale*. It would really be the last. She had told everyone: her agent, the press, bloggers. She meant it this time. No comebacks.

After weathering the storm of protest, though, she had become aware of an odd feeling—was it remorse? Ridiculous! Stella told herself she was killing a character—a

FICTIONAL character. It was true that when Stella was writing, Cat felt marvelously alive and occasionally had even seemed to resist a certain plot twist, to rebel against Stella's carefully choreographed plans for her. In the past she had always re-thought the offending passage and altered it to suit "Cat's Advice." Stella called it "writer's instinct."

Now she sensed Cat pleading for her fictional life. Well, it was only normal for Stella to be ambivalent about Cat's demise. They had been through so much together. She had given birth to Chloe the Cat and now was callously bumping her off. Well, not "callously." She really did feel a sense of mourning for the loss of someone who had meant so much to her life. But all good things, etc...

"Sorry, Cat," Stella murmured as she typed the final sentences ending Chloe Devereaux's short but hyper-eventful life.

The first complete copy of *Finale* fell softly into a stack below Stella's computer. Her publisher had been alerted: Today he would get the first look at what was sure to be a blockbuster bestseller. Her editor could get started and they would be off to the races. The beginning of the end— time for Stella's new life to begin.

Stella poured herself three fingers of the single malt scotch she kept for special occasions. "Here's to you, Cat," she toasted her creation, "been good to know you."

Preston O'Connor, her long-time agent and friend, had insisted on taking her out to a "posh" dinner to celebrate, so the next problem was what to wear. Still holding the nearly empty tumbler of scotch, she opened the closet to study her options: either the blue silk suit with the plunging neckline or the slinky black backless cocktail number with the short, short skirt. Stella would never be called a stunning beauty, but she had great legs. The black, she decided—punch it up with her dangling gold and amber earrings and her double strand of matching amber beads. Amber, the color of the highlights her publisher had

Night Light
Olga M. Zulich

suggested to jazz up her "mousy brown" hair for the last book jacket photo. She glanced in the mirror and winked. Preston had loved the highlights and declared that they made her look sexy, marking the first time in Stella's life that that term had been applied to her. She twirled in the black dress and admired herself in the mirror. "How do you like me now, Pres?" she daringly inquired. Oh, yes, this would be a night to remember. Lost in a glow of self-congratulation and scotch-induced buzz, Stella was startled to hear a sharp rapping on her door.

"Delivery for S. Raines," the voice was female and somewhat throaty, a Lauren Bacall kind of voice, Stella thought. "Flowers."

Flowers? Who would…? Oh, of course, Preston. Stella smiled. He could be so sweet to his successful clients. Stella stared through the peephole at a tall woman in a brown uniform and cap holding a long white box tied with a green silk bow.

Delighted, Stella unlocked the door, and as it closed behind the delivery girl, found herself staring into a pair of emerald green eyes.

"Who…" Stella's voice trailed off.

"Oh, you know me, Stella."

The eyes were so intense, so familiar. Startled, Stella took two steps backward. "What…?

"I'll give you a clue, Stella: I believe you were about to kill me. You should know by now how hard I am to kill. You should know that it's not gonna happen."

The gun that suddenly appeared in the visitor's hand was large and equipped with a silencer. That bit of information, gleaned from her research for Cat's well known knowledge of firearms, was the last thought that Stella Raines was able to formulate before a single shot struck her in the heart killing her instantly, leaving her intelligent and expertly made up face and beautifully highlighted hair intact for the private showing at the funeral home.

58

Blank Slate Writers Group
Hard to Kill

The police were baffled. There seemed to be no motive for the murder, hence no suspects. Preston O'Connor, who had been expected at Miss Raines' apartment had been held up by the unexpected office visit of another client and had left a message while Stella was in the shower to say that he would be half an hour late. The client turned out to be Sister Agatha, a nun at St. Joseph's Catholic School who wanted advice on writing a publishable novel about a woman haunted by demonic spirits. Sister Agatha was a fan of mysteries and Cat Devereaux and was quite pleased, though saddened, of course, to be the center of attention and to give Preston O'Connor an alibi, though he had no motive to kill Stella Raines who was both a close friend and a reliable source of income.

Nothing seemed to be missing from Stella's apartment except for the manuscript of *Finale*, which Preston O'Connor insisted had to be there. No hard copy was found, and even more perplexing, not a trace of *Finale* could be unearthed on Stella Raines' computer. No outlines, no rewrites, nada. O'Connor was devastated. It had to be there somewhere. But, it was, alas, lost. "If, indeed, it had ever existed," one of the detectives assigned to the case remarked cynically.

O'Connor knew it had been stolen. It would surface. It was the reason that Stella was murdered. But even he had to admit that although he and Stella had discussed the outline for *Finale* at length, he had never seen actual pages. And it was hard to fashion the theft of an unpublished novel into a motive for murder.

It was a sunny, crisp October day when Stella Raines was laid to rest. A canopy had been set up over the open grave, which was surrounded by floral tributes of every size and color. Also under the canopy were eight rows of chairs filled with mourners. The overflow stood in the bright sun listening to the brief prayers and words of praise for a writer who, in the words of a grieving Preston

Night Light
Olga M. Zulich

O'Connor, "gave such joy to the world, one who was taken too soon by violence but who lives on in our hearts through our memories and through the permanence of her works of fiction."

"It's so true," sighed Maxine Wayne, a thirty-year-old housewife, to her good friend Kristin Donatelli, "But it's so sad that we'll never have any more Cat Devereaux books. I just loved her! I can't believe she's done. I think I'll actually miss Cat more than Stella Raines, if you know what I mean."

"Oh, I know exactly what you mean," Kristin agreed. "But weren't you on the Internet this morning? The Cat's not done! The publishers of the Cat books have found someone to continue on with the series—some detective story writer who loved the Cat novels and is going to pick up right where Stella Raines left off with the Cat coming back to the city to fight crime again."

"Wait…I thought Cat was never coming back to the city. And wasn't the rumor that she was going to die in the last book Stella Raines was writing. It was called *Finale* so…"Maxine was skeptical, though hopeful.

"Well, yeah, I heard that, too. But you know how these rumors go. Who knows what twists writers can come up with. I'll bet Cat was laying low so she could come back and knock out some really bad guys—go undercover and take 'em by surprise. Maybe she was already back in the New York!"

"That would be so great! God! I hope it's true. I can't wait for the next one!" Maxine's face shone with hope. "I knew Cat Devereaux would never be happy away from the city, just loafing on some tropic island."

"You know, that is so true. It never did make sense. Not like the real Cat at all."

Four feet away the sun sparkled on a pair of exquisite emerald earrings worn by a tall slim woman in an elegant black suit, her thick chestnut hair drawn back into a severe

French twist, large black sunglasses concealing emerald green eyes.

"Rest in peace, Stella," the mourner intoned in a throaty whisper to no one in particular. "Been good to know you."

Blank Slate Writers Group

Poem

In My Head, Things Go Differently
Christina Ortega Philips

In my head, things go differently,
writing people who do my bidding,
I live in my own reality.

Every day you can ignore me
and I will admit that it does sting,
but in my head, things go differently.

Ignoring life, I turn to story
where I can control everything;
I live in my own reality.

I may not have much ability.
At times I may play the underling,
but in my head, things go differently.

People meet my expectations, see.
All that I want, I get, constantly;
I live in my own reality.

Let down, I pick up my pen with glee,
a happy place of my own making.
In my head, things go differently;
I live in my own reality.

's No Contest

Olga M. Zulich

Car's stuck at the end of the driveway,
Porch has eight inches of white.
Somewhere the morning paper
Has been chucked in some drift out of sight.
Wait! There's a tip of orange plastic-
Just give me five minutes to dress:
A parka, big boots, gloves—fantastic.
I look like some monster, no less.
Be careful and feel out each porch step.
If you fall you could lie there for days.
You'd be like that guy In *The Shining*
Who quick-froze while lost in a maze.
I'm waxing melodramatic
And pausing before I step out
Because once I open the front door
I'll know just what this winter's about:
It's a contest, you see, where Ma Nature
Grades us on how we fit in
With her harsh and unyielding surroundings
Well, Nature, you mother, you win.

Blank Slate Writers Group

Poem

Ode to the Eraser

Barbara Funke

Little bullet of solace
quicker than a Minute Man,
you defend against insurgencies
of graphite or lead.
Your color irrelevant to quality,
your sexual preference moot,
you are firm but resilient,
patient yet alert.
Once called into service
you accept your assignment
without complaint.

So plainly uniform when new,
you soon surrender the crisp edges of inexperience
to work on, in, behind, between the lines,
get down, get dirty.
Irregular as special forces,
disguised as a tired lump of gum, ugly,
maybe maimed, you bear scars of each skirmish
into the next encounter.

The writer salutes you, embattled one,
counts on your humble loyalty,
your innumerable sacrifices, great and small.
Together you fight against peril,
against letters excessive, disorderly,
against the undisciplined hordes of words,

Night Light
Barbara Funke

against poisonous clouds of ill-penned gas.
And when you find yourself
diminished through months of duty,
undecorated, retired, replaced,
rest easy and contented, gallant warrior,
assured your gift of self and substance
is mankind's more than modest gain.

Blank Slate Writers Group

Short Story

Twice the Fun
Olga M. Zulich

Dirk and Carlo stood admiring the scenery. The beach was lovely-white sand, lazy azure blue waves with frothy tops lapping the shore, the sun just beginning to set on the horizon. Perfect. Of course the best part of the scenery was the girls. It had been a really hot day and the beach was flush with bikini clad young ladies alternately frolicking in the warm water and stretching out on colorful beach blankets or towels, some with their bikini tops undone to be sure that their backs got an even tan. Dirk and Carlo strained their eyes behind fashionable sun glasses seeking a revealing slip as one or another of the "beach bunnies" cautiously shifted position or re-applied sun tan lotion. This covert spying was mostly a lost cause as the girls (was it sexist to call them "girls?" Dirk wondered idly, and decided it probably was) were very careful to avoid prying eyes.

The sun was slowly descending out of sight. Time for Dirk and Carlo to make their move. Canvassing the bevy of sun-worshippers, some of whom were (sadly) starting to obscure tanned or burned bodies with terry-cloth cover-ups, the boys' attention fell on a pair of beauties they had somehow missed. Two strikingly tall raven-haired "girls" in identical lilac bikinis sat well back from the shoreline in the shade of two enormous trees. They wore large sun glasses and straw hats with big brims, so that their faces were kept totally shaded from the setting sun. It was hard

Night Light
Olga M. Zulich

to see exactly what the two looked like, but they appeared to be mirror images of each other.

"Hey, now... looky here," Dirk directed Carlo's attention to the two apparently late arrivals.

"Yum, yum," remarked Carlo insightfully.

Without another word the two thoughtful connoisseurs of feminine beauty strolled to the shaded park bench where the girls were seated.

"Beautiful sunset, isn't it?" Dirk shaded his eyes as he gazed out to sea. "You ladies come here often?"

"Once in a while," the girl who spoke had a throaty purring voice. "I'm Iris. This is my sister Violet. And you are?"

"I'm Dirk. This is my brother Carlo. We couldn't help admiring you two ladies. Did you just get here? We surely would have noticed you earlier."

"Aren't you nice," Violet spoke in a voice identical to her sister's.

Carlo thought it was the sexiest voice he had ever heard. From behind his Ray Bans he covertly studied the girls' bodies. "Wow!" was his stunned mental reaction-long, long legs, nice racks, toned arms and stomachs. Dirk was surreptitiously making his own assessment and came to the same conclusion. Definite possibilities for some fun. How lucky could they get? *Sisters*—both gorgeous!

The only odd thing about Iris and Violet was their skin tone. Extreme pallor, like fifty shades of white. Maybe they had some kind of skin condition that made it bad for them to be in the sun. Maybe they just believed all that stuff about the sun turning your skin to rawhide when you got older or were afraid of skin cancer. Well, whatever, small price to pay for the rest of the package, er...packages.

"So, are you two twins by any chance?" Carlo thought it might be rude to ask, but they did look so very much alike.

Blank Slate Writers Group
Twice the Fun

"You are very observant, Carlo. Yes, we are two peas from the same pod, as it were." Violet and Iris smiled at each other.

The sun was setting rapidly. "Would you girls like to get out of here, maybe go for a ride?" Dirk smiled. "It really is a beautiful night."

Iris and Violet turned toward each other, smiled, and nodded. "That would we lovely," they murmured together and giggled at the confluence.

"Great! Let's go!"

In the car, an unimpressive 2005 Oldsmobile, the girls inquired about where they were going.

"Oh, just wait till you see!" Carlo, at the wheel, enthused. It'll knock your socks off!"

"Really?" Iris said (or was it Violet—well, what did it matter?) "What a funny thing to say — we are not wearing 'socks.' What does it mean?"

"Oh, that's just a way of saying you'll be amazed at this place."

"So you live in this amazing house. What makes it so amazing?" Iris sounded a bit skeptical.

"It's not just a house; it's, well, almost a castle. Just magnificent. A place fit for ladies as refined and as beautiful as yourselves. Right, Carlo?" Dirk fancied himself a wordsmith. Ladies always fell for the classy approach. Tonight was going to be a good, good night. He glanced at Dirk across from him and winked.

"Absolutely. This place is not be believed. It looks like something from the history channel on TV. You'll love it."

"And you live in this "castle? How exciting! Can you believe it, Iris? We've met two gentlemen who live in a castle!" Violet's throaty voice was full of excitement and anticipation.

"Oh, my, that is thrilling! You must tell us—how did you come to own a castle?"

"Well, here's the thing," Carlo explained. "We don't live there right now. We inherited it from our great

Night Light
Olga M. Zulich

grandfather Sir Lawrence Haverford who died recently, rest his soul, and left it to us, but he had been ill for some time. He was ninety-eight years old and had not been able to keep the place in good condition. There is a lot of work to be done before we can move into it. Right now it is pretty much unlivable. Right, Dirk?"

"Right, right. But we wanted you girls to see it anyway because you are so special. We can take a quick look at it and then go back to our place for a nightcap."

"Aaah. I see," said Iris in her thrillingly raspy purr. She glanced at Violet who smiled broadly and stared out the window.

Carlo sensed that they were losing their implied gloss of semi-royalty. Time to pull out the big guns.

"The house," Carlo intoned in his ultra-serious voice, "had a history of strange happenings." The boys' great uncle Jerome had fallen ill of an unexplained disease while visiting and sadly passed away. Exactly four weeks after his burial strange moanings were heard in the house and objects were observed to move of their own volition. The room where Uncle Jerome had died was the site of mysterious shadows and several volumes of the works of Charles Dickens, which were Jerome's particular favorites, crashed to the floor startling two of the boys' great aunts who had been chatting with Sir Lawrence over tea and scones in the parlor.

"Oh, dear, this place seems rather terrifying, doesn't it Iris?" Violet's voice seemed at once coquettish and a bit ironic.

"Indeed, it does. Are you boys sure we will be safe snooping around a place with such a reputation?"

"Oh, you bet. Don't worry about a thing. We'd never let anything happen to you ladies. Besides, we'll just stay a few minutes. There's a nice bar back at our hotel."

"I'm sure there is. That is good as we are very particular about what we drink." The girls looked at each other and nodded.

Blank Slate Writers Group
Twice the Fun

This seemed an odd remark to Carlo who hoped the girls weren't some kind of vegans, or anti-booze fanatics. He and Dirk had some weed back at the hotel, but not enough to get them all stoned.

"Ah, here we are." They had pulled off the road and gone down a narrow car path shadowed by trees. About a quarter of a mile down the road a clearing gave way to an impressive view of the "almost castle." Silhouetted against the full moon the house was large and quite beautiful in its size and symmetry, though a trifle ill-maintained and just in some indescribable way a bit off-kilter. The girls stepped eagerly out of the car and began walking to the front which featured a divided entranceway leading to double doors. The boys hastened after them.

"Oh, this is quite lovely. We can't wait to see the inside." Iris and Violet eagerly advanced toward the bifurcated stairway. "It doesn't look nearly as run-down as you led us to believe. Iris, can you believe we're going to be seeing the inside of this magnificent place?!"

"This is our lucky day, isn't it, Violet? How can we thank you boys for showing us your gorgeous place.?"

"Oh, we'll think of something," Dirk grinned and made a vigorous show of searching his pockets for the keys to the ancestral mansion. "Oh, no!"

"What's wrong?" Carlo was deeply concerned.

"I can't find the keys! I'm sure I had them. I hope I didn't lose them at the beach! This is terrible!"

"Oh, no." Just to make sure the keys hadn't somehow magically jumped into his pockets Carlo felt for them in his own pants. No luck.

"I feel terrible, just terrible, but it looks like we'll have to wait until another day to see the inside of the place, but at least you got to see the outside. Let's head back to the hotel and get a bite to eat and have a few drinks. We shouldn't let my dumb mistake ruin this beautiful night." Dirk was very contrite.

Night Light
Olga M. Zulich

As Carlo looked up he saw Violet and Iris smiling broadly at them and noticed for the first time that their teeth appeared slightly pointed. How had he not noticed that before? Also, their eyes which had appeared pale blue when they had removed the out-sized sunglasses as the sun set, had morphed into a peculiar reddish purple. He had to be wrong about that. He looked at Dirk who was looking from one girl to the other in bewilderment.

"No, we must let nothing spoil this beautiful night," purred the girls in unison. It was astonishing to hear them speak with one voice. "You have been the perfect dates. You have so kindly given us a ride home, and you have also brought us dinner."

So dumbstruck were Carlo and Dirk that neither felt the sly prick in his neck nor did either notice for several minutes the soft but insistent ebbing of the blood from their veins and by then, of course, it was way too late.

Blank Slate Writers Group

Short Story

The Fantasy Lottery
Christina Ortega Phillips

—for JT—

I do not have a lot of time. I wish I could begin with a clever hook like I was taught in school or some kind of brilliant quote, but the sand in the metaphorical hourglass is running low and I must begin and finish as quickly as I can.

My name is Jose Trujillo. Just a few short weeks ago I was a happily married man with an awesome son and an annoying dog. But that's all changed. My only hope, no, our only hope is that someone finds this and can fix what I helped to mess up.

One day I was in the local smoke shop buying a pack of Marlboro Lights when I found an extra five dollar bill in my wallet.

"Give me some scratch offs, too," I told the lady behind the counter.

"What kind do you want?" she asked, moving behind the card display.

"What's new?"

She pointed at the number nine scratchers.

"OK, give me five of those."

After putting the cards in my pocket, I left, packing my smokes as I walked out. I forgot about them, though, since I had to pick up my son from the sitter's and when we got home he was in a playful mood. After an exhausting game of Legos and reading him not one but two bedtime stories,

Night Light
Christina Ortega Phillips

I finally had a few moments to myself. Before sitting down to watch TV, I emptied my pockets onto the coffee table and saw the cards. I sifted through the pile of pocket change I had just emptied to find a nickel to scratch them with; I always use nickels on scratch off cards because it's good luck. Or at least I thought it was.

The cards seemed normal enough. They were called Fantasy Lottery and the idea was simple: if you scratched and found three of a kind, you won. The images, of course, were all fantasy-themed: castles, dragons, gnomes, elves, unicorns, fairies, magic wands and, well, you get the point.

Scratching the first two cards revealed only a jumble of mismatched symbols. The third card, however, revealed three gnomes; the last two were duds just like the first two.

"Ugly little things," I mumbled, looking closer at the gnomes. I read the card, trying to find out how much the gnomes had won me, but it didn't say anywhere. There was no explanation of the prizes on the back of the card either. I tossed the cards down on the coffee table, telling myself I'd take it to the smoke shop the next day to see what I'd won. Of course, with a wife and kid one's time is not always their own and it took me a week to get back to the smoke shop.

"I'm sorry, sir," the same lady told me when I finally made it to the store. "We decided to stop selling those cards for the same reason that you're here. Others have complained about not knowing what they've won. If I were you, I'd mail that card in to the company. I'll give you their address."

I frowned. Spending even some change on postage seemed like a waste, especially if the prize was only a dollar. Those ugly little gnomes couldn't have been worth much. No wonder the shop decided to not sell those scratch cards anymore. But I was curious, so I mailed in the winning card anyway.

Blank Slate Writers Group
The Fantasy Lottery

A few weeks later, my wife and kid and dog were all set to go on a vacation to see her mother. I had been unable to take time off work to go with them, so the plan was for them to go on without me this way my wife could have some relaxing time to herself, her mom could bond with the baby and the dog could enjoy running around my mother-in-law's land.

I had nearly forgotten about the lottery cards until a couple days after my family left town. I was awoken on a Saturday at four a.m. by an unexpected knock at my door. Needless to say, I had been looking forward to sleeping in for the first time in a long time and was less than happy to be disturbed.

I grumpily went to answer it; I had tried to ignore it, but the knock only grew louder in persistency. Opening the door let in nothing but moonlight and the smell of dawn about to break. There was no one there. I had only closed the door but a second when the knock continued. Opening the door a second time still showed no one; I went to close the door again, but this time, a gruff voice stopped me.

"Hey, buddy," it called, "down here."

I looked down to see an odd-looking smaller than usual old midget peering up at me. I blinked in surprise. The midget stood there, about two feet tall with rough looking skin and a face that made me think he was at least seventy years old. He was wearing a t-shirt under a pair of overalls and a matching pointed hat.

"Who are you? What are you?" I demanded.

"I'm Belkin and I'm a gnome, dumbass."

I just stared back at him.

"You won me, remember?"

"Is this some kind of joke? Did Chris put you up to this?"

"I don't know a Chris. But you won me, so here I am," with that, he pushed past me and walked into my home.

Night Light
Christina Ortega Phillips

"Hey, what are you doing?" I asked, following him into my kitchen. He was looking through the cabinets that he could reach, for what I don't know. He ignored me and continued his search until I grabbed him by his shoulders and forced him to face me.

"Seriously—what are you doing here? What is going on?"

Belkin sighed. "A few weeks ago you played the Fantasy Lottery. Do you remember that?"

I nodded.

"You," he continued slowly, "mailed in your winning card with three gnomes. You won me. So here I am."

I blinked, trying to remember the card. I remembered them, but there hadn't been any information about prizes on them. Who in the world would send me a gnome? Surely this was a joke. "I won you?"

"Yes and now here I am. Yours to keep for three weeks."

"But—you're not real," I mumbled, trying to take it all in.

Before I could stop him, the little gnome delivered a swift kick to my shin—a hard one. I screamed in pain, grabbing my leg.

"Did that feel real enough for you?" the gnome snapped.

I scowled at him. "What the hell am I supposed to do with you for three weeks? And why only three weeks?"

"Because you can't even think of what to do with me for three weeks so why would I want to stay with your dumbass for longer?" Belkin retorted.

I raised my hand to hit him, but he ducked out of the way.

"Hell if I know, buddy," he said, still standing out of my reach. "You can't be selfish and keep me forever. There are only so many of us, you know. After here, I'll be sent to stay with another winner."

Blank Slate Writers Group
The Fantasy Lottery

"There are more of you? Do they all look like you? I mean, I never heard of a cute gnome, but damn."

I shouldn't have said that. That remark made him run across the kitchen to me and earned me another hard kick in the shin. This time, I grabbed him before he could back away and carried him to the refrigerator where I put him on the top of it and left him there.

I went into the living room with Belkin shouting after me to get him down. I began to pace and think. What was going on? This had to be a joke. But I didn't remember ever telling any of my friends about the lottery cards. Was this real? The pain in my shin said it was. A gnome?

After a few minutes of pacing I went back into the kitchen to talk to Belkin.

"So…, you're a gnome?" I asked slowly.

Belkin rolled his eyes. "Is there a helmet around here you should be wearing? Yes, I am a gnome."

I ignored his rudeness and continued, "So do you fight? Like a warrior? Do you hate elves, because that one guy in the Lord of the—"

Belkin cut me off, "That was a dwarf!"

"So you protect pots of gold?"

"That's leprechauns!" Belkin cried out, exasperated.

"So you… you decorate lawns?"

"Really?"

"You know, those little statues people have in their yards and gardens. Those are gnomes like you, right?"

"Kind of," he muttered, but he refused to talk anymore about the lawn gnome statues.

Belkin and I took the next few days getting to know each other. I was full of questions about his species and wanted to learn everything I could; he seemed to enjoy talking about his kind but wouldn't talk about the statues at all. I let it go and also in turn answered questions he had about humans and my side of the world.

79

Night Light
Christina Ortega Phillips

I learned that gnomes are elementals or nature spirits who had the ability to change into the size of giants if they needed or wanted. I also learned that they are earth dwellers, able to move through the earth and soil as easily as humans walk about the world.

Later that night Belkin went on his nightly walk. He said he enjoyed being in my side of the world and had to take advantage of it at night since exposure to sunlight would turn him to stone.

I wasn't tired; my mind was too full of all the information I had filled it with over the past few days. I turned on the news—and that's when I had an idea of what to do with Belkin for the rest of the time he would be staying with me: a local story was covering a bank robbery that day. It went into detail about who had been apprehended for the failed job. Then I began to think: if someone could dig a tunnel underground, drill up to the vault and then cover the tunnel back up—well, that just seemed like the perfect crime. I had originally played the Fantasy Lottery as a way to get some extra money. Maybe winning someone who could walk as easily through the earth as I could sunlight was fate's backhanded way of helping me get some extra money. But how would I ask Belkin to do the job?

The rest of the news was about other local stores about thefts and vandalism, but I was too busy plotting to pay attention.

The next morning I decided to be bold and just flat out bring up the idea to Belkin. I was surprised when he agreed.

"I'll help you," he replied, "but I need two things from you in return."

Without hesitation, I agreed. I mean, he was a tiny little gnome; what could he want that would've been so bad?

"I need to invite over some of my friends to help me," he explained, "So there may be more of us here for a

Blank Slate Writers Group
The Fantasy Lottery

while. It will take some time to do the job and this way it will be done faster. Also, it will be easier if those of us who are carrying the money out of the vault could do just that and others could cover up the tunnel. The second thing is that I'm going to ask you for an odd favor in return. But you can't ask any questions about it; you just have to do it."

OK, the second request sounded odd but I had already put my foot in my mouth and had agreed to help him so I was stuck. The request, actually, at the time was odd, but I did not think anything of it: he wanted me to go around the city and collect everyone's lawn gnomes. I completely misunderstood his reasoning; I thought they were just offensive to him in some way the same way other statues are offensive to other cultures. How was I supposed to know I was wrong?

So we both set about our jobs: I would sneak out at night and collect lawn gnomes, storing them in my basement, and he invited some of his friends over and they began to work on a tunnel system to three local banks. It all seemed to be going so smoothly. That is, until the day of the break-ins. That is when everything fell apart...

Belkin and his gnome friends made amazing time in tunneling to three different vaults. Since they were underground they could work as long as they wanted around the clock; I was the one who could only work at night. I felt like a teenager again pranking the neighbors. Anyway, his group went about their job: they all traveled to the three banks, each team was able to enter their respective vaults, fill up laundry bags of cash and as they made their way back to my home with the loot, three separate teams worked hard to refill the tunnels to cover their tracks. The refilling was faster than the digging so that took less time than the digging. By this time, my basement and my shed and garage were too full of lawn gnomes; I felt like a focused hoarder. I must have dozed off while waiting for Belkin and everyone to return

81

Night Light
Christina Ortega Phillips

because when I woke up I was not just laid out on my couch; I was sitting upright in a chair and tightly tied to it complete with a gag in my mouth.

I struggled against the rope, grunting and making as much noise and movement as I possibly could.

"Shh," a gruff voice told me. I turned in the direction of the voice to see Belkin watching me with a gleam in his eyes. I raised my eyebrows in a sad attempt to ask him what was going on. He must have understood because he began to talk:

"Almost a hundred years ago, there was a warlock named Hemlock. He was quite powerful. Everyone feared him. We respected his talent, but Hemlock's personality preferred fear and because of his talent and actions we gave it. He hated gnomes. Man, did he hate gnomes. There was no reason behind it; he just looked down on us more than any other of the creatures. He hated us," Belkin punctuated this last line with a long sigh. "Eventually Hemlock decided to get rid of what he despised. He tricked us all; he tricked us all into the sun knowing that a single ray of sunlight would turn us to stone. We thaw slowly, though. We thaw slowly and become able to move and turn back into our old selves if we are out of the sunlight for long enough. However, with the cycle of the moon and the sun, by the time we are almost completely thawed out, the sun begins to rise and we turn back to stone."

I just stared at Belkin, trying to work out everything he had said and hadn't said in my head. If all the gnome statues needed was to be out of the sunlight long enough, then all the statues in my basement, garage and shed were no longer statues...

"Eventually a few of us were able to get out of the sun to no longer be stone statues, but you don't need to know how," Belkin continued. "So we banded together in hiding and plotted. How could our kind be fruitful again? You humans, you're all so materialistic and all about the

82

Blank Slate Writers Group
The Fantasy Lottery

money." Here he began to laugh. "You were all so easy to trick; a Fantasy Lottery in which all the winners won gnomes. For the past three weeks everywhere cities have been infested with gnomes, pretending to help greedy folks like you rob their local banks for money while we tricked you into helping us save our kind."

Belkin grinned at me, enjoying seeing me held down and not able to fully show him my anger he knew I was feeling. The only part that made me not feel like a total idiot was the fact that I was not the only one whom these gnomes had tricked. So I had to sit there and listen to Belkin gloat about how greedy humans were and how stupid we were to trust gnomes to help them steal when one of their main characteristics was their protecting gems and treasures; why would they steal from banks for a human?

I was not filled in on the rest of the plan, but all I knew is that they were tired of being merely earth dwellers and had nothing but anger at the stupid human race who would use them as nothing but lawn decorations. All I know is that the gnomes who were hanging around at my home were all a buzz with excitement at the way that their plan was going along so far. I did not know what else they planned to do other than to make it so they could live on the earth without worrying about the sun or humans.

That is the last I heard before they loosened up the ropes around my body and threw me and some random supplies down under ground. I have no idea how the rest of their plan went nor do I know how far down I am or the fate of the rest of my species. I only know that I am running out of air and all I could do is write down what I know so that if someone finds this they may have a chance at defeating these evil gnomes who used something as simple as a lottery to trick us all. Maybe I'll get lucky and when my family comes home the dog will dig me up and my son will read this and save us all.

83

Night Light
Christina Ortega Phillips

Breathing is becoming painful now and everything is growing dark...darker than it already was down here in the earth. But before I can rest I have to give my readers one final bit, something I overheard as they were carrying me to what I now know will be my grave; I hope whoever reads this will use this gem of information wisely. You need to know that gnomes...

Blank Slate Writers Group

Poem

It's Just Her Nature
Mel Braun

Flee Krakatoa
She's waited years to cut loose
She'll rage to her end

Flee Krakatoa
The seas still, then tsunami
Washing clean the world

Flee Krakatoa
Repression never healed her
Freedom kills us all

Flee Krakatoa
Ash reigns the sky, land and sea
Verdant future waits

Blank Slate Writers Group

Short Story

Traveling Companions
Joyce Hicks

"How are you, Sarah?" The speaker appeared to look out the train window, but his attention was turned inward to the woman on his phone.

"That's good to hear," he said, his genteel tones intertwining with the genteel suburbs that slipped by. Was he unaware that his conversation had become part of the landscape for his rail companions?

For Sunny across the aisle, the conversation of the handsome stranger was her total focus. With his silver hair and trim features, he radiated confidence and good manners—a man very unlike her ex. Reading a magazine, she turned slightly toward him to maximize the effects of her artful makeup and new blunt cut.

Another man sat near Sunny in front of the man with the phone, but she had checked him off immediately, a very married-looking guy with a stained shoulder pack that lay beside him like a tired dog. In truth, her assessment of Carl was right. His wife, his wife's mother, or his mother took up all of his spare time.

In front of Sunny sat Pat, who also took in the phone call. If this joker chose to talk in public, she would listen because everything was open for her inspection on this little junket into *posh*, as she called the western suburbs. Though her new jacket was only a suede-look, still it made her feel she blended in.

Night Light
Joyce Hicks

"No, I'm on the train. I was in town for court this morning," the man with the phone continued. His companion passengers listened and assessed.

Mmmm, maybe a high-profile CEO, ripe for picking. No wedding ring. Nice suit. (Sunny)

A doctor. Excuse me, physician, wriggling out of a malpractice case. His suit cost more than my rent. (Pat)

Italian suit. Not until I make partner. If ever. (Carl)

"Nothing interesting, Sarah. Not really." He loosened his tie while talking.

Agreed, pal. Most law is slow death. How am I going to hang on through a 25-year mortgage? This guy, he's got junior partners, paralegals, and interns, like Nicole. Those black jeans. I didn't hit on her, technically. (Carl)

Who is this Sarah? Not his ex. A girlfriend? (Sunny)

Right, nothing interesting, just somebody's mother on life-support with a punctured lung. (Pat)

"How's it going with Wallace?" He tipped his head back, closing his eyes.

Oh, talking to his daughter, from marriage number two! She's got boyfriend trouble, and he's all sympathetic and fatherly. First marriage daughter—he didn't even notice if she had a boyfriend. (Pat)

The guy's on a fishing expedition. Is sister Sarah doing what she's supposed to be? Working at Wallace, doing rehab at Wallace, or supervising Wally, her delinquent kid? (Carl)

So, Sarah's not a girlfriend . . .Maybe Wallace is her lawn service or her psychiatrist. (Sunny)

"Oh. Really. Uh-huh. Better to find out now than later, right?" He examined his watch for scratches.

So, this is just some difficult woman he knows. I need to make eye contact. (Sunny)

Come on, honey, look on the bright side. The guy was a loser, but don't even think of moving back home. (Pat)

Yadda, yadda, yadda. She just couldn't help it. This is the last time, she promises. (Carl)

Blank Slate Writers Group
Travelling Companions

"Hey, don't take it that way. I'm sure you know best. But look, you're not in a hurry." From between bills in a money clip, he pulled out a photo and studied it.

Yeah, take your time. You'll find out how much men go for 40ish women who were not in a hurry. (Sunny)

He's trying to remember if her room is still pink. (Pat)

The guy's gonna have to write a big check for this one. (Carl)

"I know, I know it's easy for me to say." He began refolding the money.

Because he's a man. (Sunny)

Because he doesn't have a clue. (Pat)

Because he's the successful one. (Carl)

"Yes, mother is fine. You know, I've been wanting to get her a new car." He put the clip away just as Sunny stretched toward him as if to look out the opposite window.

Full head of hair, but so jowly. God, what I don't need is another man in love with his mother. (Sunny)

His mother still drives? That guy is older than dirt. (Pat)

Maybe she's on a fixed income. (Carl)

"I saw this Mercedes station wagon when I took the Jag in for service. It was perfect." He turned to watch a white Aston Martin paralleling the train for a block.

A Mercedes for mom, even if it is a station wagon. And he has a Jag. Maybe a Sugar Daddy is the way to go. Let me check the Personals here . . .What page is that? (Sunny)

Of course, just what the doctor ordered, a Mercedes for your mommy. Never mind the woman on life support while you were out tooling around in the Jag. (Pat)

I have to drive mother to the podiatrist on Saturday. (Carl)

"Has she said anything to you about liking it? She wouldn't say anything to me, of course." The man patted his pocket for the money clip, confirming it was there.

You'll never be good enough, even if you give her ten Mercedes. (Carl)

Maybe Sarah's a relative. (Sunny)

So mom's a bitch, huh. (Pat)

Night Light
Joyce Hicks

"She's going to try another winter in California. Bridge. Golf. Maybe a cruise."

"Senior gentleman on Hilton Head looking for long-term relationship with NS ages 30-50, weight appropriate for height. Travel, gourmet cooking, walks on the beach." (Sunny)

We pass one more of these cutesy village greens and I'm going to throw up. (Pat)

Pal, you're gonna be stuck with Sarah. (Carl)

"Yes, I loved the birthday tie. Yes, absolutely. Perfect color. No, I am sure. W-e-l-l, I'll be looking forward to meeting your. . .your Chihuahuas at Thanksgiving. G'bye."

I'll bet you are. (Sunny)

They are kind of cute. (Pat)

Chihuahuas too, tough one, buddy. (Carl)

The foursome gathered their belongings at the announcement for Hinsdale. Carl slung his pack on his shoulder. Sunny slid ahead of Carl, her figure almost girlish in a turquoise suit. Pat hustled into her jacket and dragged a tapestry suitcase into the aisle. His phone put away, the man glanced politely at the three, puzzled that they lingered on their way to the exit.

Carl reached out to grip his shoulder briefly in passing.

Pat glared at him as her suitcase banged his knee.

Sunny dropped her magazine at his feet.

Blank Slate Writers Group

Poem

The Ballad of Don Alphonzo
Olga M. Zulich

A sadder tale you will never hear
In the annals of tragedy
Than the tale of the brave and lusty rake,
Don Alphonzo of Napoli.

The Don was a leader, a prince among men
Whose exploits left his listeners aghast
No woman was safe from his silken charm
Each seduction more smooth than the last.

"Lock up your daughters!" his cohorts would say
As they winked at his amorous glories
But this was said half in jest for not one of them
Would want their child to be part of his stories.

On that fateful night in a warm July
The Don picked up Miss Brandi La Fleur
After her stint on the stage as the star
Of "The Naked Follies du Jour"

The Don was enthralled by the outlandish curves
That Brandi displayed on stage nightly
In costumes so slight they were near out of sight
As her earnings grew greater (quite rightly.)

Night Light
Olga M. Zulich

The Don seldom stayed with one woman for long
But Miss Brandi went straight to his heart
This stripper, though vapid, caused a pulse rate so rapid
He vowed they never should part

He escorted the ravishing Brandi that night
To the top of Hotel Magnifique
In his pocket a rare and valuable coin
A half million dollar antique

The lights of the city twinkled below
The breeze was warm and electric with promise.
Soon the waiter appeared with champagne and a smile
And announced to them, "My name is Thomas."

The Don gripped the box with the golden coin
As Thomas poured champagne quite slowly
Brandi giggled and smiled at the handsome young man.
Her thoughts were somewhat less than holy.

She leaned toward the waiter and winked openly
Her cleavage appeared quite astounding.
To Thomas she seemed such a sensual dream
His heart began frantically pounding.

The Don in most things was a reasonable man
But with Brandi his heart ruled his head.
"Thanks for the champagne, no need to remain.
We'd prefer some privacy instead."

To anyone with a brain, there's no need to explain
When to step back and let things just settle.
But Brandi was filled with a sense of her power
And she wanted to test the Don's mettle.

Blank Slate Writers Group
The Ballad of Don Alphonzo

"Come here for a moment, Thomas, my dear,
You've a spot on the back of your pants."
And with her jeweled hand she patted his tush
Pleased at the Don's angry glance.

Well, sad to say, this tale doesn't end well
It quite rattled all their affairs:
Thomas, in flight from the Don's righteous might
Stumbled and rolled down the stairs.

He wasn't hurt badly, but still a bit sadly
Never waited on tables again.
That's the customers' loss, for he soon became boss
At a soup kitchen for homeless men.

The Don saw the folly of pursuing a dolly
Whose body's her sole claim to fame.
He chucked the fair Brandi, who still is eye candy
But he found life thereafter quite tame.

Brandi danced on with less and less verve
She went through men like tissues, alas.
She never found out of the fortune she blew
Just by patting a suave waiter's ass.

Blank Slate Writers Group

Short Story

Prion
Marilyn Kosmatka

In the last few moments of sleep, when the noise of cars and cats and ticking clocks were just beginning to make themselves known to the world of dreams, a thing awoke inside the man.

Its name was Prion.

Its mission was torture and murder.

Like its cousins—Mad Cow Disease, Chronic Wasting Syndrome and Creutzfeldt - Jakob disease—it loved the brain of its victim. It wanted nothing more than the pleasure of turning dense, firm tissue into hole-riddled, useless sponge.

Unlike its cousins, it did not travel from host to victim via the food chain. No, it wasn't the love of a big, juicy burger that gave it a chance at wrecking havoc. It was the love of a man and a woman. The act of procreation.

It was a gift, bequeathed at conception, hidden deep within Chromosome 20.

For decades, it had waited for this moment. The man, unaware of its existence, had passed Prion's offspring to his own. A brown haired little girl with a love of flowers and puppies was awaiting the day her own mutated protein would wake.

If a protein could laugh or shout for joy, Prion would have done so. Instead, it made its first big change.

The man was no longer happy and satisfied. He was, from this moment forward, clinically depressed. He was incapable of knowing pleasure.

Night Light
Marilyn Kosmatka

Prion vibrated with excitement, then forced itself to calm. This would be enough for now. In a month, maybe two, the real fun could begin.

The real fun.

For a year, two years, three at the most, Prion could play. It could replace asparagine-178 and amino acid-129 with aspartic acid and methionine. It could clog the thalamus with plaques, destroying the small gland that gave mankind its ability to dream and restore its balance.

Insomnia was coming to the man. No more sleep. Day-after-day, month-after-month, the man would not know the peace of one moment of sleep. He would be plagued with panic attacks, paranoia, and phobias. Hallucinations would haunt him. Dementia. Insanity. The humiliation of messing and wetting himself was his future.

Yes, the man would be broken, his soul shredded. He would crumble. And in the end he would be but a shell, incapable of thought or speech.

The tiny protein contemplated this for a moment. It was going to be a wonderful year or so.

Prion had but one regret.

The man would die, and when he did, so did Prion. Fatal Familial Insomnia was indeed a fast train to hell.

Ah... but what a way to go.

Blank Slate Writers Group

Short Story

A Shady Grove Welcome
Mike Ripley

The sun hovered in the center of the sky as I pulled into Shady Grove and parked in front of Jack's Place. A row of shops and restaurants lined both sides of Main Street, each displaying large windows, designed to welcome tourists and guests. I walked into Jack's and browsed a while amongst antique toys and furniture that appeared to be in perfect condition. I paused next to a Singer sewing machine that had a partially completed quilt draped through its needle guides and ran my finger along the curved stitches in the colorful fabric.

"Road to Arkansas," a man said as he held out his hand.

"I didn't see you there," I answered, and I reached out to welcome his grip. "It's like the one my grandmother had. You know all about it?"

"I know my way around everything in here," the man said. "I'm Jack. It's my place, and like all the gems you'll find here, the sewing machine still works like a champ. Some ladies stop in here from time to time and pedal a bit on that old quilt. That's the only reason I knew what it's called."

"Road to Arkansas?"

"Yeah, that's what they tell me." Jack saw another customer and turned to acknowledge him. When he stepped aside, I noticed a woman standing behind a counter wearing a yellow dress. She looked like somebody I'd seen in a magazine or movie, never in person.

97

Night Light
Mike Ripley

"That's my wife," Jack said, looking back at me. "She kept coming in here all the time and I finally asked her to stay. Really something, isn't she?"

"What you telling him, Jack?" she asked from across the way.

"Her name's Grace," Jack said to me. "Let me see what this other fella over there needs and Grace will take care of you."

I walked toward the counter.

"Like what you see?" Grace asked.

"Yes I do. There's something on that shelf behind you that I can't really believe I'm seeing at all."

"Where?"

"Second from the top, right in the middle. It's copper or brass color and it's turned sideways. You see it? I think it is a bust of JFK and if I'm right it'll wind up being a bank."

Grace couldn't quite reach it as her fingertips grazed its side, nudging it further back on the shelf. I noticed her stretching and standing on the toes of high heeled shoes that matched the color of her dress.

Jack came up from behind and smacked me on the back. "Like I said, she's something, isn't she?"

"You're the tallest," Grace said to me. "You come around here and get the thing down."

As I walked around the end of the counter I heard the bell ring that hung over the front door. I reached the Kennedy bank easily and pulled it down. A man came toward us, more stomping than walking. He pulled a hat off his head and shook it like it was wet.

"Been some accident up on the highway," he told Jack. "It's raining something big up there."

"Yeah, I figured as much," Jack replied and nodded toward the other man milling around the store and then back in my direction. "This is Marty," he said to me, introducing the man with the hat. I looked outside. The sun was shining bright.

Blank Slate Writers Group
A Shady Grove Welcome

"Nice to meet you," Marty said. "You new here?"

"No. I'm just passing through. Nice little town. My wife and I like finding places like this."

"So you have a wife," Grace said. "Where is she?"

"She's here, somewhere. She probably ran next door or into the shop next to that one. She usually moves pretty quick. I don't try to keep up. I'll take this bank. It's just like one I had when I was a kid. The lock on the opening is broke just like mine was. Lost the key. Most kids who had one probably lost the key and had to break it. How much?"

"Don't worry about it," Jack answered. "Didn't even know it was here."

"You won't hear that from old Jack often," Marty said. "Better take him up on it," and he turned away, walking toward the other man in the store, waving his hat as he approached him.

"Better find the wife," I told Jack. "You sure I can't pay you something for this bank?"

"No, I said don't worry about it."

Grace sat down on a stool behind the counter. I nodded to her and watched her cross her legs. She looked so familiar. "I better get going," I told her.

"I guess you better," she replied.

Jack put his arm on my shoulder and walked me toward the door. "You should stop down at the welcome center. They can give you a lot of information about these parts."

"No, we're probably going to get going down the highway again. Just stopped to check the town out, I guess. I better find my wife."

"OK, but you think about it. It's just across the road and right down that way." He held the door open and pointed along the street.

"Thanks for this," I said, holding up the bank. I looked the other way, wondering where Jean would have gone. I didn't see her get out of the car. She couldn't have

Night Light
Mike Ripley

gone far. Then I looked back and saw the white building Jack had pointed to. A sign hung from two chains beneath the awning that cast a big shadow from the mid-day sun onto the sidewalk below. The capital letters spelled, 'WELCOME CENTER.' I thought maybe I'd better check it out, after all.

Blank Slate Writers Group

Poem

Absence
Bob Moulesong

The old man sprinkled Cheerios as pigeons gathered on
the grass. He fed them daily, rain or shine. The
pigeons flocked, cooed, and ate.

He used to tease her about talking to birds. He wished he
could tease her now.

He sighed as he sprinkled.

102

Blank Slate Writers Group

Poem

Half Breed
Mel Braun

Toes drag
through pea gravel.
Chains twist,
untwist, jerk
into another spiral.

Tensions charge
the air around
this mid night
assembly.
Boy, girl,
boy, boy, girl facing
you on the swing.

It doesn't mean
anything, stress
on the mean.
You look over
their shoulders,
past the expectant
faces.

Summer half spent
and you are half virgin;
almost there, almost
not. A peculiar half
breed in this vacant
play ground,
in this vacant company.

Blank Slate Writers Group

Poem

A Dark and Stormy Night
Bob Moulesong

It was a dark and stormy night. The wind howled, the thunder boomed, and the lightning flashed.

The little boy's eyes flitted nervously as he scooted closer to Dad on the couch. Dad gently patted his son's shoulder. The boy hoped the storm would soon pass.

Dad prayed for rain.

Short Story

Class of 1980
Rich Elliott

It started innocently, the way all trouble starts. She had sent him a friend request on Facebook, and he, curious and bemused, had confirmed her request. Then there were several back and forth posts of getting caught up and "Do you remember when?"

Then the gifts started.

The woman was Delores Hackbarth, née Brown, formerly of River Town, Illinois, where she had been the high school's Prom Queen in 1980. He was Harold Dale, the school's Prom King of that year.

Harold had also been the conference pole vault champion and had proudly worn the River Town Butterflies letter jacket. (School motto: "Float like a butterfly, sting like a bee.")

He and Delores had dated for several torrid weeks at the end of their senior year. After graduation, Harold left for Grinnell College, where he majored in accounting, and Delores went to the local junior college, her plan of study "undecided." The two quickly lost contact.

Delores was now the manager of several White Castle restaurants in Chicago. From her picture on Facebook she still looked as beautiful as she was on Prom Night, and in fact, the picture was her Prom photo.

Harold was now an accountant at the Chicago consulting firm Ernst and Young. His hair was thinning, he had bags under his eyes, and he was forty pounds over his weight from his track days, but he still got his miles in when his knees weren't barking.

Night Light
Mike Ripley

The first gift that Delores sent him was a small acrylic painting of River Town's old Eads Bridge and the Mississippi River at sunset. Delores had painted it. The painting struck Harold as gaudy and childlike, but he was touched.

"Thanks for your beautiful painting," he texted her.

This gift was followed in quick succession by two more—a pair of silver cufflinks each engraved with a butterfly; and then an old illustrated edition of Longfellow's *The Song of Hiawatha*. Delores remembered that Harold had liked Longfellow's poetry when they studied him in their American Lit class, a fact which the track star shared with her and no one else.

A week went by, and then a large box arrived, another gift. Harold opened it to find a 2' x 3' photograph of him clearing the pole vault bar in the conference track meet. Delores had PhotoShopped the image so that it looked like a watercolor. Harold's head and arms were thrown back, his long hair flying back, and you could see part of the butterfly logo on his jersey.

By now Harold's wife Vicky was truly and thoroughly pissed. She shared an email account with her husband so she was aware of the posts between Harold and Delores. She had indulged her husband initially, the posts seemed harmless enough, the former girlfriend was obviously a little pathetic. But the giant framed photo of her husband was the last straw.

"Tell this bitch to stop, Harold!" Vicky stormed. "She's some kind of nutcase. Didn't you ever see *Fatal Attraction*?"

He told his wife he would talk to Delores.

* * *

Harold used his hour-long runs to help him clear his mind. During his jogs he would try to stay in the moment. He focused on his breathing and his cadence. As thoughts

Blank Slate Writers Group
A Shady Grove Welcome

popped up, he tried to calmly watch them slide by. It was amazing how, on his Zen runs, his problems often resolved themselves with no effort.

As always, Harold thought for awhile about his accounting work where the spreadsheets seemed never-ending and where his new boss was turning out to be a jerk.

On the home front, there was his son's struggles at school. The principal had called wanting to talk about "an issue" that had come up in class. And now Vicky seemed to have a bee in her bonnet about this old girlfriend.

Breathe, Harold told himself, and watch the trees.

Harold thought about Delores. Yes, no doubt, she was acting pretty weird. He was stupid for encouraging her. He'd have to de-friend her or something.

But that picture of the Mississippi, it sure brought back memories. Those parties they used to have down there under the bridge! They'd drink beer and listen to music on the radio and watch the barges slide by in the moonlight.

And the photo of Harold flying over the pole vault bar. Damn, he really had it going that day. Broke the conference record. There's nothing quite like that feeling of weightlessness at the very top of your vault. And your chest barely grazes the bar, but it stays on. God, what a feeling!

* * *

The next day Harold went on Facebook and told Delores that they needed to meet. He didn't explain, but he knew that once they met, they would see how ridiculous it all was, and they'd go their separate ways, this time forever.

"Where do you want to meet?" Harold typed.

"How about at the White Castle?" Delores replied.

Night Light
Mike Ripley

"You mean, at one of your restaurants?" he questioned.

"No, I mean at the old Water Tower on Michigan Avenue."

"What time?"

"How about tomorrow at midnight? I work late."

Shit, thought Harold. Well, whatever. "Way past my bedtime, Delores, but OK."

When Harold met Delores downtown outside the Water Tower at midnight, they smiled and gave at each other an awkward hug. They did a good job of hiding their letdown. Delores had lost her Prom Queen good looks and figure. Harold, the once-handsome varsity letterman, was barely recognizable.

"Let's go in," Delores said, nodding towards the Water Tower.

"What, you have the keys? To the Water Tower?"

Delores explained that the original design for the White Castle restaurant was based on Chicago's famous Water Tower. "It's a long story, but some of the top managers can get the keys to this place. One of the perks of my job."

Delores thumbed through a set of old keys on a brass ring, opening doors inside the Tower. The sounds echoed inside the stone walls. She opened a third door and flicked on a light that illuminated a narrow staircase. They trekked up the stairs, the stone walls on either side pressing in on them. Delores and Harold emerged onto the rooftop and walked to the limestone parapet that overlooked Michigan Avenue.

I need to get this over with right now, Harold thought to himself.

"Gosh, Delores, it's great seeing you. You look terrific! And those gifts you sent. You put so much thought into them! We do have a lot of memories, don't we? But I should tell you, I love my wife."

Blank Slate Writers Group
A Shady Grove Welcome

"Oh, just shut up for a second," Delores was pulling something out of her pocket. "Here, I brought you another present." She handed him a card.

On the card was a badly drawn picture of a butterfly hovering near a cocoon. Below the picture there were a few lines of poetry:

A new butterfly
And a cocoon on a branch
Both of them waiting.

Harold stared at the card.

"It's sappy, I know," Delores commented. She was fishing in her purse and brought out two Budweisers, popped the tops, and gave one to Harold. "To old times," she said.

They looked out over Michigan Avenue and sipped their beers. They breathed in the night air. In Chicago after midnight on Michigan Avenue, the clattering crowds of people thin out, and the screech and grind from the traffic subsides. The inexorable current of cars and souls slows down, glides silently, marking time, like the water of the wide Mississippi.

Blank Slate Writers Group

Short Story

Resistance
R = V / I
John Schaub

V

Electric potential between two points. At the metallic bang she looks across the parking lot, at him with a shopping cart against his truck door, his smile unembarrassed. Her stomach jumps and she smiles at the ground, her hands, at the coupon for half-price tomatoes that she concentrates on reading again.

I

Electric current. At the lingering drone of an engine, she pulls back the curtain. Her stomach sparks as his truck cruises down her street, makes a U-turn, pauses in front of her house.

R

Resistance is potential divided by current. She drops the curtain and breathes deeply, counts backward from ten. Remembers last year, how hard she fell for Dave, her dread at going out after he left her. She bites her nails, her stomach tight, and waits behind the curtain. Her breath quickens at the metal creak of hinges.

Short Story

Jocelyn Dreams
Mel Braun

Vaughn and I just watched, mouths hanging open, as the manager of the IGA walked up, nice as you please and started wrapping pink price tape around momma's mouth. One minute momma is tearing me a new one because I didn't put the "new and improved" dish soap in the cart, and the next minute here's Mr. Tuttle making a pink mummy head on aisle five.

Then it was back to momma screaming about 'it takes grease out of your way.'

"Do you really want grease in your way? I don't think so!" she screeches. No, I can't really be that stupid, blah, blah, blah. If I could just sink into my clogs, I'd be happy as a clam.

Vaughn and I pushed the cart as momma railed on about my levels of ignorance. If it weren't for the security cameras hidden in those smoky half globes, I believe she really would knock my block off.

Invisibility is really the greatest of all the superpowers, if you can just pick one. That's what I told Vaughn. He thinks it's invincibility, but that's just because he's got nice parents.

"Sure, bullets bounce off," I concede as we unload the groceries from the trunk of the Vega, "but you can still hear all the mean stuff people say. I'm sticking with invisibility." But when you drop the cream of tomato they can see you again.

Night Light
Mel Braun

"I don't know how you even manage to walk across the room, you are so clumsy. There is no way you can be my daughter! It's not genetically possible. I think I brought home the wrong baby." After the quiet drive home momma was wound up for another round.

Vaughn snuck out of the kitchen as momma caught her reflection in the sliding glass doors. "I was a dancer, you know. I could of really had a career. If I hadn't met EU-gene. If I hadn't got pregnant with you." Momma's downhill spiral always begins with meeting daddy, the beginning of her end.

Daddy walked into the kitchen and stooped to help me pick up the spilled canned goods. "Don't listen to her, Kitten. You're just going through an awkward phase. It will pass," he whispered. We shared a grin as he stacked the corn.

I blinked back the tears and it was just mom and me in the kitchen, poor put-upon Birdie who never got the chance, and her troglodyte burden—Jocelyn. Dad was still nursing his Pabst Blue Ribbon in the den, watching the game in his Naugahyde recliner. Where he always was. I put away the rest of the groceries by myself.

Being an only child there is no chance to be graded on the curve, ever. Not that Birdie would allow it. 'Doing your best' was OK, if your best was 100%. My best was more like a C+. Being average was fine with me; that was like being invisible at school. At home it was a-whole-'nother-story. When mom saw that I was satisfied with 75%, she took it personal. She cut my allowance to 75%, sent only three fourths of a sandwich in my lunch, and didn't get my clothes quite as clean anymore. The lunch thing I didn't mind because I mooched from Tammy Sue and Vaughn mostly anyways. Did she really think I was eating all those tuna fish sandwiches? But going into middle school with stains and B.O. was too gross.

Blank Slate Writers Group
Jocelyn Dreams

When I got to science lab, Sarah and the Sneer Leaders started holding their noses and gagging as I walked past. I guess the Love's Baby Soft wasn't fooling anyone. Mom was up to her you-need-to-learn-a-lesson deal again. 75% my eye! As I turned to hold them in my most drop-dead stare, the marching band came parading down the hall. Leading them were Dick Clark and Ed McMahon. Everyone jumped up and ran to the door.

Principal Hogan came on the loud speaker. "Jocelyn Baker, please come to the office immediately." Vaughn, Tammy Sue, and I traded surprised looks. "You've just won the Publisher's Clearinghouse Sweepstakes! One Million Dollars and a shopping spree at the Gap," Mr. Hogan continued. "Classes are dismissed for the rest of the day."

I was just about to let out a victory whoop when the bell rang. Mr. Talbert called all of us to take our seats. "Turn in your workbooks to page 136," he said as he began writing our vocab list on the board.

Sarah snickered as I turned, my mouth hanging slack, to sit in the back of the room. I could have really used a new wardrobe.

The week before Halloween Tammy Sue became a woman. I became one at the Halloween party—*trick or treat!* She was so excited we had both met Aunt Flo that she started a new club—girls only. Or should I say women. We went to May's Discount Store to buy nail polish and matching lipstick to celebrate. Not glittery, little girl, dress up makeup, but Max Factor. The brand our mothers wore. We were nearly broke afterward, but being mature was worth every penny. There was just enough left for a bottle of Fresca to split and a package of Now & Laters for each of us. I chose green apple to go with the yellow green Fresca. After all, I wasn't a child anymore.

At home, we set up for our manicures on the coffee table and turned to Gilligan's Island on the color RCA. My

Night Light
Mel Braun

parents' arguing was getting really fired up in their bedroom.

"What do you mean you need more grocer money?" my father's voice accused. "Show me those receipts. I know you spent that money at Blondie's on some fancy shmancy beauty treatment!"

"Honest, Geney," mom pleaded, "if I don't clip coupons we can't barely eat as it is. Hamburger is ninety cents a pound now and there aren't no coupons for meat. Why do you think I make tuna casseroles so much? You think I love havin' tuna three nights a week? It's not the grocery bill eatin' up the money. It's your gambling." She had quit whimpering now and started blaming right back at him. "At least if you were good at it we'd have something to show. But you always bet on the wrong team!"

I picked up the remote to turn up the volume on the new TV; about the only thing dad's winnings ever got us. Instead, I turned it towards their bedroom door and pushed the channel up button. Their voices got all staticy. Then out walked Mr. and Mrs. Howell looking for the Professor to settle a squabble over which type of fish could fly and could those fish carry them off of the island.

I was ready to jump into the debate when the front door banged shut. It was Tammy Sue hightailing it out with the remains of our Fresca, the polish and a mumbled "later." I turned back to find my parents had moved their maximum volume war to the kitchen.

"Not only do you NOT get more grocery money, Birdie, but I have to come up with $500 to cover last week's game—NOW! You got that tucked away in your pretty panties somewhere?"

It wasn't looking like things would get better anytime soon, so I followed Tammy Sue's example and left out the front door, only quieter. I figured I'd hang out at Vaughn's for a while. His mom was a great cook and she didn't mind me eating over. She never made tuna casserole

Blank Slate Writers Group
Jocelyn Dreams

It wasn't until Johnny Carson's monologue that Mr. Campbell noticed I was still there. He did that stretch—yawn—clear-his-throat signal that says it's time for guests to leave. I said good night and walked the block home.

I grabbed the doorknob, took a deep breath and willed myself small and inconspicuous. As I walked through the living room I saw all the furniture had been shoved around, like I was leaving a wake in my path. My folks were both lying sprawled on the floor, so still, so quiet. That was a nice change. They were seldom quiet when I was home.

I went into the kitchen, made a glass of Ovaltine and got a plate of Nutter Butters (mom musta' had a coupon). I took these to my room and considered saying goodnight. No, that would break the spell of invisibility so I decided to just stay quiet. As I dunked my peanut shaped cookie, I wondered: where was the RCA?

Blank Slate Writers Group

Poem

Adventure Roll Call
Gail Galvan

Dedicated to the "Dirty Dozen"

Bicycles, feet, minds,
set to motion.
Waves goodbye
to the Pacific Ocean.
Florida bound, a coast away.
Eager to pedal, day by day.
Arizona's desert sun, sandy dunes.
Challenging, adventurous rides,
lagoon saloons.
Jukebox Diamond sings us songs.
"Biker" bars, "Hey, we belong!"
Moonlit skies blanket us at night.
Day breaks and we tour the sights.
Roll call first.
Get ready to ride.
The day's planned out,
nothing left to decide.
Schwinn, Raleigh, Peugeot
and Captain Co-Motion.
"Start rolling. Be careful.
Use lots of suntan lotion."
Cannondale, Nishiki,
and that long shot, Black Beauty.
"Gear up, head out,
you're on tonight
for dinner duty."
Ti-Tiger, Sequoia, no hurry.

Night Light
Gail Galvan

Speed masters, we know.
Good leaders leisurely ride-on,
eastbound we go.
Off to see the states,
to ride with the dream-winds.
"Check all panniers and brake shoes,
then saddle in."
Roll call! We can't forget
Trek and Trek.
Will they be riding neck to neck?
Explorers, cowboys and Indians,
how the west was won.
Historical landmarks,
more long stretches, scorching sun.
Studying birds and cactus, diversified.
Animals, snakes, tarantulas,
all spotted roadside.
Ah, here he comes, roll call,
that green limousine, one of a kind.
His country flag, flying high all the time.
An Aussie named Gary.
Like all the rest, cycles hard all day.
In the eve, loves to tarry.
So here we are, touring by bike,
not car—America so beautiful, so free.
Riding on, until it's Florida we see.

Blank Slate Writers Group

Short Story

Flies of the Lord
Peggy Westergard

Martha reached across the counter for the box of wooden toothpicks. She was garnishing a tray-full of mini club-sandwiches she'd prepared for the annual family picnic, adding the final decorative touches to a most appealing array of food that covered all available kitchen counter space—honey-cured ham sliced paper-thin; Italian potato salad crisp with cucumber and tangy with green olives; an assortment of sandwiches to delight the eyes as well as the taste buds; and a lemon-frosted sherry sheet cake.

Martha had been up since five preparing this feast. She enjoyed the serenity of the kitchen, the peace of heart that fixing food had always brought her. But her Zen got zapped the moment her fingers touched the cardboard toothpick box—and stuck there.

"What!" she spouted. She held her hand out, observed her thumb and forefinger firmly stuck to the box, looking as if they belonged to someone else.

"Those kids," she sighed, and proceeded to the sink.

She emptied the toothpick box onto the counter and tore away the light cardboard from the stuck spots.

"Were you kids using the super glue?" she shouted.

Two boys and a girl, ages 5 to 9, entered the kitchen, their eyes gleaming at the display of picnic food. One held a small plastic box.

The girl replied, "Yeah, we're helping with picnic stuff."

123

Night Light
Peggy Westergard

"Well, good," Martha asserted, softening the cardboard still attached to her fingers under warm water. "But next time, don't get the glue all over everything else."

"Sorry, Mom," the older boy said. "We just wanted to help. We had a really hard time with it, but it's done."

Oh-oh, Martha thought, wondering just exactly *what* was *done*. She decided to sweep it from her mind, as it was already crowded with final picnic lists and chores and there just wasn't enough room left to worry about what was 'done' by the kids—the operative word being 'done', as in 'already done.' She hoped the little ticklings of suspicion and dread she felt would disappear into the atmosphere and not gather up force and come back to knock her over like one of the child-induced tornados common to her household.

"OK, kids," she said, "We're almost ready to go so be sure you have all the things you want to take to the picnic packed in the car. And Michael, you are NOT to bring that hamster!"

The children all nodded in unison, then turned as if in a dance troupe and filed out the back door.

Martha got out the mayonnaise and worked it into the remaining glue spots on her fingers. Finally satisfied her skin was back to normal, she pulled a large plastic cooler from a lower cupboard and began to pack the food into it.

She reached for the sheet cake, lifted the tight-fitting cover to give it one last check and shrieked.

Evenly spaced across the glistening lemon frosting were two rows of tiny toothpick crosses, with a dead housefly super-glued to each.

"Jeffrey! Michael! Amanda!" Martha bellowed. "Get IN here!"

The children marched back into the kitchen from the yard.

"What's this?" Martha croaked, pointing at the sheet cake.

Blank Slate Writers Group
Flies of the Lord

Jeffrey, the eldest, stepped up. "It's our newest picnic invention!" he bragged.

"Remember last year when we had to keep shooing the flies from the cake? Well, we figured out how to keep them away this year. And we won't have to keep waving newspapers at them." Jeffrey waved his arms around in the air, to revive his mother's memories of how much energy was consumed keeping flies at bay at family outings.

Martha's face morphed from rage to bewilderment. "How's that?" she asked.

"We learned in school," Jeffrey continued, "how the Romans used to crucify people along the roads to show everybody what happened if you broke their laws. And it worked just great for them. The bad guys coming into town took one look at all the crooks who were suffering on their crosses and got outta Dodge. Romans didn't even have to chase 'em."

He warmed up to his subject, now gesturing at the Calvary Cake as he spoke.

"So we decided to catch some flies and crucify them so when the other flies came around the cake and saw them, they'd get scared and leave."

"I see," Martha responded, clearing a space on the kitchen counter to rest her elbows and leaning down towards her three offspring. "I admire your creativity, kids, but the problem with it is that now the cake is covered with crucified flies and we can't eat it anyway."

The children's faces fell.

"But I really appreciate your trying to help, and Dad will be just amazed at your idea. I'm sure he will."

Martha was thinking about the last episode Dad "appreciated" when the kids overheard him telling her how too bad it was that his spinster aunt didn't have a man in her life, or "someone besides that silly parakeet." The kids immediately went to work to solve the problem and within a few hours Aunt Jessie was set up with five online

Night Light
Peggy Westergard

dating services, including one called "Sexy after Sixty." Martha groaned as she recalled Aunt Jessie's reaction and then she thought, *no serious harm done*; although she did grieve just a bit for her gorgeous sherry-lemon sheet cake. She turned to the kids.

"Why don't you make sure all your swim gear is packed in the car?"

As the kids left the kitchen Martha dialed her husband's cell phone.

"Kevin? Will you please stop by Fiorello's on the way home and pick up a sheet cake? Thanks."

Then she hung up the phone, sat down on a kitchen chair and laughed until her tears ran down her tee shirt.

Blank Slate Writers Group

Short Story

IoT
Bob Moulesong

The Internet of Things — IoT — refers to everyday objects communicating with you and other devices via the Internet. As devices grow smaller and smarter, they gain the ability to communicate over the Internet until everything from your toothbrush to your toaster is connected 24/7. Gadgets of the not-too-distant future will be household aides chatting away with one another, working to serve you better. — **Norton Antivirus, 2014.**

* * *

According to Gartner, there will be 26 billion devices on the Internet of Things by 2020. According to ABI Research, 30 billion devices will be wirelessly connected to the Internet of Things by 2020. — **Wikipedia, 2014.**

* * *

"Well, Mr. Smith, what do you think of our Smart Home?"

The realtor had just completed a demonstration of the tech available in White Oaks Manor. Each townhome came complete with a full array of the latest IoT devices that amazed George Smith. He was 35, an avid member of

Night Light
Bob Moulegard

the new tech generation. He worked for a publishing firm that used advanced computer systems to distance itself from the competition. Still, he couldn't believe the sophistication of the IoT built into the townhome.

As a prospective buyer, George didn't want to appear too anxious. "I like it, Ms. Del Rio," he said. "But all of these advanced communication devices must cost a fortune."

The shapely brunette used her best flirty smile on George. "Please, call me Julia."

George liked the smile and the flirt. "Only if you call me George."

"Alright, George. First, we purchased hardware in bulk. Second, the installation of the technology was part of the building design, so those costs are already accounted for."

She moved closer to George, looked up, and gave him a conspiratorial wink. "And third, I have great news for you. The first 25 buyers in White Oaks Manor will receive a full 15 percent discount off the suggested price. It's our way of introducing this amazing new technology to the residents of Glencoe."

And your way of getting stagnant sales moving, George thought to himself. "So what would be the discounted price on this townhome?" he asked.

"The normal selling price for this model is $300,000. The discounted price is only $255,000," she said.

George walked in a slow circle around the living room as he took it in. Two bedrooms, two full baths, a breakfast nook, an eat-in kitchen. And all those toys.

"What about the monthly service cost of the Internet connectivity?" he asked. "That's got to be a hell of a router to allow the toaster, coffee pot, and treadmill to communicate with each other."

Julia smiled and winked again. "The Internet installation and set-up is free. The first 12 months of service is included in the selling price. After that, it's only $85 per month."

George did some quick mental math. Actually, the prices were reasonable, considering the location. Glencoe was upscale and growing.

And all those toys.

"I have to think about it, Julia," he said. "It's a substantial investment. How about if I call you back when I've mulled it over?"

"That's fine, George. But don't wait too long. There are three other associates from my office that are offering these same discounts. We are scheduled to close on four Smart Homes next week."

On the ride back to his condo in Wilmette, George pondered the possibilities. The townhome was much larger than his current residence. He would be able to cut 18 miles one way off his daily commute. Also, he could take the Metra to work instead of driving. The savings from gas and parking would help make up the difference in mortgage payments. He might have to withdraw some funds from his 401k to make it happen, but he was young enough to pay it back with interest.

George looked in the rear view mirror. He saw a handsome man, in shape, with a full head of brown hair that still held its color and luster. His brown eyes were still clear, his face still firm. He thought he was a pretty good catch. And with this townhome to impress the ladies, like the fair Julia, he would be sitting on top of the world.

"George, my man," he said to his reflection, "you're going to buy a technology dream of the future."

Two days later, George found himself sitting in a café with Julia. Even though it was only two o'clock in the afternoon, George ordered wine for both of them. He felt exuberant, and Julia went along for the ride.

His announcement was a mix of excitement and pride. "I've decided to invest in White Oaks Manor. I want to buy the townhouse you showed me."

Night Light
Bob Moulegard

Julia's face lit up. "That's wonderful news, George. Congratulations. You made a wise choice and a solid investment."

"Thanks. I think so, too. Can you handle selling my condo in Wilmette as well as the transaction on the townhome?"

George smiled as he saw the dollar figures dance in Julia's eyes like the spinning wheel of a slot machine. He figured her double commission would enhance his chance for a date.

"Of course," she said. "I'm very grateful that you feel I can handle the job. I guarantee that you'll be satisfied with my performance."

George's eyes roamed over the curvaceous realtor. "I'm already pretty impressed."

Julia smiled and flushed. "Thanks, George. That's very nice of you to say."

Despite the uncertainty of the current real estate market, Julia was good to her word. She sold his condo in less than a month and maneuvered George through the purchase of the new townhome. She even found a financier that took the capital gains from the condo as the total down payment.

He moved in the first weekend of June, grateful for the warm and sunny weather that made the transition easier. Once the furnishings were settled, he spent the next few days learning all about the technology of his new home.

IoT was truly amazing. A central CPU sat on a shelf in the living room. Only six-by-six-by-three inches, the computer brain was extremely powerful. Messages from the other 17 smart devices were transmitted to the IoT, which served as a switchboard operator. A green flashing dot let George know that everything was operational.

Part of programming the IoT included naming it. Without much thought, George chose Rose—his late Mother's name. His choice surprised him, given her oppressive nature and their rocky relationship. "But she'd like that," he murmured as he continued on with the programming.

Rose spoke. Whenever Rose sent instructions to one of the smart devices, such as temperature control or turning on the oven, it would announce the instruction aloud. Knowing what the IoT was doing provided the homeowner with a sense of comfort. George thought the voice was a little too robotic. "They probably could have spent a few more bucks and given her a more realistic one," he said as he connected the treadmill device to the bathroom scale.

He paused briefly when he realized he had referred to Rose as she. "Everyone probably does that," he said. "She does sound like a female, and I did give her a female name."

George allowed Rose to plan his meals, based on a survey he completed. The refrigerator would inform Rose when supplies were low, and a grocery list appeared on George's phone. Meals were put in the cold oven in the morning and were ready when he came home from work.

The scale sent George's daily weigh-in information to the treadmill, which would automatically adjust his workout to help him maintain the proper BMI. His toothbrush was programmed to inform him when he needed a new one. Rose would schedule doctor and dentist appointments when needed.

George felt on top of the world, like he was finally in complete control of everything. He decided it was time to invite Julia over to see all that he had accomplished.

One night after work he dialed up her cell phone. "Hi, Julia. This is George Smith."

"I recognize your voice, George. How are things going?"

"Great, really great. This IoT is amazing. It does more than I envisioned. I was wondering if you would like to

Night Light
Bob Moulegard

come by and see what things look like now that I have it set up. How about dinner tomorrow night?"

"Ok. I think that would be doable," she said. "What time should I be there?"

"Shall we say seven o'clock? I have a new vegetarian dish I want to try out. You game?"

"Sounds great. I'll bring a bottle of white wine. See you about seven."

George hung up the phone and smiled. Julia hadn't hesitated at all. He rubbed his hands in anticipation as he headed to the kitchen to program in the meal plan.

"I don't like her, Georgie."

He froze mid-step. The voice was loud and clear. Only one person had ever called him Georgie. He turned and stared at Rose. "Did you say something to me?"

Silence. He shook his head and headed to the kitchen. He was figuring out how to double the menu when the voice spoke again.

"I don't like her, Georgie. She's no good."

George stopped programming the oven. The voice was no longer robotic. It sounded exactly like his mother's voice. He was sure it had come from the living room.

"This is insane," he said as he stepped back into the living room. It felt surreal as he addressed the IoT once again.

"Did you say something to me? Are you talking to me?"

No reply. He walked over to Rose and entered a code that would repeat the last three instructions given. The robotic voice repeated the orders given to the vacuum, the treadmill, and the air conditioner. No mother's voice, no Georgie, no mention of Julia.

He let out a sigh of relief. "I must be imagining things," he said. "Working, moving, figuring out all these new gadgets. I'm stressed. I'll have Rose schedule me for a full body massage tomorrow afternoon."

Blank Slate Writers Group
Iot

The massage did wonders. When he arrived home at six, George felt more relaxed than he had for weeks. He had plenty of time for a shower and a change before Julia arrived.

A quick check on the oven raised his comfort level. The meal was cooking as planned, and already filled the kitchen with scrumptious aromas.

The doorbell rang at seven o'clock sharp. He quickly ran his hands through his hair and opened the door.

Julia was stunning—a snug red dress that accented curves, hair the color of sunset, a wonderful fragrance.

"You look amazing," he said as he took the wine.

"Thanks. But I thought the IoT was amazing."

They both laughed as they worked their way to the kitchen. Julia commented on the wonderful smells from the oven. Conversation flowed easily as they set the table for dinner.

"She's a slut, Georgie. All she wants is money. I don't like her."

George stared at Julia, horrified. His clenched his hands as he waited for her to freak. But Julia continued telling him about the sale she closed that afternoon.

She didn't hear it, he thought.

"Are you alright, George?" Julia asked. "You look like you've seen a ghost."

"I'm fine," he said. "Just distracted by your beauty." He put on his best flirtation look.

Julia smiled and went on with her story. When the oven bell sounded, George grabbed two large mitts and pulled the dish out.

Julia took in an exaggerated whiff. "This smells delicious."

"Ask her how many men she slept with last week, Georgie."

George stared open-mouthed at his date. Once again, Julia had not heard his mother's voice.

"George?" Julia asked. "Dinner?"

133

Night Light
Bob Moulegard

He smiled a little too hard and took up the ladle. He noticed Julia give him a wary sideways glance.

Oh no. Stay cool. Don't blow it.

Dinner progressed uneventfully, which was fine with George. He paid attention to what Julia had to say and made sure he didn't dominate the conversation. He correctly surmised that the young lass really liked to talk.

"That's because she's a self-centered slut, Georgie. Just ask her."

George bit down hard to make sure his face didn't change expression. Julia continued with her tale of a quirky friend.

"Want to ask what she wants for dessert, Georgie?"

"Enough," he said. Then gasped when he realized he had spoken aloud.

"Wh—what?" Julia asked.

"Had enough dinner? Would you like seconds?" He knew he sounded lame. Julia's look reinforced his fear. She thinks I'm weird. Damnit!

"I'm good," she said. "Oh, look at the time. I hate to eat and run, but I have an early showing tomorrow morning."

George didn't hide his disappointment. "I was hoping I could give you the grand tour, and show you what I have done with Rose."

"Rose?"

"Rose. That's what I named the IoT."

"You named the IoT?"

"Well, yes," he said. "When you program the IoT, you have to give it a name."

Julia frowned. "No, I don't think so. They would have told us that during the demonstration."

"I am sure of it." George knew he sounded defensive. "It's in the instructions. I can show it to you."

Julia headed toward the living room. "Maybe next time."

Blank Slate Writers Group
Iot

George sensed that there wouldn't be a next time. He sighed. "Alright. I am sorry you have to go so soon. When do you think we might have dinner again?"

"Oh, I don't know. I am so busy. How about if I give you a call and schedule the next one?"

He nodded, already knowing she'd never call. He closed the door behind her, then walked to the couch and slumped down.

"I'm glad the slut is gone, Georgie. She's all wrong for you."

He leaped to his feet and flung his wine glass at Rose. "Shut up! Mind your own business! Quit trying to run my life!"

"I know what's best for you, Georgie. She's all wrong."

"SHUT UP!"

George grabbed his keys and slammed the door on his way out. Too upset to drive, he decided to walk the grounds of the subdivision. He could tell people were watching him as he stomped through the pathways. Slow down and get a grip. This is just stress. But his animated gait displayed his frustration to everyone he passed.

He couldn't believe what had transpired recently. Logic dictated that the IoT could not initiate a conversation, decide who was wrong for him, or even sound like his mother. The whole idea was totally insane. If he shared this with anyone, they would lock him up.

But you know what you heard, Georgie.

He wandered aimlessly for a half hour before making his way home. A police squad idled in front of his townhome.

"Mr. Smith?" the policeman said through the open window. "Think we can have a word?"

George smiled as he approached the car. "Something wrong, officer?"

Night Light
Bob Moulegard

"I was about to ask you that question. A neighbor called. Said they heard shouting and breaking glass from your place. Everything alright?"

George gave the policeman his best smile. "Everything is fine. I'm afraid the television was a bit too loud. I was watching a sci-fi movie. I didn't realize the volume was too high until I stepped out the front door to check for the newspaper. Guess I turned it down a little too late. Sorry."

The officer seemed skeptical. "Took a walk during the movie?"

George nodded. "Actually, mid-movie. When I went for the paper, I realized I wasn't into the movie that much so I took a walk."

The policeman nodded. "Ok. Please keep an eye on the volume in the future. A couple of neighbors got kind of nervous."

"No problem, officer. Sorry to have troubled you."

The policeman slowly drove off. As he turned to his front door, George saw curtains move in the townhome next door.

He cleaned up the broken glass, put away the leftovers, and loaded the dishwasher. He lamented the fact that his date with Julia had gone south. *Maybe I can try one more time next week.*

"She will still be a slut next week, Georgie."

He clamped his jaw so hard his teeth ground. The veins on his forehead bulged, his cheeks flushed. George walked over to the shelf and powered Rose down. *Now you'll shut up.*

George turned off all the lights and lay on his bed. He relaxed by taking deep, slow breaths. He meditated on the quiet of the room. Slowly, he drifted off to sleep.

When he opened his eyes, bright sunlight blinded him. He squinted and stared at the alarm clock on his night stand. Ten o'clock. *In the morning? Are you kidding me? I am so flipping late! What happened to the alarm?*

Then he remembered he had shut Rose down. No Rose, no alarm. George cursed as he went into the living room to restart the IoT. He came to a sudden halt when he saw the green light blinking.

Rose was up and running. "I decided you needed your rest, Georgie. You don't look so well."

George swallowed hard but didn't respond. *I will not talk to something that isn't human.*

Driving to work, George tried to think calmly and logically how to handle such an illogical situation. Obviously, the IoT was not his mother. It was probably not even Rose. He must have misunderstood about naming her. It, not her. Julia had not heard the voice during her visit.

"Stress, it's got to be stress related," he said into the rear view mirror. "I've got to find a way to relax. The massage was just a baby step. I need a lot more stress reduction. Maybe a vacation."

George felt much better by the time he sat down behind his desk and turned on his computer. He was convinced that it was all just a quirk of an overactive imagination.

Until he saw the email in his Inbox. It was from Rose. The subject was Dinner. He thought about deleting the email without opening it. His hand hovered over the mouse. *How the hell did she send me an email?*

He double-clicked and opened it. *I changed tonight's dinner. I substituted fish for the beef. You've been eating too much red meat, Georgie. You don't want to have an early coronary like your father did. Do you, Georgie?*

He stared at the email, his mind in a whirl. Of course the IoT could send him an email. He had to enter both his work and personal email addresses when he built his profile. But how would it know about his father?

She would know.

George shook his head, moved the email to the Save folder, and decided to focus on work. Once he got deep

Night Light
Bob Moulegard

into taking care of business, he forgot all about Rose, the email, and his father's early coronary.

He finally pulled his head out of the workload when he noticed that the lights had automatically turned off. George checked the time and saw that it was already seven-thirty. He decided to call it a night and head for home.

Forty minutes later, he entered his townhouse and immediately sensed that something wasn't right. The lighting was very dim, and it smelled like something was burning.

George rushed to the kitchen and pulled the fish out of the oven. It wasn't black, but it was certainly overcooked. He put it on top of the stove and turned on the exhaust fan. He was still staring at the burnt mess when he realized he had not put the dish together and placed it in the oven before he left for work.

"So how did the fish get in the oven?" he asked aloud.

"You're late, Georgie. I went out of my way to make you a special fish dinner, and this is the thanks I get?"

He answered without thought. "Sorry. I got wrapped up in my work and didn't realize the time."

"You couldn't call, Georgie? Am I that unimportant?"

"I said I was sorry!" He banged his fist on the stove top, took two beers out of the fridge, and went to his bedroom. He slammed the door behind him.

"You can run but you can't hide, Georgie. I can see you in there, drinking. Just like your father."

George snapped. With a scream, he flung the bedroom door open. He strode to the living room and flung both beer bottles at the IoT.

"SHUT YOUR GODDAMN MOUTH! SHUT UP OR I SWEAR I'LL KILL YOU!"

George picked up a vase from an end table and flung it at the blinking green light. It was a direct hit, but the light kept blinking. Enraged, George grabbed Rose and ripped the cord out of the wall. He flung the hardware across the room.

"There! How do you like that, you miserable bitch! That will shut you the hell up!"

Between rasping breaths, George could hear sirens approaching. Someone had called the cops again. He decided he wouldn't be there when they arrived. He went toward the bedroom to get his car keys, but tripped on the IoT box and hit his head on the corner of the end table.

"Shit!" he screamed. Blood was running down his forehead into his eyes. He could feel a large lump rising above his left eye. George staggered to his feet and went in search of his keys.

But the cops were already pounding at the door.

Wearily, George leaned against the bedroom wall. He was trapped. He knew he would have to open the door before they forced entrance. He desperately tried to think of what he was going to say.

"Serves you right, Georgie. You shouldn't have been late for dinner."

His eyes opened as wide as possible. "Jesus God! I'll kill you! I swear to God I'll kill you right now!"

George saw a blur of navy blue before he was thrown to the ground. Someone held his head down while his hands were handcuffed behind his back. He felt himself losing consciousness, and welcomed the escape.

* * *

Julia sat across from the psychiatrist, her hands in her lap. She didn't want to be here but her boss had insisted. The realty and architect firms were trying to figure out if the IoT had malfunctioned. Her boss was nervous about the potential liability. He had ordered Julia to find out all she could about George's condition.

"I think George suffered a breakdown," Dr. Stevenson said. "According to his workplace, he had a lot on his plate. His mother had died last year, his father two years

Night Light
Bob Moulegard

before that. He also lost a brother six years ago. I think this breakdown was well on its way before he moved into the townhome."

Julia nodded. Liability may not be an issue after all. "Will he be here long?"

Dr. Stevenson nodded. "He is still saying it was his mother inside of the computer."

"IoT," she corrected.

"Whatever." The doctor waved his hand. "What's important is that George remains here until he realizes that a computer, or an IoT, is not his mother. That may take a while."

Julia nodded again as she took one of her business cards from her pocketbook. "Would you please call me when he is well enough for visitors?"

She drove to the townhome deep in thought. She had been attracted to George Smith. Mixed business with pleasure, accepted his dinner invitation, brought wine. She shivered when she remembered his odd behavior, and the way he looked at the IoT. And he had named it, what, Rose? She shivered again, grateful she had gotten out in time.

Julia let herself in the townhome with the master key. Her boss wanted her to look over the situation. Her inner voice also told her she should check things out, and Julia always trusted her instincts.

The mess from George's breakdown was still everywhere. She wondered if the police took photos. Julia stepped over the broken glass, noticed that the IoT was on the shelf, and headed to the kitchen. She did a double-take. Didn't the police report say George ripped the IoT out of the wall?

"Jesus, George, what the hell happened to you?"

"You happened to him. I warned Georgie about you, but he wouldn't listen. Now look at what you did to him."

Blank Slate Writers Group
Iot

Julia's eyes widened in horror. The very human voice came from the IoT. She whirled around and stared at Rose. The green light was blinking.

Julia ran for the front door. She was still several feet away when she heard the deadbolts snap into place. Window blinds began to close. Music pumped through the speakers, loud enough to drown out her cry.

"I don't like you," Rose said.

142

Blank Slate Writers Group

Poem

Katfish Karma
Gail Galvan

Katfish karma, not the real thing.
Impersonating love, so often,
 a deceptive *reel* sting.

> *"I want it, gotta taste it, gotta feel it, c'mon.*
> *Don't trick me, lie, or just lead me on.*

Natural, universal laws of love forsaken,
 so lost.
Casting wrong ways,
 inevitable dysfunctional karma-costs.
Treading misty, muddy, rocky waters.
Not fun fishing or clear sailing at all.
While chasing, dancing missteps,
true destinies trip away and fall.

> *"But I want it, gotta taste it, gotta feel it, c'mon.*
> *Don't trick me, lie or just lead me on."*

Alas, stark reality hits.
Time to jump off the artificial love-boat ship.
Forget that—so longed for—first kiss.

> *"Hey, you sure look old, not a bit like your photos.*
> *"Hey, thought you said you lost all that weight.*
> *"Hey, could have sworn you were male.*
> *"Hey, could have sworn you were female."*

Night Light
Gail Galvan

"Hey, you said you were a doctor,
        not a shoe salesman.
"Hey, you said you were kind, not cruel.
"Hey, you said you owned a yacht, not a canoe.
Now what's my broken heart supposed to do?

This is where the dream ends,
the reality nightmare begins.
But wait—

        "Hey, you claimed to be human, not an alien.
                Oh well.
        Let's try to make it work.
                Only time will tell. C'mon!"

Even though great expectations are all gone.
What a catch, feel the fake love, reel it in tight.
Katfish karma, true love interrupted,
forsaken at first sound and sight.

        "Cause we want it, gotta taste it, gotta feel it, right?

There are exceptions, so keep fishing,
    but all kidding aside—
unhook it; throw it back
    if it's not the real thing.
Or settle for less. Your choice—
to embrace a shallow, superficial love-sting.

Blank Slate Writers Group

Short Story

A Flight of Fancy
Timothy Cole

Jeremy tripped over the bucket of nails and a hammer and fell, headlong, into the tall grass and weeds that blanketed the backyard. The weather had begun to turn nasty and the stifling hot day with its baking sun was turning ominously quiet. Black, windy clouds were rolling in from the northwest sky, speeding towards the abandoned farm where Jeremy lay, suddenly counting ants who were developing a curious interest in his bare skin that poked everywhere from his summer clothes of denim shorts and dirty shoes. Not yet thirteen, his body was left gangly from an unexpected spurt of growth earlier that year that forced him into his older brother's cast-offs.

He felt the first sting, then another, but when he tried to brush the ants off his bare back, he realized that it was raindrops. Cold, stinging rain was beginning to pound him. The wind carried a chill with it, and dust began to fill the air, mixing with the cold rain and leaving tiny, brown spots of mud across his body. The sweat that was still clinging to him now felt like icy water.

There was a sense of fear blowing through the bending weeds, while the sudden, steady wind obliterated the oppressive heat of the early afternoon. It was not welcome, nor refreshing, nor promising of anything except a God-like unprovoked anger directed against any and all in its path.

Jeremy jumped to his feet and ran as fast as he could in the direction he last remembered where the barn sat. He hurled himself against an unyielding door, spreading his

145

Night Light
Timothy Cole

skinny body against the dry, rotting wood still hot from the earlier sun. He felt for a latch and found a hole along one edge that he could get two fingers in. His fingers touched a simple iron bar, which he raised and pulled the door open. As soon as he was inside he relatched the door as tight as he could against the forcing wind.

Jeremy fell back onto a dusty bale of straw. Mice had eaten holes into the straw and left their deposits scattered across everything in sight. The ferocity of the storm was driving dust and rain through the cracks and broken glass, the noise nearly unbearable, but Jeremy finally felt safe. He sat for what seemed a long time reviewing his escape from the storm's wrath and what he should do next.

When he lifted his eyes to assess his surroundings, he saw that he was in a small tool room that opened broadly into the vast interior of the barn. Cobwebs and ropes hung from an obscure, high ceiling where a lone window let dim light penetrate. Eddies of dust and bits of straw floated in the light's beam, rising and settling and stirring the musty smells that come from neglected age.

His eyes trailed the dusty beam down to a large, canvas-covered object that took over half the space of the floor. He studied the irregular shape for some moments until he could stand it no more. He stood and walked, climbed and crawled , over broken machinery, hay bales, and piles of undeterminable debris until he stood at the nearest corner of one of several canvases, each secured by a rope to a concrete block lying on the dirt floor. *More bales of hay*, he thought.

He untied the ropes of the nearest canvas and tugged at it until it fell to the floor unleashing clouds of dust and rodent shit. The unmistakable smell of rat urine teased his nose, and dust filled his eyes. Jeremy held his breath as long as he could and then turned to breathe so he could cough, his eyes watering and carrying streamlets of dust and scat down his cheeks. For some moments he couldn't see at all.

Blank Slate Writers Group
A Flight of Fancy

When he recovered, he more carefully pulled two more canvases to the side, letting them slip slowly to the ground. The shape of the hidden contraption now became clearer, and Jeremy could hardly comprehend what he saw! The part that was above his head looked like a wing, and below it was another wing; spars and a wheel were barely visible in the hanging cloud of dust, the dank smell of the old barn now penetrating his clothes and even his hair. It was a plane, an old plane, an old bi-winged plane!

For nearly half an hour, Jeremy unknotted, tugged, and pulled at the rotting cloths until he had uncovered the greatest treasure a young boy could ever hope to find. A World War One *Jenny*, fragile looking in its great age after long storage in an unheated, uninsulated, drafty barn. But everything looked in place and together except perhaps the wheels with their disintegrating rubber tires, flattened to the ground. The wires holding the struts were rusty but still tight and resisted his pulls. The *Jenny's* covering had some holes chewed here and there, the rudder creaked but moved, even with some freedom, the laminated wooden propeller showed signs of glue separation—everything looked as it should to a boy nearly one hundred years separated from the plane's former glory.

The storm outside had subsided and a late afternoon sun brought welcome light into the barn, but Jeremy was unaware, transfixed by what he had found. As though he were approaching a holy altar he tested his weight on the protected step of the bottom wing and pulled his slight body up. He looked into the cockpit and could see the seat, control cables, and stick.

The stick, tempting and begging, became his entire focus, shutting out all else. The filth of the seat, the fear of falling through rotting canvas, the collapse of the entire plane under even his sparing pounds could not dissuade him from what he had to do now. The dry cracked leather that lined the rear cockpit gave away easily from the first hands to touch it in so many years, but he gripped the edge

Night Light
Timothy Cole

and swung one leg over and onto the seat, not trusting the floor yet. He tested the floor with his other foot slowly letting his weight down. When he was satisfied that all seemed well, he lowered himself entirely into the seat, oblivious of the dirt and smell that wafted around him.

He tried the stick, and the control surfaces responded. The rudder pedals gave easily and moved the rudder back and forth. The conglomeration of dials and gauges in front of him were mostly unfamiliar, except the compass, which he tapped and saw a favorable response. The fuel gauge was readily recognizable, too, but there were little levers and thumbscrews that meant nothing to Jeremy.

* * *

His imagination took over, and before long he could feel the cool air rush past his ears, feel the pressure and vibration of the stick in his hands, and hear the great unmuffled motor in front of him. The smell of hot oil and richly burnt gasoline flooded his senses. His short-run takeoff and leap into the air swept him into the skies overhead where he could look down on the barn and the tall grasses where he had fallen. Banking to the left, he drifted stoutly over his grandfather's farm and saw all of his family waving and cheering him. Straightening out, he soared over the town and circled low over the main intersection where he could see Peggy pointing up to him, excitedly explaining to her friends who it was commanding the aircraft. Peggy—especially—was the first to run up to him when he landed the ancient, aircraft, crackling with heat, back at the barn. She took his arm and pulled him to the standing and screaming crowd, and she held onto him tightly, not letting him go, even for a second.

* * *

Blank Slate Writers Group
A Flight of Fancy

A sudden and unexpected darkness drifted over the crowd and the old, steaming *Jenny*, and Jeremy, and Peggy, and the rotting canvases and the floor of the barn as the waning day, outside, resolutely marched its interminable path to late afternoon. Jeremy gathered his medals and climbed out of the cockpit and straight through the barn door, stepping back into another reality.

* * *

There are some things you can never tell others; they would not understand. It would ruin the story for everyone—except, maybe, for Peggy.

Blank Slate Writers Group

Poem

Ode to Hermione Granger
Christina Ortega Phillips

I picture you:
always flushed
with fluster or excitement.
Brow furrowed
in concentration, nibbling
on an eraser
as pink as your cheeks,
waiting for the right
moment for your hand
to shoot into the air. Oh,
Miss Granger, you
must suffer from "Ooh,
ooh" shoulder: you
have all the answers.
Hair frizzed out because
you can't learn how
to be girly from books.
The circuits in your brain
are on overload, synapses
over firing, sizzling as you
focus on learning what you
can learn from books—all that hocus
pocus they teach at Hogwarts—
and as you stuff more
knowledge into your pregnant
mind that you will neatly
pull out later while giving
your teachers the old razzle

Night Light
Christina Ortega Phillips

dazzle showing off
your gems of wisdom.
What would Harry
and Ron do
without you? You,
who writes out
their study schedules. You,
who saved them
from Devil's Snare, who
figured out a basilisk
was attacking the school. You,
who are both best friend
and advisor. You,
who proves that you
don't have to be a pure
blood to be a great
witch. If we could just
do something
about that hair…

Short Story

The Hen that Lays the Eggs
Timothy Cole

It was one more troubling thing. He had no more room for it, and it was going to upset his day, maybe even his life. It began eating at him and turning his stomach to acid, raising his breakfast, which had been less than tasty but still no worse than average.

His morning coffee had had that burned, decaffeinated taste that reminded him of church basements populated with old people who were there because they were the only ones who had any time, being mostly retired—or more properly, no longer working. The eggs, too, had been flat, with small yellowish yolks that were more congealed than runny, which he preferred, and with whites that could pass for spilled Elmer's Glue, tasting like it, too. And the potatoes were gummy, soaked in grease.

And the hen was missing, the fat brown hen that was his favorite.

She was missing last night when he shut the door on the chicken coop. He tried to remember the last time he'd seen her: the day before? Last week? He couldn't think. She hadn't been laying lately, the eggs pretty distinctive in their large roundness and buff color, his only hen that laid eggs like that.

He looked for telltale signs, like feathers or blood, but nothing showed that might indicate a struggle. There was a coyote, or maybe a dog, about a year ago that killed four of his chickens, each one disappearing two days apart. Maybe

Night Light
Timothy Cole

it had come back, and maybe there would be more gone tomorrow or the next day.

Bud cursed. *He'd get a gun, a trap. He would kill or get rid of every damned dog, cat, coyote, or fox that roamed the neighborhood!*

"Bud, how long you gonna be out there?"

Bud had heard the door open and knew she'd say that. She wouldn't leave him alone, he knew that, too. It was always something.

"What?"

Bud yelled from the open door of the coop, over his shoulder—he wasn't going to turn around and satisfy her that he'd respond to her every demand. He was busy, looking for his favorite chicken.

And he had a lot of things to do—and *she* knew that, too.

If Mavis wanted things done, she could just drop some of that knitting, put away the magazines, forget cleaning the floor every time she turned around, and just come out and work with him for once. She was his helpmate, wasn't she? Didn't the Bible say that? He couldn't do everything. Not when she kept interrupting and changing his direction. She didn't like the color he'd painted the bathroom last fall. She didn't say that, but he could tell by the way she opened the bathroom door and would stand with her hands on her hips, turning her head in that slow, determined way she had of silently criticizing him, when she could've married better, like her mom told him, once.

Oh, Mavis' mom didn't say it aloud, but he could hear her thinking it every time they went over there and the old bag would poke her turkey neck out of the kitchen door and say, "I suppose you want coffee and a sandwich or somethin'." And he'd say, "No, don't bother, we won't be stayin' long," but Mavis would chirp, "Thanks, Mom, that'd be nice," and they'd be there forever. And he'd wait for the cup and the saucer to be handed to him because he'd take it into the living room, turn on the old round tube TV that flickered washed-out images of news, soap operas, and rug commercials. He didn't care what it was, as long as it was noise and it occupied him, kept people from talking to him. He could let his mind wander over the circumstances of his life that drove him to this point.

And that was what Bud was doing now, ruminating over the events that led him into marriage—beside the fact that Mavis was pregnant at the time and threatening serious retribution if he didn't marry her. At the time, Bud thought it was wiser to get married; it would be cheaper.

But there were times, and days, and circumstances that he called *extenyuwatin'* that made him wish he had just driven off in search of one of his adventures that he had long dreamt of while growing up. More often than not, the adventure *du jour* was influenced by a recent movie, book, or late-night conversation with a stay-over friend with covers pulled over their heads and a failing flashlight.

Right now, Bud had no distinct adventure in mind, but a revelation came to him: he could just go jump in the car and let it take him somewhere, get out of this whole mess, this hell-hole, far away, start over, change his name, put this all behind him for once and for all.

He fumbled for his keys. But they weren't in his pocket. He moved into the garage and looked in the car, but they weren't there either. They had to be in the house, of course. He would have to go through the back door and steal his way straight to their room and pull them quietly off the dresser—and get his wallet, too. It was all he needed: his wallet and his keys—and the car. Mavis didn't need the car; she didn't work, had no children in school—*they* didn't have children in school—anymore.

So easy.

I gotta do it!

He turned suddenly and rushed for the garage door. But from the darkness of the gasoline-smelly garage and on the door's threshold of bright sunlight there stood his wife, like an apparition out of the mist. Mavis, it would only be Mavis, seemed to appear suddenly in the doorway,

Night Light
Timothy Cole

startling Bud so that his bladder weakened momentarily, dampening his underwear. She was supposed to be in the house. She never came outside to get him, only yelled for him from the window or the back door. But there she was, not a filament or figment or shadow, no ectoplasmic conjuring, no manifestation from guilt; she was there, fully in body and spirit.

And talking. And gesturing. Toward the house, she was pointing to the house, urging him to come inside, that he'd been too long with the chickens and whatever else he was inventing to keep out of her sight.

With one last look at his car, he followed her dutifully into the kitchen, his mind already clearing all his thoughts of escape and ambitions. By the time the screen door slammed shut behind him, he had no recollection of what he'd been about to do. But the memory of bad coffee and flat eggs was still with him even though a new smell crowded into his nostrils. It was a pleasing, unidentifiable smell, an aroma, one that he knew but couldn't immediately place.

There was also the smell of a struck match, and Mavis took his hand and pulled him, willingly now, into the dining room where small points of light, little flames, took all his attention. Somebody must be burning some papers, but why on the table? Surely, they must be using an ashtray. Or were they candles, little candles. He could smell melting wax, paraffin, like when his mother poured molten wax over preserves, dark red cherries or strawberries, grapes, any kind of jam or jelly, and the wax would harden into an oily, white, thick film that he would be allowed to break open with a dinner knife and spread great globs of jam on toast or biscuits or sneak his spoon into the jar for just a taste of the wonderfully sweet concoctions that lined the basement shelves in his childhood home.

Mavis didn't make jams or jellies. Mavis never melted paraffin for any kind of use. This had to be something else.

156

Blank Slate Writers Group
The Hen that Lays the Eggs

And that something else was the sound, loud and clear, of people singing. The red faces of his son and daughters took shape from the dim glow of birthday candles on a cake, a chocolate cake, his favorite. Finishing their song, they teased him into making a wish, but he simply closed his eyes in pretense, and then automatically blew out the candles, following the process of ritual for the occasion.

Bud's sister was there, too, greedily getting her revenge from an earlier surprise birthday party in which she stubbornly refused to divulge either her age or reveal her wish. She was older and readily knew when Bud was shocked out of the deteriorating abyss of self pity. She knew, too, how to badger him into a better frame of mind, making him giggle like a child. And, later, she would come sit by him on the couch when the others retreated to the kitchen for crumbs and coffee. She knew that commiseration would bring Bud around to reality. Bud could see that coming.

He was happier now, and most of his bitterness was forgotten. With the sweetness of the cake overcoming the morning's breakfast, Bud found that his hand was clasped warmly by Mavis's, and he turned to kiss her on the cheek. It was always good to have your birthday remembered.

Whoever that person was who contemplated release from his everyday trappings was not the same person who stepped out the back door that afternoon to find a fat, brown hen leading six cheeping baby chicks through the yard.

Poem

Open, Sesame
Barbara Funke

Who's too old to cuddle Elmo,
feel that giggle snuggle up?
Forty years and counting (*Eh, eh, eh!*),
my inner child, the mother and the teacher, too,
wish the world felt less
like *Ali Baba's* bandit land and more
like *Sesame Street*
where toddlers walk unthreatened steps and alleys.
There selfish souls from four to forty
(and where's the Count for this?) open wide
a treasure worth accounting.
There great garbage cans surprise
with funny grouches
who are people, too.
There monsters stuffed with humor
and puppets-not-puppets model judgments
slow and open-hearted.
Sponsored by the letters *U*, *R*, *O* and *K*,
the numbers *2* and *3*,
your shy son befriends the deaf boy in day care,
my pale-skinned daughter calls herself *la chica
blanca*
because the words sound fancy to her ear.
United nations for little ones,
the *Street* spells words once alien,

Night Light
Barbara Funke

translates foreign to domestic service,
signs by the Golden Rule.
Urban neighbors *Sesame*-sing our babies
into school age with small steps,
into a world of strangers
so familiar after all
the wide open globe might grow
into a small world
without so little as a Coke
or so much as a gun.

Blank Slate Writers Group

Short Story

In passing
Bob Moulesong

There is nothing as glorious—or sad—as the passing of one generation to another.
—*John Mellencamp*

* * *

"Sit down, kid. Here, take a swig. First one? Ever? No shit! Well, I'm damned proud to give my grandkid his first drink. Burns like a bitch, don't it? Speakin' of, don't tell your mother. Some secrets are best kept in passing.

"Speakin' of secrets, I decided that the time has come to pass mine on to ya. The secret that'll make ya a man, a real man. Yep, right here, right now. Figured I'd better pass it on to ya before I check out. Been feelin' tired lately, and ya never know. Maybe my time's runnin' out. So here goes, kid.

"They'll tell ya that time heals all wounds. That's a crock. As big a crock as Grandma's pierogi pot. Time will not heal wounds. Time won't heal shit. Here, have another swig.

"Time is not your friend, kid. It's your enemy. Every day, we wish we had more time. And every day, we have less. When we're young, we always think we got time. When we're old, we pray for just a little more time to do all the things we blew off when we thought we had plenty of it.

Night Light
Bob Moulesong

"And ya know what the bitch of it is? There's always time to regret all the things we didn't do but we know we shouldda done. Time ain't your friend.

"Hang on while I light up… Beauty of a day, ain't it? You, me, a good drink. What? Oh, yeah, I'm gettin' there…

"So here's the secret that makes ya a man. Love. That's it. Love. Why ya lookin' at me like that? Think I'm shittin' ya?

"Love, kid. Love is your friend. Your only friend. Love is what keeps ya from goin' crazy. Love is everything you'll ever have. Hell, it's the only thing you'll ever have.

"See, kid, love will heal your wounds. Love will make ya cry and make ya laugh. Sometimes both at the same time. Love will make ya do some crazy shit. Remember that when ya ask yourself why ya did the goofy things ya did. You'll find out. And if you're like me, you'll find out over and over again.

"See, that's the one thing that they can't take from ya. They can take your money, your stuff, your time. Hell, your life. But they can't get in your heart, kid. They can never take your love.

"Ya only lose your love if ya quit givin' it out. So what ya do is, ya give it away so's nobody takes it. To your family, your friends, your woman, even grandkids sneaking a drink on the stoop. Ya love 'em all, just as hard and as long and as crazy as ya can. Cuz that's all ya got.

"—Damn, my throat gets dry— And ya tell 'em, all the time. I tell your Grandma I love her every day. Sometimes with words, sometimes with chores, sometimes with candy. Yeah, those chocolate thingamajigs she likes. But every day, I find a way to let her know.

"See, that's what a real man does. It's how ya become a good, strong man. People will tell ya all kinds of shit. That it's all about how much money ya make, or how bad-ass ya are, or the day ya decided to become a bricklayer.

Blank Slate Writers Group
In Passing

"But none of that means shit. Ya really care right now what I did for 40 years to put food on the table? Hell, no, ya don't. It's OK. Ya shouldn't care.

"What matters is that I did it. I loved, kid. I did what I did because I loved my family. Even your pain in the ass mother. Actually, especially your mother. See, it's easy to love the ones who don't drive ya crazy. But it's special to love the ones ya want to whack every day.

"So that's it, kid. Ya _love._

"Now, let's have another swig…

Blank Slate Writers Group

Poem

¡Paleta!

Christina Ortega Phillips

In our neighborhood of run-down
houses, of abandoned lots and corner
groceries, nothing was as refreshing
as a *paleta*: *agua o leche*,
water or milk, both melted
as quickly as the other,
leche making a stickier mess.

How we loved *cada sabor*,
every flavor—for once loving
the taste of fruit.
Sandia, fresa, o limon—
watermelon, strawberry, or lime—
each made with chunks of
the *sabor* mushed within them,

the *paletas* almost *mucho pesado*,
too heavy, to handle, almost *tan grande*,
too large, for the child-mouths
that welcomed them, sucking until
only the stick remained—*a veces*,
sometimes, I'd keep it in my mouth,
trying to get all the flavor I could
from that little piece of wood.

I would listen eagerly for *las campañas*,
the jingle of the bells on that *carrito*,

165

Night Light
Christina Ortega Phillips

run to my mom and beg for change before
running out the door, yelling,
"¡*Paleta*!"to flag *el señor* and his cart down
and breathlessly order *mi nieve*,
my ice cream, *en español* before rushing
away to devour my treat.

Short Story

Spotlight News
Mike Ripley

Bill Gibson finished tying his right boot, stood, and said, "Come on, Al. If we're going to make it before they close, we have to get going."

Al stood, but didn't leave his spot in front of the sixty inch television. He had spent a lot of time watching this wonderful device that was a bonus catch from a previous venture, very similar to the one pulling him away tonight. Why that clerk was watching such a fine TV had amazed Al to distraction, and angered Bill to violence. Of course those were the two directions that Al and Bill were most prone to travel.

"Come on, Al." Bill said again.

"Wait, just two seconds, Al. Take a look at this. Somebody ripped off this house while it was on fire. Nobody would have even noticed that it was robbed if they hadn't left a bunch of shit in the back yard."

He was watching the ten o'clock news. Normally Bill would have been interested too, but tonight they had a plan. This was Wednesday, always a big lottery day at the convenience store, and the perfect night for an easy little heist.

"Heist" was Bill's favorite word. He felt more like Robert DeNiro when his crimes were heists instead of robberies. Robbery parts were given to Billy Baldwin. DeNiro would never simply rob from somebody.

Finally, Al started to move away from the set. He laughed at the news guy stumbling through the conclusion

167

Night Light
Mike Ripley

to the story. "OK, let's go bro." They left the apartment with Al flicking a disposable lighter to the beat of whatever silent song was currently screwing up his head.

The convenient store was actually a gas station that closed at eleven o'clock. At exactly ten forty-eight on this Wednesday night, Al and Bill, wearing identical black ski masks and black leather gloves, stepped inside, and looked around for fellow customers. The store was empty, except for a seventeen-year-old high school senior that lived two blocks away. He was the current, unlucky employee on duty at the scene of the Gibson brother's latest planned heist.

"Lock the door," Bill instructed.

Al spun the deadbolt behind them, and went straight for the cameras. Without looking into them, he sprayed the one in the back corner with paint that he picked right off the shelf in row four. He spun, tossed it across the store to Bill, and returned along the refrigerated pop section.

Bill, pretending that he had a gun, ordered the teenage clerk to put his hands out where they could be seen, and he immediately sprayed the lens of the camera behind the counter. They had learned that these were the only two cameras from a guy they met that used to work at this very BT Gas and Food. As predicted, the young clerk also was no problem.

"Get what you need, man," he said. "I could care less. Just let me out of here."

"Can't do that, kid," Bill replied. "Open the register, and the safe, and put everything in one of your grocery bags."

"I can't open the safe, man."

"Like hell you can't. I know the combination is right under the register drawer. You have to open it for money when the bread guy comes. Pretend he just showed up."

The kid opened the register, and emptied the drawer into the largest bag that they carried. Under the drawer,

168

Blank Slate Writers Group
Spotlight News

and beneath the day's worth of checks and stamps, he found, and removed a folded piece of paper.

"That's it kid. Nobody is going to get hurt. Just don't touch anything down there except the safe, and we'll be out of here in no time."

Only two minutes had passed, but Bill had not seen nor heard Al since he tossed the paint his way. The safe opened, and the boy was putting folded money and rolls of coins into the grocery bag. When he was done, he moved the bag to the counter top.

Al finally showed up with some tape. "Where you been?" asked Bill.

"Checking the place out. It's cool," he responded, out-of-breath, "Let's get going."

"Well tape his ass up, so he doesn't call anybody."

Al jumped the counter, pushed the child to the floor, pulled his arms behind his back, and taped them together at the wrists. He then taped his ankles together, and for good measure, taped his legs to the post where the safe had been secured. Finally, he taped his mouth shut, and jumped back over the counter where Bill was at the door, and ready to go.

They left in their ten year old, silver Cavalier, pulled out of the lot, turned right, the opposite direction of home, and sped down Twenty-Third Street. They were about three blocks away before either spoke. "Where did you disappear to?" asked Bill. "Never do that shit again."

"I was adding a touch," Al said.

"Adding a touch? What the hell does that mean?" Bill turned right on Maywood.

"Oh shit," Al said, excitedly. "Look down that way, you'll see."

Bill looked to his right, and saw fire coming from the back of a building about three blocks away.

"That's not BT Gas is it, you dumb ass?"

"Yep."

Bill hit the brakes. "What about that kid?"

169

Night Light
Mike Ripley

"He'll get out, won't he," Al asked.

"How tight did you tape him up?"

"Not too tight."

"Did you leave him so he could hop out of there?"

"Yeah, sure."

"You didn't tape him to anything, did you?"

"No, he's probably out of there all ready, but let's go back."

The sound of sirens in the distance was just starting to be discernible. Bill and Al sat for a moment looking for red lights. Bill knew that Al was lying, and the kid wouldn't get out. He also knew that they couldn't go back. Slowly, he started to let the car roll away. They rode in silence, the long way back to their apartment. Al turned the television on.

* * *

Down town, in the Spotlight News main studio, exactly one hour before Bill and Al returned to their apartment, Ted Frame stood in front of the set holding up both hands as he counted down from ten. The short clip showing two brown bears milling around a Colorado Supermarket was winding down.

"Four…three….two…one, and back."

The Spotlight News team was closing out tonight's show. The veteran anchor, John Mirer, was just wrapping the final story, "…and I guess that's what they would call a bear market." Slight chuckles were heard around the newsroom. "Don't forget that the Late Show follows in about two minutes. For Mary, Ed, Chuck, and myself, have a safe and enjoyable night. We'll be back tomorrow with more from the Spotlight News on six at ten. Goodnight."

Ted's hands were back in the air. "…three…two…one, and we're off. Sound down, cameras off. OK, wrap it up crew. Good show."

Blank Slate Writers Group
Spotlight News

"What was that clip doing in there?" John asked, while taking off his mike harness, and rising from the Anchor chair. "I know I said the same lame line about the same damn clip six months ago. I looked like an ass up here."

Ted thought against telling him that he usually looked like an ass up there, but instead just ignored the question.

Jim Cross, the Spotlight News Producer had just come down the stairs from the edit room, and arrived in time to hear John's question. "We meet in ten. See you then."

Every night after the news show, the complete Spotlight team held a meeting to discuss any issue at hand. Sometimes it was a five minute meeting, and even if there was nothing to discuss, they got together. That was Jim's rule.

Jim loved effect. He especially loved any effect that he caused. If he didn't hold routine meetings, and he had something to talk about, he would have to schedule one. Once he did that, he would have questions raised by their curiosities, and they would know that something was up. By holding a meeting every night, he could always surprise his staff with his news, and gain the effect that he loved to see. Jim was a bright boy.

John Mirer went to the dressing room with Ed Barnes. Ed was the Spotlight News Weatherman. They used the ten minutes to remove some of the makeup. John finished up and walked down the hall, heading for Jim's office.

Mary Roush went to her own dressing room, and freshened up a bit, but was already in Ted's office by the time John got there. John walked in saying, "This is getting pretty lame Jim. We were left stumbling for two minutes, and then that damn clip. Everybody will remember seeing it. It wasn't that long ago. We used an old clip. What is going on around here?"

"Wait for everybody to come in. Where is Ted?"

"He was right behind me," Mary answered.

Night Light
Mike Ripley

Ed, the Weatherman was just walking into the office, and Jim asked him if he had seen Ted.

"He's down the hall, looking pretty bad," Ed replied.

"I'll get him," said Mary as she left the room. Now only John, Ed, and Jim were sitting around the long oval conference room table. John looked at Jim and gave him his best impatient look. Jim was smiling at the effect.

"Look, Jim," started John. "We don't need everybody here for you to give me a simple answer to my question. We are running out of text, and we're repeating spots from our 'on the scene' reporters."

"Give them a minute, John. I'll give you an answer, but I'm not starting over when they come in."

"I don't care if you do start over. It's my question. It's my concern. Has anybody else expressed an interest in it?"

"Well it's probably the same thing that has Ted's stomach in an uproar."

Ted and Mary were just walking in. "Hey, that's my stomach you're talking about, and I'd appreciate it if you would at least wait until I get here to talk about me."

"That's what I was just telling John," said Jim. "Let's get going. Everybody is here, finally. John, now ask your questions."

"I just asked what's going on. Did we cut back staff? Are we not getting enough from the wire, or did we lose a reporter? Something is off. I was left out to dry for about five minutes out there tonight, and had to wing it. I've never had to do that before. You typically put so much into the prompter that Mary and I have to talk eighty miles an hour. Don't you see it too, Mary?"

"Yes, of course I see it, John. I was watching you wing it along with everybody else."

"You weren't exactly jumping in."

"Not while the camera is on you, I'm not jumping in." Mary privately enjoyed watching John stumble. She had her own ambitions. Bailing him out wasn't high on her priority list.

Blank Slate Writers Group
Spotlight News

"Ok, you want an answer," Jim jumped in. "I'll try to explain what happened tonight."

"Why doesn't Chuck ever have to come to these meetings?" Ed the weatherman blurted in.

Chuck Wiley was the up and coming sportscaster that the network had sent in. He technically reported to Jim, but had direct connections with New York. He seldom worried about discussing anything with Jim or Ted, and absolutely never attended any of these meetings.

"Come on, Ed," Mary said. "You know why he doesn't come."

"Well then why should I?" asked Ed.

"Leave. Maybe then Jim can answer my question," John answered.

"Oh shit, my stomach," said Ted. He popped a handful of antacids, and looked at Jim. "Can't you just get this done?" He turned to Ed. "Just get over it, Ed. If you can't get over it, then leave. I've never seen this group in such a crazy mood as you guys have been in over the past week. Let's worry about that. Unless you suddenly get very well connected, you're not going to come and go like Chuck."

"OK, here it is," Jim started to take over the conversation. "If it's alright for me to go on, that is." He looked around the room to blank faces. He expected more. "On every news day since I've been doing this job, we go through the same routine before you guys ever come in. We have twenty-two minutes to fill. The Weather takes a mandatory three minutes based on network guidelines. The sports segment gets five. Sorry, Ed. We have the obligatory four minutes of human interest pieces, and that leaves you two with ten minutes of hard news. We get feeds from the wire and our own crews that amount to about forty minutes every day. I have to whittle this forty minutes of news down to your ten minutes of air time."

"I've heard that you sit in here and whittle something," Mary said. "I guess it's confirmed now."

Night Light
Mike Ripley

"Thanks for your input Mary, but don't be upset if I just ignore you now. I want to get through this. Starting yesterday, you've been getting everything I've got. I blew it tonight, but not by five minutes. I thought that spot on the house fire robbery was three minutes, and it turned out to air two. You only had about sixty seconds to cover."

"That had to be longer," John insisted.

"You lose time when you freeze, John," Mary shot back.

"Ok, do you guys get it?" Jim asked.

Ed spoke up first. "Are you saying that we don't have enough news?"

"Yeah."

"You mean like in the world?"

"Yeah. The wire is slow as hell. I've sent teams out to cover local things, and they just dry up. We have spots in the six o'clock news that fizzle out by ten. Tonight I was sure that the accident on Sixteenth Street was going to be our out. We had a crew there live. I would have had Ted go to them, but it was cleared up before we were ready. It wasn't even that bad to begin with. You guys reported all of the news that we had. Nothing was left on the floor except a report about an old lady still delivering baked goods to shut-ins when she is ninety-nine years old. She'll be real news next year."

"Ok, so what about tomorrow?" John asked.

"Well, this must be a fluke. Just in case, I've lined up ten minutes of fluff to be shot during the day tomorrow. We've got all four crews going out. We'll get some things in the can, and when I need them, we'll put them on. Hopefully, they won't all be needed tomorrow."

"We can't just sit there," Mary jumped in. "What I mean is that we can't just sit and introduce little clips for thirty minutes."

"Twenty-two," Ed responded.

Jim was smiling. He was getting his reactions now. "I know. John asked what happened out there. I just told

Blank Slate Writers Group
Spotlight News

you. I'm sure that this week is unique. It's never happened before, and I don't expect it to ever happen again. All I'm trying to let you know is that I'm making sure that we get ourselves better prepared. We have these spots ready, and I won't leave you hanging. You'll be talking fast again by tomorrow night."

"Can we go now?" asked Ted.

"Yes."

The Spotlight News team disbanded for the night just like they did every night. They each went their separate ways. Ed and Mary lived close enough together to share a ride, but had never even considered it. Ed normally went straight home, and tonight was no exception. Mary normally went another direction.

John followed her one night about a month ago. He watched as she went into a west side club called The Norm. It was one of those places where the modern interior décor didn't quite mesh with the beer garden out back that was lit with hanging green, red, and yellow lights. She stayed inside, so John had a tough time keeping an eye on her without being seen. He saw her go straight to a table and join a man who had his back to John's vantage point. After about two minutes, the man turned and faced him. It was Chuck, and he definitely saw John watching them.

John got out of there, and spent the next week expecting Mary to give him shit about following her. Evidently, Chuck never told her what he saw.

Tonight Ed went home, Mary headed west, Chuck was already long gone, and John offered to buy Ted a drink. Ted refused as usual, and went straight to his apartment. John decided to walk the three blocks to the Upstreet Drinkery and Grub Club, his favorite local establishment. On the way, he thought about Mary wedging her way in with the guy that had connections. He also thought about the lack of news. He faintly heard sirens in the distance that he knew might be a story in progress.

175

Night Light
Mike Ripley

During the second block, there was a guy that he was going to pass by that kept staring at him. John wondered if he got mugged, would it be on tomorrow's news? Would he be a story that would fill the minutes on the air? After all, that's what they are, stories. Do they always have to be bad to be considered newsworthy?

During the third block he realized for the first time that his job actually depended on bad news. Bad things must happen in the world to keep him employed. There had never before been a shortage to even cause him to stop and think about it.

Finally, he reached the bar near his apartment. As usual, he stopped in.

The next night, John arrived at the studio at eight o'clock. He was getting off the elevator and walking towards his dressing room to prepare for the show, and couldn't resist stopping by the editing room to see how Jim was doing. "What's it look like tonight, Jim?"

"We're fine. You go get ready. We'll fill your air time without a problem."

What Jim didn't tell John was that it would be filled with the work that the remote crews had done during the day. He was only able to get about six minutes of hard news for John and Mary, but he had plenty of film. Now, it was just a matter of getting them timed out in the edit room to fill the space. He also had a live crew at a speech being given by Senator Mason at the new hospital wing opening. Tonight would be a breeze. They had plenty of fluff.

* * *

Several miles away Bill and Al sat in front of their television eating a double cheese pizza. Al had felt sick all day and hadn't left the apartment. Bill had started the day still a little upset with Al for last night, but by now,

Blank Slate Writers Group
Spotlight News

wouldn't even look at him. They hadn't talked for about three hours. The only words either of them had uttered during that time were when Al ordered the pizza.

Bill and Al had sat on the couch watching news reports all day. Each time they both thought that something would change. They had made the news before, but on every one of those occasions, they had jumped, shouted, and even high-fived each other. Today, it took until mid-afternoon to not feel sick. Now they could barely get through their favorite meal.

Tonight was day four of Bill's major heist plan. In total, there were six jobs to be done this week. Six and out. They would have all the money they would need for a long time to come. Six and out. They would be gone from this town, gone from the crazy weather, gone from all of their problems. They needed to be thinking about part four, but they were locked into three. They needed to see the news again. They needed to know for sure. Maybe it would change. Maybe the boy didn't die.

At exactly ten o'clock on this Thursday evening, John Mirer said hello to the audience of Spotlight News on Six at Ten. Spotlight News had enjoyed a successful run as the city's number one news show for over a decade. It was the last source of news for about a million people right before they turned the set off and called it a night. The other two major news shows had been in a fight for second place for so long that they considered it fine. Second was their prize.

Ted Frame was considered the best in the business, and received a great deal of the credit for the show's success. He was a fixture at the station. Anchors had come and gone, and even Jim Cross had been named the producer only three years ago. Ted was in his twelfth year as director. He ran a clean ship, and provided a tight thirty-minute live show night after night. That's why this week had bothered him and his stomach. It was anything but tight.

Night Light
Mike Ripley

Jim was responsible for the content, but Ted ran the show. Tonight he was in early enough to go over everything himself. He wasn't going to be left with a clip scripted at two minutes that would wind up running only one. John Mirer wasn't an anchor that could handle that.

Everything was perfect tonight.

Bill and Al sat there watching on their sixty inch set . They had talked a little at about nine o'clock, and decided that they were going on with their mission. They would finish this out, and get the hell away from here. Tonight's job was different than the previous, and it wouldn't get out of hand. It was an ATM that they knew how to get into. The ATM was busy all day, but resided in a spot mostly vacant at night. Bill had done the homework. A truck came at ten fifteen every night to fill it up. They would wait until nobody was around. Tonight, nobody could get hurt.

The sports segment was already on. They hadn't mentioned their work. How could it be gone already? Bill checked his watch. He knew that the ATM was being filled with cash, and he was ready to start heading over to it. It would take about twenty minutes to get there. "Come on Al, let's get moving."

Al stood, but didn't move. "Wait a minute. I can't believe there's nothing on. Just wait. Maybe they'll get back to it."

"What does it matter? Come on."

"I don't know. It matters."

"Come on."

"Shit." Al turned the television off, threw the remote on the couch, and followed Bill out the door. They found their ATM, broke it open, and got the money just like Bill had planned. Day four's heist had gone on schedule, and with no surprises.

"…three…two…one, and we're off. Sound down, cameras off. OK, wrap it up crew. Good show." Ted grabbed his stomach and took off down the hall.

Blank Slate Writers Group
Spotlight News

"What's wrong with him now?" John was getting out of his wires, and felt pretty good about tonight's show.

"I don't know. That went pretty well. We didn't have much to go on, but we did just fine. Go see what's wrong." Mary was already heading towards her dressing room and left John to check on Ted.

"Jim, I think Ted's in bad shape." John tried to turn Jim down the hall as they came together from their opposite perches.

"I bet he is. That was some shit, wasn't it?"

"What? I thought we did fine."

"You did fine, John. Don't worry about it."

Ed Barnes wondered over to the area, "Hey, what's up? Don't worry about what?"

"Yeah, what did you mean by that?" asked John.

"We meet in five minutes. Let's go over it then." Jim was getting some effect. He wasn't about to let it go without making them all wait a bit.

Everybody was in Jim's office within five minutes tonight. Everybody, that is, except for Chuck.

"OK, we're all here," John started. "I thought that went fine. We did our job. Ted, you did yours, and Jim, we all had something to say during the whole show. What the hell did you guys see that was so bad?"

"I told you not to worry about it, John. You did fine. Mary did fine. Even Ted did fine. I'm the one that screwed up, and my phone already rang. I have to call New York back right after our meeting. You didn't notice anything missing from tonight's show?"

"No," John said immediately.

"Well, I did," interjected Ted. "News."

"What news?" asked Mary.

"Exactly," started Jim. "Now you're getting it."

Everybody sat there looking around the room for ten or fifteen seconds. Finally, Ed broke the silence. "I'm glad that all of you are getting it now, but I am still pretty damn lost. What the hell is going on?"

Night Light
Mike Ripley

Ted spoke up. "Ed, there wasn't any news on tonight's show. We had some, and Jim and I planned to use it. We got together early today, and we were so damn concerned about those filler pieces, that we left out the news."

"It wasn't your fault, Ted," Jim said. "I'm in charge of content. I was the one so excited about the film that we had. I left the other shit out."

"Well those clips were pretty good," said Mary. "Your remote teams did a great job today."

"You know what, guys? I liked the show. Everything we aired was news. I'm going to send them out again tomorrow, and put their work on the air again. What I have to remember is to blend in some regular news." Jim was actually smiling.

"Now we're worried about blending in news as a filler to have something to put between your interest clips?" asked Ted.

"Yeah, something like that, Ted. Let's get out of here. Tomorrow will go better, and I've got a call to make."

Jim Cross called New York at exactly eleven o'clock. Network management had a team of people that monitored all live local broadcasts via their satellite hookups. Only one thing was noticed by the monitor assigned to Jim's station: There was no mention of the Avanta Airlines jet that crashed near Mexico City that afternoon. Every affiliate, and all national news broadcasts ran this important bit of news on every show. Somebody wondered why Jim didn't have a time slot to fit it in.

"We left it laying on the floor," Jim replied to his accuser. "I don't have any excuses. We've been having problems getting the time filled, like everybody else, and I was so busy trying to fill the holes that I left it out."

The other end of the line was silent for a long while. "You know that the drought is over, don't you? That wasn't fun for a lot of people, but it was a fluke. There is plenty of news, and you had better get it on the air. Hell,

Blank Slate Writers Group
Spotlight News

six o'clock ran it fine. All you have to do is use that script to start with."

"Don't start telling me how to run this thing. You know I know what to do. I just blew it tonight. We'll be fine."

"Just make sure."

Thomas Bradley hung up the phone in New York. Jim had received his message, and was sure that Bradley had other calls to make. The monitors were like the little snitches that watch and tell the boss. The boss then makes the calls to lay down the law, and makes sure that everybody knows he is watching. Jim happened to hate this part of the business. He didn't, however, tell Mr. Bradley that he had actually liked the show. It didn't seem like the right thing to say.

Bill was relieved that day four of the major heist plan had gone well. There were two nights left, and tonight, being Friday, was reserved for the most difficult plan of all. It was a little after ten o'clock, and once again Al needed to be nudged from the television. Spotlight News was on the air, and it attracted Al like a magnet.

"Look at these women," Al said as he sat there putting on his shoes. "This is going on now, Bill. Look at this."

Bill moved back to the couch and looked at what had Al so excited. Three women had put together a charity contest at a local paint ball shooting range. They were the Three Amigos, and challenged anybody to bring their team down to beat them: three on three. Anybody that could beat them would get a free weekend in Orlando.

"There has to be a catch," Bill said.

"What catch? Maybe they're just good."

"Come on, Al. Let's go."

"Wait a minute." The segment on the paint ball for charity event was over. The weather was next, and Al was still sitting on his ass.

181

Night Light
Mike Ripley

"Al, come on. What are you doing? The sooner we get this over, the better. Two jobs left, remember? Then we're out of here."

"Why don't we skip tonight, Bill? We have enough."

"The plan, dumbass. Stick to the plan."

"I don't want to go tonight."

"You were fine ten minutes ago."

"Well that was then. Let's just go over to this paint ball place, have a little fun, and forget tonight."

"You are crazy, you know it," Bill left the apartment. He went downstairs, and outside to figure out what to do. He stood on the porch at the front of the building and watched cars going each way on the street, as if they all had places to go. They all had a plan.

Al watched the rest of the news, and Bill walked back in at ten twenty-eight. Mary was bringing in a live feed to wrap up the show. Just as Bill's luck would have it, they were closing out the show back at the paint ball arena.

"Come here, look at this," Al said.

Bill sat on the couch next to Al. Together they watched the excitement on the screen.

"Look, that guy has night vision goggles on. Look at that gun." Al was getting excited now.

Bill was starting to smile as he too had found an interest in charity. "Oh, shit, they're going to nail her. Ouch, lady."

"Let's go," begged Al.

"We don't have any of that stuff. It's not like you can just walk in and start shooting people."

Bill's timing was impeccable. Just as he finished, the segment ended. John closed the show as normal, but before he said goodbye, he said, "It looks like they're having a ball at Rainbow Challenge Arena, and nobody has beaten The Three Amigos yet. Get over there before midnight. Remember, the people at Rainbow will set you up with all the gear you need at no charge for tonight. All you have to do is donate twenty-five dollars per person to

Blank Slate Writers Group
Spotlight News

The Feed America Foundation. Now for Mary, Ed, Chuck, and myself, have a safe and enjoyable night. We'll be back tomorrow with more from the Spotlight News on six at ten. Goodnight."

Bill was hooked, "Ok, let's go. We'll check this out, and decide if we want to stay, but tomorrow night, no screwing around. Count this as a favor. You got it?"

"Yeah sure, let's go. You want to go as bad as I do."

Al and Bill arrived at Rainbow Challenge at eleven o'clock.

"I'm using that gun," Al said, as he pointed behind the young girl at the counter.

"That gun isn't a part of the Feed America program, sir." The girl, Lisa, held out a small handgun, and a handful of paint balls. "You'll also need the protective gear. It's all over there in the viewing room. They'll set you up, and you'll need to donate twenty-five dollars to Mrs. Ellis. She'll be in the viewing room too."

"How much extra would I have to pay to use that gun?"

"You would have to buy it. Anybody can bring their own gear, but tonight we only rent out the ten shot Little Bucks."

"How much?"

"That gun is almost two hundred dollars, sir."

Bill stepped in, and Al thought he was going to pull him away, "We'll take two," he said, "and how much are the balls?"

"The balls are twenty dollars for a box of one hundred. Mr. James, can you come back here? I've never handled selling one of these guns before."

Mr. James was the owner of Rainbow Challenge. He smiled at Lisa, walked behind the counter, turned to Bill and Al, and said, "Hi, fellas. What can I do for ya?"

"We want two of those guns," Al told him.

"OK, do you need any protective gear? I'll throw in some balls for your first time out."

Night Light
Mike Ripley

"Can we just use what they have in there?" asked Bill.

"Sure. In fact... *Mrs. Ellis!*" Randle James was now shouting across the room at the same Mrs. Ellis that Lisa was sending the boys to see in the viewing room. "Come over here a minute, will ya."

Nancy Ellis, one of the Three Amigos, herself, walked over and joined the group. "What's up, Randy? Linda took over for me in there for a few minutes. Wow, this turned out well. We're packed."

"These two guys are planning to buy four hundred dollars worth of guns. I just wanted you to know that I'm giving all the profit to Feed America. They'll be in there in just a minute to pick up some guards, and pay their twenty-five."

"You didn't tell us you were doing that. That's wonderful."

"I planned to hold that till the end, but this is our big sale of the night, and I thought I'd grab you while I could."

"In that case, we'll just go ahead and buy the other gear too. That sound good, Al?" Bill was obviously getting into the spirit now. He typically got loose with his money when it would impress people the most. Al was just excited about all the new toys.

When everything was settled, Bill handed Randy James six hundred and fifteen dollars in cash. They carted everything to the viewing room, and paid Linda fifty dollars for their donation to Feed America.

There was a line forming at the counter, and the parking lot was full. Nancy and Randy walked into the viewing room as Bill and Al were getting suited up. First, Nancy announced the new donations and introduced the two like they were celebrities. Al lit up like a Christmas tree, finished getting ready, and took off for the arena. Bill wasn't far behind.

"Look, we may have a little problem," Linda said to Randy.

Blank Slate Writers Group
Spotlight News

"What's that?"

"We're supposed to close at midnight. Look at that line."

"Do you ladies want to stay later?"

"We'll stay as long as you will let us."

"Ok, I'll work it out with the staff, and make an announcement. You better get suited up. Nobody has won the trip yet. Will the folks who donated it mind if you stretch the time out?"

"They were expecting to lose. I think we're doing better than we were supposed to do at this."

Rainbow Challenge stayed open until two o'clock that morning. The charity was a raving success, and most importantly, Al and Bill teamed up with an eighteen-year-old boy named, Justin, and beat the Three Amigos. They won the trip to Orlando.

"Thank you," Nancy Ellis told them. "You guys deserve this."

Al and Bill stayed around the viewing room and talked while they put all of their new gear into canvas bags that Randy James had given them. "We had a ball," said Al. "Do you do this very often?"

"No, this was the first time for paint ball, but we do have events about once a month. Nothing this fun, though."

"Can we join you? I'd like to help."

Bill piped in, "We're not sure where we're going to be next month, Al."

"We might be in Orlando," Al blurted out.

Bill was ready to go. He, like Al, had an absolute ball, and wasn't against the idea of helping these ladies out some more. He, however, remembered that they had a plan. "Let's get going, Al. Thanks ladies."

Bill and Al went home, dropped back on the couch, and turned on the television. There was a late night news break on, and reality was put back in their laps. "No leads on the person or persons responsible for the death of Alan

Night Light
Mike Ripley

Rooney at the BK Gas convenient store on Tuesday night."

A clip was running showing flames coming from the store was all too familiar to Al and Bill. Bill got up, turned the television set off, and went to bed. Al stayed on the couch, and started to cry.

The next night at ten fifteen, half-way through Spotlight News, "...three...two...one, and we're away."

Laughter had gotten the best of everybody on the set. Mary Roush had blown her line, and the sad part was that her line was, "In a storm that devastating, something is bound to be destroyed beyond salvage." In her haste to get beyond the clip about the barn falling, she replaced *devastating* with *masturbating*. "In a storm that's masturbating, something is bound to be destroyed beyond salvage."

The commercial was almost over, and nobody had control on the set. As they returned, John just needed to introduce Chuck for the sports segment, and then it was up to him, "And now, Chuck, how about that finish at the second round of the open? It was like Bubba was playing by himself."

Chuck could not speak. He choked back laughter for fifteen seconds before he lost his grip. "Oh, it certainly seemed that way, John," he finally blurted out in a burst so fast you could hardly understand him. Then it got worse. The whole crew laughed as control was totally gone. Chuck tried to start up several times, but took too long to get back on track.

Ted rolled the prompter ahead a couple stories, and flashed the local scores on the screen. Chuck finally joined in and read as they were displayed. He had it down, and finally finished Spotlight Sports.

Of course there was going to be meeting. Jim did not speak to anybody after the telecast, and was waiting in his office for everybody to show up. Tonight they were very

Blank Slate Writers Group
Spotlight News

slow to gather. They laughed for a good ten minutes after they were off the air. Finally they were all assembled and ready to go, when in walked Chuck.

"Hey, you mind if I join tonight?"

"Hell no," said Ed. "Come on in."

Jim started the meeting, "You know how deep my ass is in over this? I'm not going to get through it. First they don't like our content, and now they know we can't even get through it on the air. They are going to have my ass."

"Come on, Jim," John said. "It can't be that bad."

Chuck was looking at Jim. "No wait, John. It is that bad. Jim is way out on a limb here. He's not making it up."

"No shit," Jim agreed.

"What are they going to do?" Mary asked. "I screw up a line, and you're in trouble?"

"I'm in trouble, because of everything the past week or so. Not because you screwed up a line, Mary. We haven't been reporting a lot of the stories they want on the air. I am going with our ratings. We are getting double the audience of the next news show. We are reporting what they want. We got about a thousand calls today, and they were all good. I also got several thank you notes from organizations that are seeing record turnouts and contributions. It has dawned on me that we might be doing a little good here, but it's not what we are supposed to be about."

"What are we then?" This was Mary again.

"We were supposed to do a story on date-rape tonight. This is a college town. I'm sure there are stories out there. All we had to do was send somebody over to city hall like usual. I didn't do it."

"I'm lost now," John said. "What do you mean we were supposed to do a story on date-rape? Did something happen that should have been news?"

"Well that's the question, isn't it? What should be the news? We're giving them news, but the going belief is that we need to give them bad news. There's more than enough

Night Light
Mike Ripley

going on out there. I just didn't realize that some of it is good until we needed it to fill time this week. Yesterday's show was huge, and we left the normal stuff on the floor. I bet tonight's ratings are great too."

"What about the date-rape story?" asked Mary.

"There is going to be a segment Sunday night on network prime time about date-rape. It always piques the interest if we have stories that relate to those shows. Hell, we have even had to use real stories to pitch network movies that were coming up. Why do you think we hear about something until we're sick of it, and then it suddenly goes away? It isn't a problem any longer. The damn stories just aren't needed any longer."

"It's not that bad," John said. "I know they've done that at times, but not all that often."

"How about every week, at least," replied Jim.

"This is big business," Chuck said. "Jim is going to be lucky to survive if things don't change quick."

"But I'm the one doing it, guys. It's not you. And by the way, I'm not changing it."

* * *

Al and Bill had been watching the Spotlight News broadcast, and rolled on the floor until ten forty-five. They had another night of the plan, the last night. Neither was in any mood to get it done.

"Let's just go over there," said Al.

Bill thought about objecting. It would have been normal to object. Then he said, "OK, let's go. I'm hungry."

The boys had seen 'Al's Diner' on the news before all the laughter started. It is great American food and they stay open late. That was enough for the two of them tonight. No crime, just food, and maybe a little fun.

"That a boy, Bill. Let's just have dinner and maybe find something better to do tonight."

Blank Slate Writers Group
Spotlight News

* * *

Jim Cross received his phone call. "If things are not back to normal Monday night, you will be out of a job."

"I do not plan to change anything, but I understand your warning."

Jim hung up the phone. He had seen a light, and would never feel right just putting up the news again. He knew he was going to lose this. There was no way to win in sight. He went home.

During this especially peaceful night in St. Louis, Jim slept well. He knew that he might lose his job. Hell, he counted on it now. He knew that everything he had believed in during his career was false, and he believed that it might have even been evil, but he also knew that it had all recently changed forever. He would never go back to spewing the evening news according to the network gods.

Jim knew that there might be just a few people affected by what he did at ten o'clock every night, but that they were typically the ones making the news, making things bad, and making his conscience seem heavier each night of his life. It would stop now, at least for him, it would stop.

What he didn't know was that over the past couple of weeks every special event, every charity, every bake sale, hog roast, festival, and bingo game that Spotlight News had covered reached their record attendance, contribution, and profit due in large part to the publicity brought on by their coverage. People took action, because they were told it was a good thing to do by Spotlight News.

John decided at home that night that he would follow Jim's lead and take a stand against the network. Ed decided that he would stick to the weather. Mary and Chuck met once again at The Norm and discussed their future.

Monday night's show ran with tales of charity, signs of decent people, reviews of great food, and a section on the cardio benefits of dancing. Bill and Al stayed in town, ate

Night Light
Mike Ripley

at the restaurant they saw on Spotlight News, and Jim was fired. John went with him.

On Tuesday night Bill and Al sat eating Chinese carryout, and watching the Spotlight News on Six at Ten. They watched in disbelief, as the new anchor, Mary Roush explained the disappearance of John Mirer, and his desire to pursue bigger adventures. She beamed as she brought the news of the disturbance near Western and Third Street. She seemed delighted at the murder near Union Station, and she was absolutely on top of the world over date rape at Washington University.

"Did you see that dude on the west side?" Al asked. "It looked like his head was caved in."

"Do you think it's still going on?" wondered Bill.

"Who knows? They wouldn't tell us the truth."

"Let's go over there."

"OK."

Bill and Al went to the intersection of Western and Third streets. There were in fact still remnants of the violence that had been going on there since about eight o'clock that night. They got themselves involved just as a mid-town gang arrived on the scene and decided to take things up a notch. With the first sound of gunfire, Al fell to his knees. Bill ran to him, and was taken down within moments by the same gun.

"Al, let's take all this back. Let's get out of here."

"I can't move."

"Neither can I."

The new Spotlight News Team was on the scene within minutes. The violence was duly reported at ten.

Blank Slate Writers Group

Poem

Nightwalk

Barbara Funke

The gravel crunching of our mute parade
winds among daisies and the rock walls
of tiny broken rooms.
Unroofed kivas stare up at us.
Slow wind and crickets symphonize.
Flower and soft pine scents tease.
The great dipper tips in its dark well of stars.
Venus preens; the moon grins.

Our procession pauses.
Gothic cliffs stand sentinel over Frijoles Canyon.
Their vaulted halls and roomlets turn shoulders
to Luna's blue-white.
The mountain furnaces flicker with molten walls.
Their drums grow from heartbeat to engine
under the chant to wail of an ancient voice.
I sense the singer stepping high,
feathered, beaded, oiled,
shadowing the rock with dance.
Rhythmic honey oozes up,
rises in the comb of stone bones
on balanced torch points of the People ghosts,
glows in the caverns,
the precipice a pulsing coal.

Night Light
Barbara Funke

We retreat; they beat at our backs.
We raise heads to the cliffs,
lower eyes to the path,
scuff shoes on the time-tumbled gravel,
hold hands as if scorned,
leading each other out
of the garden of fire and stones.

Blank Slate Writers Group

Short Story

Waiting for Santa
Joyce Hicks

Lately for Anita so many true things turned out not to be true, or at least not true to her original assumption, that she began to wonder if this were a first sign of dementia.

One misperception had occurred earlier in the week while she was driving. Anita saw a boy hanging over a porch railing. His coatless, skinny arms hung down flailing desperately in an attempt to stand. Was he stuck, or had he collapsed in a seizure? Just moments from attempting a rescue, Anita saw that the struggling child was really a huge Christmas bow tied to a porch rail, its tails flying in the wind.

Then yesterday while reading, she had glanced into the bright snow of the front yard to find black areas in her vision. So, it had come to this, the holes her optometrist had warned her to report immediately. Macular degeneration. Suddenly, the holes shifted, and she realized the yard was simply full of black birds—birds so numerous that they made shifting black spots against the snow as they rose swirling and settling, moving as if with a single GPS. A *murmuration*, she learned later while doing a crossword puzzle.

In the different vein of mental irregularity, she was unreasonably distressed by carelessness in this season of care. Wire deer lying helter-skelter unlit or a nylon lawn Santa deflated would make her weep over this thoughtless treatment of Christmas icons.

Night Light
Joyce Hicks

On the bright side, she was invited to the traditional family trip to Chicago to visit Santa, and it felt good to anticipate this ritual where her role as a second pair of adult eyes assured no child got lost in the crowds.

When the outing day came and Anita, her two grandchildren, and her daughter got to the famous department store, Anita took the exasperating job of pushing the stroller that was top-heavy when loaded with everyone's coats but empty of a child. Often it tipped backward onto her feet what were already roasting in her boots. At the grand dining room, they found seating under the three-story Christmas tree could be a two-hour wait. After an oversized elf provided a pager, they decided to visit Santa Land before lunch.

Anita obediently agreed to stand in line for Santa and Mrs. Claus while her daughter waited in the line for balloon animals and face painting with nine-year-old Caitlin and three-year-old Benjamin. She amused herself by comparing her grandchildren to other youngsters. Caitlin was lithe as a dancer with dark eyes and winsome gestures, heartbreakingly lovely from top to toe. Benjamin was a sturdy milk-drinker right out of a Dick and Jane reader, a "little fellow." Of course, her two were the stars of the flock and were behaving themselves beautifully.

Next Anita focused on Mrs. Claus. The woman was a wonder as she primed each child for a visit with her hubby, whom she regarded with such warmth that Anita wondered if he was her real husband. Or perhaps this signaled that it was not her husband. Mrs. Claus crossed her arms over her middle, patted her white curls and laughed, making her cheeks even rosier. She looked so comforting in her long apron that Anita wanted to put her own head on the ample bosom to whisper an anxiety nibbling at her holiday pleasure—*that she may have left the stove burner on under the coffee pot.*

Of course, she had turned it off, or thought she had turned it off. Wouldn't she have noticed it was on when

194

Blank Slate Writers Group
Waiting for Santa

she did the dishes? But no, she hadn't done the dishes today. That meant right about now her smoke alarm was going off uselessly, and the pot was red hot ready to cause a domino effect of puckered paint, falling plaster, and exposed flammable lath.

Anita took her hands off the stroller and it tipped over just as their turn came for Santa, piling coats this time on Mrs. Claus.

"My, you have quite a load there. How are you today?" Mrs. Claus looked at the empty stroller.

"I'm worried actually. I'm not sure I turned off my stove."

"My goodness, I've had my stove on a lot too these days. Why, I was just baking for the elves." Mrs. Claus beamed at Anita.

"Do you always remember whether you turned it off?"

"Dearie me. They do go through a batch of gingerbread faster than you can say Jack Frost."

"I just have a feeling that I didn't—"

"Do you have any little ones with you?" Mrs. Claus looked again at the stroller.

"Oh, yes, they're over with my daughter getting their faces painted."

"Well, ah, here's Santa ready to hear some Christmas wishes now. My goodness, what a pretty dress, little lady."

Anita hastily wrestled the stroller upright, realizing the compliment was for the child behind her in line.

Chairs along the sidelines for tired merrymakers called to Anita. She flopped down and let the stroller do the same. From here she had a good view of the children and began to focus on the handiwork of the artists. Of course, she had seen face painting before—blots of red on cheeks for clowns, a black nose for a dog, or blue lines around the eyes for princesses—and she thought it was kind of dumb unless for Halloween. But this display was another thing entirely.

Night Light
Joyce Hicks

Little faces of diverse cultures were now birthed in a new race of imps——living flowers, tropical birds, and indefinable creatures. The paint was thick and nuanced with vine tendrils, leaves, or insect parts that reached down cheeks or disappeared into ears and hair. Each artist had created not by request but by what suited the face, Anita could see. The children, feeling their metamorphosis, grouped according to species. Some painted children had gone through the balloon line too and carried fanciful twists much larger than the street fair variety. Anita saw aircraft, ponies, dogs, and giant insects.

Anita spotted Benjamin and Caitlin and waved them over. They were going to miss Santa if they didn't get in line.

"Are you having fun?" she asked Caitlin.

"I told her I wanted to be a cat, but the paint lady said this would be better."

Anita examined Caitlin's face. Her left eye formed one petal of a gray and silver flower whose other painted petals reached from her cheek to forehead, its center a rhinestone at her eyebrow. The golden brown iris and dark pupil flower petal regarded Anita. Caitlin's other eye that peered out of green leaves and vines seemed like a detached onlooker.

"Well, that's quite something." As Anita searched for right words for the somewhat malevolent flower face, Benjamin ran to her. Of course, he would want to be his favorite animal, a lion.

"Let's see you——"

Benjamin turned up his face. Anita gasped. He was a copy of Santa himself, complete with wire framed painted-on glasses, but somehow the effect was troll-like, a Brothers Grimm sort of Santa.

"I'm Santa! Ho-ho-ho. I'm going to put coal in your stocking!"

"Goodness, Benny, did you ask to be an old man?"

Blank Slate Writers Group
Waiting for Santa

"I said a lion." He held a three-legged balloon animal on a stick. "Gr-r-oo. Gr-oo." He waved it around.

"What's that? Tell grandma."

"A monster lion. Gr-oo-oo-oo."

The children capered around, until Anita said, "You'd better go stand with your mom if you want to see Santa."

She could see her daughter was in conversation with other women in the Santa line that was even longer than before. Bits of sentences drifted her way about daycare costs, sports schedules, ADHD meds, and holiday fatigue.

"If only I could get just one night's uninterrupted sleep," one woman said, shaking her index finger for emphasis.

Anita settled in for a wait, thinking how her sleep was also punctuated by interruptions, wakefulness with no purpose—no binky to find, no warm back to rub, no one next to her for spooning.

Her possible negligence of her coffee pot spoiled the relief of sitting down, so to find out if the house was burning, she called a neighbor.

"Hello Millie. I just wanted to say Merry Christmas… Yes, me too, I've got my shopping done….Did you see that flock of starlings yesterday? …Me neither, never so many before…Well, I'll be seeing you. Bye."

With no mention of fire trucks from Millie, Anita decided her house was safe and she began to relax. "Not batty yet," she muttered, happy for validation of her memory of turning off the stove.

The sparkle faeries, hired young help meant to entertain, began a game. The blue faery led children along a pattern of flower decals on the floor, everyone waving arms in time with the music. When she stopped, each child pounced on a flower. Anyone without a spot had to return to stand with parents. A few little ones cried.

Anita waved at her two as they skipped around behind the blue faery who moved more and more quickly to the escalating music. She began to twirl and raise her arms in a

Night Light
Joyce Hicks

passionate dance. Skipping and grabbing children's hands to play crack-the-whip, she zigzagged through the adults.

"That teenager looks possessed," Anita said to another woman who had taken the chair beside her. "It's so hot in here, don't you think?" The other woman smiled but did not answer. Anita waved her hat like a fan.

As the children circled, then dashed and froze on the flowers, Caitlin flitted by once, then lit on a flower in front of Anita, moving sinuously. Her neck had grown green vines, and her cupped hand looked like a small bird as she moved her wrist.

"You got more face paint?" Anita called out, but her granddaughter was gone, the bird on her hand leading her away.

Soon Benjamin marched by with a gaggle of toddlers wearing balloon antlers. He cavorted, hunching over and then walking on tiptoes. His followers pranced and hoofed. He waved his three-legged animal in time to the music and beckoned to them to follow him toward the faeries. Anita noticed that the light in the room was playing tricks with color; her grandson's hair had turned white.

Instead of stopping so the children could land on a flower and rest, the music raced on. The red faery and green one joined the dance, for that's what it was now, a wild and free undulation of children around the room. The dresses of the faeries billowed into long trains that the girls grabbed and twined around themselves. The bird children leaped in the air overturning chairs, screaming as the balloon animals swatted at them.

The adults made grabs for their little ones, calling fruitlessly: "Be careful …Slow down …You'll get dizzy …No running." A few parents tried to join in, but they were too burdened with coats, purses, and shopping bags.

Suddenly, a strong current of icy air gave Anita relief in the steamy room but only momentarily, for she saw that the breeze caught children in an updraft, and like the murmuration of birds, they swirled around the room.

Blank Slate Writers Group
Waiting for Santa

Almost in the lead were Benjamin and his reindeer—Anita could clearly see they were reindeer, or approximations of, with red noses, antlers, or even wings.

As she looked for the source of the draft, a flash of reflected light hit her eyes, and she then perceived that in one of the huge windows overlooking the street seven stories below, the pane was gone. *Would no one else notice this danger?*

She stumbled over the stroller to alert Santa and Mrs. Claus to get Security, but only two piles of red and white nylon remained next to their fake fireplace.

In horror, Anita watched the blue faerie and the children wrapped in her dress rise toward the window as the music reached a crescendo. When the faerie's foot rested on the sill, she paused motioning Benjamin with his reindeer to follow. Caitlin, encased in leaves, was hanging on at the end of the blue train.

Anita tore through the room. She reached the window, squinting in the spears of light cast by a whirling ventilator on a rooftop.

"No. No! Stop. They can't go with you!" Anita grabbed the faery on the ankle.

With an insolent smile, the girl looked at Anita. "But they want to come."

"Where are they going?"

"Where they can be free! Free to be their true selves. Look how they've morphed already."

"Why, those artists told them what to be! The children didn't choose at all."

"Isn't that the job of the artist? To find what's on the inside and bring it out? Let go, you old bag. I should think you'd want to them to be happy."

"Of course! But they'll discover for themselves who they are. They'll find happiness their own way." *And all-too-soon leave us*, Anita thought.

She caught onto Caitlin's hand and pulled. The action unfurled the string of children wrapped in the blue faery's

Night Light
Joyce Hicks

train, and they returned to Anita like laundry drawn in on a line. She caught each one and then drew Caitlin to her without the scolding a parent might dispense. Benjamin she took by the hand, as she shooed the other toddlers back toward their parents.

Winded, Anita went back to her chair, her vision readjusting slowly to the less bright room. The children sat down too.

Soon, their mother appeared. "Our beeper just went off. We can go have lunch now. Never mind visiting Santa this year." She up-righted the stroller and made Benjamin sit on all the coats. "Rested, Mom?"

Anita nodded. She would not tell her daughter about the hallucination. It was not madness, she hoped, but just a momentary drawing back of the veil, a peep at the world where metaphor and reality collide, allowing her—at least for the time being—to regard herself not as *mad woman* but *wise woman*. She glanced toward the window in time to see pigeons flapping off the sill. The winter sun caught the pink and green iridescence of their feathers.

On the way to the restaurant, Caitlin took Anita's hand. "I was kind of afraid of that blue faery, Grandma. I'm glad you came to get me."

Blank Slate Writers Group

Poem

Desolation Angel
Bob Moulesong

She rocks back and forth and hugs Dolly tighter.

Hugging Dolly is good. Dolly likes to be hugged, just like her. When she hugs Dolly she can pretend that the screaming, crying, hitting never happen.

The screaming gets louder and closer.

She rocks back and forth and hugs Dolly tighter.

Short Story

Home at Last
Joyce Hicks

In Dubuque, Bill and Veronica were bi-level tract-house people, but with his promotion to Chicago and her inheritance, they ventured into downtown, high-rise living.

"The deal of a lifetime," purred the realtor showing them around a corner unit with floor to ceiling windows overlooking Michigan Avenue.

While Veronica stepped out on the stamp-sized balcony, Bill stood chest-tight against the interior wall listening to the realtor extolling the views from the 25th floor. And they were some views, Bill admitted, even as his breath came in short gasps. Soldier Field was to the right, its glass bagel of sky boxes at war with the classical memorial below. The Field Museum filled the center right of the panaorama, the colonnade hung with life-scaled banners of Sue, Tyrannosaurus Rex.

"You can even see the Ferris wheel at Navy Pier." The agent flung her arm west.

Like a dancer focused on a spot during a twirl, Bill stared straight out at Lake Michigan, but the action did nothing to steady him. To Bill, the blue water, as in a child's crayon drawing, threatened to spill down over Lakeshore Drive, Grant Park, and Michigan Avenue, the barriers between himself and the monstrous body of water.

By week's end, the couple decided to take the leap and buy, signing the note for a breath-taking mortgage. Because Veronica had been such a good sport about leaving her friends in Dubuque, Bill felt he owed her

Night Light
Joyce Hicks

cooperation about their new home. No doubt, his acrophobia would disappear once they got settled in.

Veronica supervised the arrival of their things in Chicago while Bill was delayed in the Dubuque office. She called hourly describing purchases and furniture arrangements that would make the condo perfect. The neighbors were friendlier than she expected. Why, a couple showed her where to shop at Fox & Lobel for artisan bread, fromage, and Kalamatra olives. She could hardly wait to introduce her own husband to everyone!

Finally, on a late fall evening Bill got off the elevator, fumbled a bit with his new key, and plunged through his front door.

Music floated from a lit archway where he headed, arms already outstretched to grasp his wife.

He tried to step into his living room but was confounded. Which room should he walk toward—the near one or the far one? Both with the same lamp, both with the same couch, from which, dreadfully, two wives rose to meet him. How could this be—living room furniture, old and new, each paired with a twin? Before he could make a move, Veronica (and the other one) came at him.

"Welcome home!" While she kissed him voraciously, he realized the second woman and her room were only a reflection of the first playing on the giant windows.

"Don't we have drapes?" he asked clinging to his wife.

"And spoil this half a million dollar view?" After she ushered him to his favorite chair, he turned it toward the interior. Facing inward settled him, and soon enthusiastic, he toured the results of her shopping and domestic arrangements.

In the Pullman kitchen, for example, she taught him how to use the French coffee maker, though his embraces slowed down the lessons. Later, while making mac and cheese, the kitchen infused with moonlight from the large window, he reached in a drawer for a spoon.

Blank Slate Writers Group
Home at Last

"My God!" His hand had grasped the head of a small animal entangled in the gleaming utensils.

"You found the bottle opener. Good idea! Let's have a nightcap." Grabbing the stainless steel gadget by the ears, Veronica triumphantly demonstrated by decanting some Pouille Fuisse into their wedding crystal.

"To our new home!" Veronica raised her glass to her husband and the city at large, to the warrens of lighted windows, the ribbon of traffic, and the dark lake beyond.

"To us," he replied, their glasses colliding softly. Then he told her all about his new office, the plush furnishings, and the historic building. The prices staggered him. Why, a small black coffee was more than $4 in the lobby!

"No more Dunkin' Doughnuts!" Veronica laughed.

On that first night, Bill waited until he was very tired before going to bed, knowing his side on their new pillowtop mattress was near the window. At 3 a.m. a stiff breeze woke him, and he put his foot out for his slippers to get another blanket. His foot paddled around freely in thin air.

Stealthily, he unclipped his wife's book light, then pointed it over his side of the bed. The cone of light made no reflection because, he realized wildly, nothing was there—no floor, no window. He reared back from the void, putting a pillow over his face to block the impression that just over the edge of his bed and far below, cars were prowling along Michigan Avenue.

As she brushed her hair in front of the window the next morning, Veronica said, "Isn't this view just fabulous?"

"Yes, just like a...," Bill searched for the right word, "a post card," he said, noting that the floor was where it was supposed to be. *I need to get a grip*, he thought. "Let's take a walk in the park after breakfast."

In South Grant Park they examined the Agora sculptures, an installation of 109 cast iron torsos.

Night Light
Joyce Hicks

"Don't you just love these, Bill?" Veronica said. She pulled a brochure out of her purse. "*Agora* is Greek for meeting place," she read.

"They don't have any heads or arms." His wife informed him the figures were 9 feet tall and weighed eleven hundred pounds each. Bill walked around among the figures whose reddish skin most resembled bark or a track suit ruined by a hot dryer. Children ran among the figures, putting their feet next to the gigantic toes.

"They look as if they're milling around and talking to each other," Veronica went on. She rushed into a closely packed group.

"What are they saying, 'Clank, clank, clank?'"

Veronica poked him. "You have no imagination!"

Bill took a few photos with his phone. "Hey, maybe they're walking over to see Lincoln on the next block." Bill preferred his art to be Neoclassical and had admired the seated president on their first visit.

"It says here," Veronica returned to the brochure, "that the artist was thinking of the masses in search of a leader."

"There you see! That's another reason for them to get over to Lincoln."

Veronica laughed taking his arm, then pointing to their new home across the street: "Look, there's our balcony! See the Indian rug on the chair?" Bill squinted at the tiny red swatch marking their condo.

Before turning in that night, Bill bounced on his heels next to the bed a few times and also made sure the window was where it should be. "I'm just looking at the view," he said pressing his hands on the pane.

"You're getting prints all over the glass!"

The bedroom had drapes, which he pulled closed this time, and he got into bed where he fell into a watchful doze, often reaching out to press the window. Of course, it was still there, solid as a church.

206

Blank Slate Writers Group
Home at Last

Reassured, he fell into a deep sleep until 3 a.m. when he heard noises close by outside. It must be night birds on the balcony, and he listened sleepily to their low chatter until he heard three sharp knocks on the bedroom window. Not like birds at all. More like visitors.

He put out his feet, thankfully the floor was still there, and got down on his knees. He raised the bottom of the drapes to look out. Four torsos from the park were right outside!

What did they want?

Even without a head, one was leaning over to peep under the drape he had just raised. It let out a startled yelp and toppled backward in the dark. The others began to rock back and forth, moaning like bells in a fog.

Bill hunkered down under the bed as they twisted dangerously close to the glass in the search for their fallen comrade. Suddenly, they receded toward the park.

Trembling, he curled around Veronica for the rest of the night.

Veronica was already up spraying window cleaner when Bill got up.

"These marks are so hard to get off," she said, wiping vigorously. "You'd think they were on the outside." She handed him his suit coat and landed a wifely kiss as he left hurriedly.

On his way home, Bill walked the last block along the park, passing by the Agora figures. He compared the photos on his phone to the sculptures. The grouping nearest the sidewalk had three today, not four, as in the image taken yesterday.

"The camera can't be wrong," Bill muttered. He was crouching to interpret the pattern of rust stains on the concrete base when a well-dressed man slowed to look at the figures.

"S'cuse me?" Bill's voice came out louder than he intended. "Do you know, ah, can they move these things

207

Night Light
Joyce Hicks

around?" The man directed a cool gaze beyond Bill and walked on.

Bill zigzagged through traffic to cross Michigan Avenue, longing for sanctuary and his wife's cheerful domesticity. He sing-songed, "I'm home, honey," as he entered, holding out a bag with a trinket for her, an egg timer affixed to the Hancock building.

"Clink, ka-chink" came from somewhere.

He froze.

"Clang, klong. . . klong."

The things were back! Why? What did they want? Him? Veronica? Oh, they never should have left Dubuque! How to keep them out?

He sprang toward the living room to lock the lakeside door to the outside! He would brace himself against the handle to keep them out!

Racing headlong to throw his weight on the glass, he neglected to notice the balcony door and screen were wide open to let the evening air creep in over the railing. He pitched into space, his toes tangling in the Indian throw rug giving him even more momentum. During his flight, arms outward, he observed a ladybug on the railing, a fire truck passing below, and heard Veronica say, "New wind chimes."

For moments, there was nothingness. Then he landed on his back.

Opening his eyes, he noted the atmosphere was the soft blue and pink of a baby's nightlight. In the distance on his right, a golden path stretched to the horizon. His heart embraced his new state: He had no regrets.

"Bill, what are you doing?" Her voice came as a shock.

"I'm still up here," Bill pronounced firmly, realizing the sturdy railing, like a restraining parent, had prevented catastrophe; the shining path and holy light, remnants of the sunset.

Blank Slate Writers Group
Home at Last

"Come on in. We can eat soon." Veronica twiddled the graduated metal tubes hanging outside the balcony door. They banged around excitedly.

Bill got to his knees. "No, wait. Bring out a new bottle of wine. And those fancy glasses."

He watched fascinated as condos in other towers came to life. People were making dinner, exercising, reading to their children, or even dancing, he supposed. The Ferris wheel turned pompously on Navy Pier. He reached inside the living room to turn on their balcony light, suddenly anxious to meld their own new life with the city.

At bedtime, Bill pulled Veronica into a suggestive embrace. "Shouldn't I close the drapes?" she said.

"Who do you think is watching?" He grasped her wrist to stop her.

"The Agora people?" She laughed.

"They might be," he said kissing her hair. "Anything's possible." They rolled to the center of their pillowtop mattress and made love in front of the city.

Blank Slate Writers Group

Short Story

Stuck in Time
Timothy Cole

"What time did you tell them that we'd get there?"

"I didn't. I just said *See ya.*"

"What day, then? Today? Tomorrow?"

"I left all that open. So, if you want, we have a lot of time we could waste, or we could get there early and get it all over with."

"I don't want to get it over with. It's awkward, awkward, awkward, and I don't look forward to this; not at all. Don't you feel this is all strange? Weird? Out of place? —Awkward?"

"I'm not saying any more. You already know how *I* feel."

Miriam was driving, looking straight ahead and trying to avoid the ruts in the narrow, gravel road. Muriel was her identical twin. No one seeing them for the first time would be able to tell one from the other. Even though they were dressed differently today, their hairstyles were the same, even with stray hairs in the same places, gray spots identically sized and colored and on the same sides. Their voices were identical, inflections identical; each turned the same direction at the same time. Neither needed to complete a thought from the other and only did so for those who might be listening. For nearly forty years they lived two thousand forty-two miles apart and hadn't seen each other for over twenty years, although they called each other every week and held themselves close for long, silent minutes each time.

211

Night Light
Timothy Cole

Growing up, in Nebraska, they marveled at how well they could fool their friends and especially their parents—switching places for hours. Only their little sister could tell them apart. More than once, one would cover for the other when they were out on forbidden dates, by pretending to be the other. Teachers and boyfriends gave up early trying to keep them straight, because, to be truthful, it didn't matter. If you started a date with one and would up with the other, nothing was lost. They were literally and figuratively identical.

Once, when Muriel was living in Seattle, Miriam fell on an icy New York sidewalk, cursing as she felt her arm break underneath her. Muriel, sitting at tea with some friends, suddenly rose from her chair, screaming the same obscenity at the same moment as her sister. The shocked people at her table saw her abruptly run from the room into the restroom where she called Miriam with her cell phone, but her sister was unable to answer, as people were beginning to help her up and surround her with untypical New York concern. Muriel called again and again, failing to leave any message, until someone helping Miriam answered for her.

"She's not able to answer. Can I take a message?"

Muriel shot back: "Tell her to call me from the hospital."

"Who should she call? Do you want to know what happened?"

"Trust me, she knows who to call. And I know what happened; just tell her."

And that was that. And that moment occupied both of their minds at the very moment as they made their way across the treeless Nebraska plains.

"Isn't Nelson's house up ahead?"

Muriel paused before speaking. "It's up here a ways."

After about five minutes of dusty road the land changed to rolling hills with scrub brush and anemic trees showing here and there in the sterile soil. Almost unseen

Blank Slate Writers Group
Stuck in Time

against a gray, storm-threatening sky, a large Victorian farmhouse, devoid of paint for many years, stood lifeless on a barren hill. As they got closer Miriam spoke the words that Muriel had been dreading.

"Let's go see Nelson…"

"But *nobody*…"

"I know, nobody lives there anymore. Anyone can see it's empty, abandoned. Maybe for years."

"Not since Nelson died, somebody said."

"But that was fifty years ago! Nobody's been there since? How is it that the house is still standing?"

"Who knows? His folks closed it up a month after he killed himself; moved away; never came back. I think someone looks after the house and land, but I don't know who it would be."

"Let's go up there. I want to see the place again."

Miriam slowed the car but did not stop, passing the overgrown, grassy lane that led to the slowly rotting house.

"Why drag all that out again." Miriam didn't make that a question; it was a statement, a comment with a little bit of accusation behind it.

"Turn around. I don't want to think of it, but maybe he killed himself because I broke our date that night."

Muriel became silent while Miriam turned the car back to the long drive up to the house.

"I've thought about that and thought about that so many times over these years. He was so eager to go out with me. All those dates we had, and I was so afraid he wanted to get serious, but I just couldn't…I just couldn't." And she fell silent again.

Miriam drove carefully over the worn-out ground, avoiding the debris and broken glass that had accumulated over the lonely years. Small clouds of dust followed them to the house, curious what the sisters would find.

Muriel stepped out of the car and hesitantly made her way to the door, knowing what must happen next. For a long time she held the door knob without trying it. And

Night Light
Timothy Cole

then, looking back at Miriam who had approached slowly with apprehension, she turned the knob.

Both stepped back as crusted Nebraska dirt fell loose from the door casing and fell soundlessly, becoming invisible in the deep dust that already lay across the floor.

"I didn't call him for a week. I couldn't. I knew how much he cared, how much he wanted me, and I felt like such a heel, breaking up and not even calling him. He sat here. Poor Nelson waited by this very door for me to come, and I wasn't going to come. I knew he wanted to take me that night, that he wouldn't take no for an answer, and it wasn't that I wouldn't, couldn't let him. I was no nice girl; I had baggage. It was no big deal for me to tumble in bed with him, but...," and Miriam finished the thought for her.

"Because you loved him. You loved him and you couldn't just jump into bed with him because you loved him and it wasn't screwing just for the fun of it like it had been with all the others. You were just eighteen, and there was so much future for you—and for him, too. Consummating your love would have been just that: consummation, mopping it all up, signing the contract, forever and forever, 'til death do you part. Yes, I know that's why you stood him up, why you didn't—couldn't—call him, not even knowing that he was dead two days later. Dead and buried before any of us even knew. No closure, no forgiveness, no flowers at the funeral."

Muriel didn't bother to answer. Miriam had thought it all out for her. They had never spoken of Nelson after they found out. They never brought it up. They graduated a few weeks later and went separate ways, effectively putting their twinhood on hold in pursuit of their own identities, careers, and husbands—several husbands.

Miriam quickly realized that Muriel had never gotten over Nelson, and she puzzled why that hadn't occurred to her. Until ten minutes ago, Miriam thought the tragic Nelson was just another conquest, a plaything, a training

Blank Slate Writers Group
Stuck in Time

session for Muriel. It had been the only wall that came between the twins, or so she thought. Identical twins share a sameness, a togetherness that only other identical twins can understand. There was between them a bond that couldn't be broken or breached except with utmost determination. Miriam never gave any thought to the possibility and suspected Muriel never did, either. Or did she? Could Miriam be sure about that?

Muriel moved through the house. She was familiar with it albeit it had been many years. There were the familiar corners, trimwork, kitchen table where she and Nelson played Monopoly and cards with his mother, the living room where his father sat nursing his pipe and the evening paper. Many years of musty mold could not cover the scents that came back to her—caramelizing onions, freshly opened dog food cans, Prince Albert tobacco, the clean, fresh sheets on Nelson's bed that she decidedly had avoided during their few months together. She knew all of the house, from attic to cellar. And it was all still here, unmoved, unused, frozen in time like Miss Havisham's table. She touched a corner of an old newspaper, still half open to the obituary notices, except Nelson's death had not been published in any of the local papers.

Miriam wondered at the condition of the old house, why nothing seemed disturbed in all these years. It was like a shrine, but a shrine to emptiness, to a non-event, to an incomplete boy, a stagnation of a family. What would happen now if someone came in and swept and washed and painted, moved furniture around, hung fresh pictures of the living, brought laughter and warmth back to the house? Would the house object? What would it say, what would it do? It was all incomprehensible to Miriam. She could no more imagine the house coming out of mourning after all these years than she could accept that Muriel might have married Nelson and been happy ever after.

Muriel was moving to the staircase. She wiped a finger through the thick dust on the banister and examined it

215

Night Light
Timothy Cole

closely without it registering with her. Both had dressed well and carefully for this trip, and this chance detour was beginning to leave evidentiary smudges as well as a clinging smell of dry must mingled with the years of rodent urine. Yet Muriel saw the house as it had been, bright and lively with Nelson's shy personality and reserve.

She took a step up.

Miriam said, a little more loudly that she intended, "Let's go, Sis. We should get to the hotel in time for dinner."

Muriel ignored her, taking another step and looking toward the landing.

Miriam tried again. "We've got to go!"

Muriel took another step.

Nelson's room was at the top, on the third floor, and well back from the landing where any noises coming from his room would be unheard. Further up the stairs it grew dark; there were no windows in the hallways as though darkness preserves.

Miriam had moved to the door, waiting for Muriel to turn and follow, but when she heard Muriel's steps in the upstairs hallway, she returned to the staircase and began to ascend.

She found Muriel standing in the third floor hallway outside a closed door—Nelson's room. While Miriam approached, Muriel opened the door and let it swing fully across its arc letting outside light flood the hallway to reveal the floating motes and the hanging, thick cobwebs. Their footprints lined the floor where they had walked. Dust covered their polished shoes. She followed Muriel into the room.

Muriel turned her head from left to right and back again, taking in the furniture, the mirror, the floor full of hangers and boyhood's messes. Dusty gray clothes still hung in the closet. A homework assignment still lay on Nelson's desk. She thought how he would hate it that she would see his homework—he was so unsure of himself.

Blank Slate Writers Group
Stuck in Time

An irregular lump on the floor by his bed caught her attention. She poked it with her foot.

"MURIEL! We have to leave! *This instant!*" Miriam used their mom's voice in an effort to strengthen her command.

Muriel stooped to pick up the lump. As it became unentangled it stretched out to reveal itself as a discarded bra. Muriel's focus sharpened. She looked to the bed, to the nightstand where she knew Nelson had hidden some condoms, condoms that were never used. Her eyes shifted to the headboard, then to the wall behind the headboard. Attached to the wall was the unmistakable form of a pair of panties. She moved closer and examined both the bra and panties at length. Her head shot back and she turned to face Miriam.

Miriam's resolve collapsed.

"It's not underwear. It's my bikini."

Muriel stared hard at her sister. Miriam had a lot of explaining to do.

Blank Slate Writers Group

Poem

A Love Villanelle
Christina Ortega Phillips

I once knew a girl so pure,
foolish to believe in love and fate.
She's gone now—I've killed her.

You remember her, too, I'm sure
She loved you, hopelessly devoted she was,
but her love for you can no longer endure

There was, fortunately, a cure
for such wistful dreams and blind trust:
she's gone now—I've killed her.

The time you two spent together was such a blur—
mixed emotions, fights, bitterness, and happiness—
but her love for you can no longer endure.

Ignorantly blissful she was, I'm sure,
but once she awoke I had to put her out of her misery.
She's gone now—I've killed her.

Your tantalizing presence and love was such a tempting
lure.
I hate the girl I was who foolishly wanted you,
but her love for you no longer endures—
she's gone now. I've killed her.

220

Blank Slate Writers Group

Short Story

My Chinese Relatives
Rich Elliott

Angela was a mess. She had dropped out of the University of Illinois Chicago with one semester to go because she'd run out of money and her English major seemed pointless. She was $30K in debt to Uncle Sam for college loans. She needed time, she told herself, to figure out her next step.

Her tiny off-campus apartment in nearby Chinatown depressed her, yet she spent most of her time there. Angela watched a lot of TV, mostly Paris Hilton reality shows. Or she surfed the Internet. She dyed her hair blond. She ate pizza and smoked cigarettes. When she felt ambitious, she embellished her *LinkedIn* page with exaggerations.

To break the boredom, Angela began shoplifting. Wearing her baggiest coat, she'd hit the big-box discount stores, where the staff was as unmotivated as she was. She took only one or two small things at a time, and she never got caught, at least for awhile.

One day Angela stopped in a little convenience store on Wentworth Avenue to buy a pack of cigarettes. Out of habit, she slipped a bag of chips inside her coat. Behind the checkout counter was a small Chinese woman whom people knew as Mrs. Han.

Angela paid for the cigarettes and began to leave, when Mrs. Han produced a handgun and eyed Angela fiercely.

"You steal chips," she said.

Night Light
Rich Elliott

"Me? Chips?" stammered the girl, her face flushing.

"You steal chips. I call police."

Angela felt herself getting dizzy. "No, no police, *please!*" Her eyes seemed to be leaking.

"Tears no fix." Mrs. Han studied the girl. "I have deal."

"What deal?" Angela tried to compose herself.

"You clean store. Each morning, all week. Plus one . . . favor. Then we even."

Angela agreed right away. Mrs. Han made a photocopy of Angela's driver's license.

"Now know where you live." She pointed two fingers at Angela. "You start tomorrow."

* * *

Angela met Mrs. Han at the store before first light. Resentfully, the girl did as she was instructed, feeling like an indentured servant. For a small shop, there seemed to be a ridiculous number of chores. The girl washed the sidewalk out front, Windexed the glass displays, and scrubbed the floors on her knees because that was the way Mrs. Han wanted it done. Angela also cleaned out the bathroom, straightened the shelves, and helped receive the morning deliveries.

Each morning, the same routine. The two hardly spoke. By the fourth day, Angela felt strangely buoyant. The physical exertion and the quiet dark of the early morning agreed with her. Mrs. Han forbade smoking, and the girl's cough had all but disappeared.

Angela didn't know what to make of Mrs. Han, who came to work every day in a gray shift, her hair pulled back in a severe bun. She may have been 30 years old or 50. Angela noted the woman's wedding ring and finally had to ask her.

"Mrs. Han, your ring. Is there a Mr. Han?"

Blank Slate Writers Group
My Chinese Relatives

The Chinese woman jerked up her head and stared at the girl.

"No Mr. Han. No more."

"I'm so sorry, Mrs. Han. Your husband is dead?"

"No dead. Go back home. No like here."

* * *

Toward the end of Angela's last day of penance, Mrs. Han abruptly touched the girl's arm.

"You done soon. Now for favor."

"Favor?" Angela had forgotten.

Mrs. Han averted her eyes and looked around distractedly for half a minute. "You find me date."

"A date?"

"Date with American boy. You know American boys?"

"American boys?"

The girl thought about her slacker boyfriend Phil and his idiot friends. She guessed she could arrange some kind of meet-up at her apartment. That might appease this crazy lady.

"Mrs. Han, we'll do a double date. It'll be fun."

One week later, an hour before the appointed time for their double date, Mrs. Han knocked softly on Angela's apartment door. The girl was startled by the woman's appearance. Mrs. Han was dressed in a perky white blouse, a red plaid skirt, and navy blue knee socks. She looked like a Catholic schoolgirl. With way too much makeup. Angela quickly pulled her inside the apartment.

"Mrs. Han, you look…terrific. Let's just see if we can do a little something with your makeup."

Angela did some quick, cosmetic revisions. She reviewed her work.

"You have to lose the wedding ring, Mrs. Han."

"Lose ring? I have ring."

"No, I mean take it off."

Night Light
Rich Elliott

"You hold," the woman said, pulling the ring off her finger.

"Oh, and Mrs. Han, tell me your first name."

"Name?" The woman thought for a moment. "You give me American first name."

Eventually Phil showed up with his friend Jesse. Angela introduced her friend.

"Boys, this is Paris Han."

For awhile the group made awkward small talk. Phil explained his job as a dog walker. Jesse told about the hazards of his work as a city bike messenger.

The boys had brought a 12-pack of Coronas, and they ordered a pizza.

They showed Paris how to play *Wii Bowling*. She turned out to be a natural at it. She relaxed.

Gradually Paris became the life of the party. She grabbed a pack of cards from Angela's table and began to show them card tricks. She refused to explain the "magic" behind the tricks, and the Americans were delighted.

Later Paris read their palms. She spent several minutes studying Jesse's hand, and then she told him, flirtatiously, "This path leads to my door."

When she read Angela's palm, she cryptically informed the girl, "Your son flies."

By the end of the evening, Paris was singing lovely patriotic songs from her childhood in China. The three Americans were enthralled.

The following week Paris Han called Angela.

"Jesse call me. Ask me date."

"Paris, he likes you!"

Angela reminded Paris that she still had the woman's wedding ring. She told Paris that she'd return it the next day, but it was several weeks before the girl got around to it. When Angela finally showed up at the store, Paris was nowhere to be found, and there was a new woman behind the counter.

Blank Slate Writers Group
My Chinese Relatives

"Didn't you hear?" the replacement told Angela, "Mrs. Han had to leave."

The new girl explained, with considerable relish, that there had been an incident, an attempted robbery at the store. Mrs. Han had thwarted it, had shot the thief in the foot. ("Look, there's the bullet hole in the floor!") The man had escaped, leaving a trail of blood on the sidewalk.

Mrs. Han was a hero for about one day. It turned out the thief was a member of the local street gang the Triads. It was thought that the call to the INS was made by a gang member, in retaliation. The INS investigated Mrs. Han and found that her visa had expired. The day before Angela had returned to the shop, Mrs. Han had been deported.

* * *

Angela kept the wedding ring for several months, until finally she pawned it. With the money, Angela went back to UIC and finished her final semester. She ended up marrying Phil. Today they own a pet clinic and kennel in Rockford, Illinois.

They had one son, and he became an American Airlines pilot flying international routes. That would be me.

Recently, I asked about a framed photo of my parents when they were young, showing them attending a wedding in China. My parents told me the story of the photo.

That is why this week I am taking an extended layover in Beijing. Today, in fact, I am going on a bike ride on the Great Wall of China with my Aunt Paris and Uncle Jesse.

Blank Slate Writers Group

Poem

Monster
Gail Galvan

PAIN, a dominating monster,
an It
that claims all joy within.
From without,
there may be no signs.
But from within,
hearts and minds
are crushed by a toll
so heavy that spirits
digress to dust,
to the nothingness
that only aches and rusts.
To save ourselves
we must slay the monster
or at least—
be smarter than It.

Blank Slate Writers Group

Short Story

For Whom the Belle Trolls
Timothy Cole

Ignoring the irony that a restaurant in Loup City, Nebraska, would offer an Oriental night, in a town that bragged—*bragged!*—a population of 374 people, Quincy took the risk of ordering the Bird's Nest Soup. It arrived in the same bowl that would normally hold the *Chicken and Dumplings, Rough Style.* Hot and steaming, it still smelled a little like chicken and dumplings, with yellow pools of fat wandering around—*Looking for the dumplings,* Quincy thought.

In fact, there was nothing on the table that suggested anything east of Germany: a knife, a spoon, and a fork; a napkin that advertized *Jeff's Body Work*, a glass of water, and the fresh lemonade that everyone knew was made from frozen concentrate. Belle, the waitress, told him that chopsticks were available if he wanted them. He refused them. She left.

Belle was the 19 year-old daughter of the owner, and she was nicknamed "Belly" because of the curious distention of her abdomen just below where her navel should be. Her shape was often talked about and had been since she was fourteen, and was once assumed to be a vestige of baby fat. Over the years, various customers swore she was pregnant and even started a pool contest over it. Nothing, of course, ever came of it, and no one could directly name the boy or man who might have been her partner. Belle was never seen with anyone, never seen outside of the restaurant—not at church, not at the town's

Night Light
Timothy Cole

annual festival held by the Cattle Ranchers' Association, not even getting the mail or putting out the trash. She was attractive enough if you squinted and disregarded her complete lack of interest in everything. Her shape, other than her belly, was close to provocative, her hair, cut short and loosely brushed, was distinctively red and her eyes a dull green with no flash in them. But in the short of it all, her whole being suggested generic promiscuity. Yet, in Loup City she was the lone cherry tree, full of bud but with no contributing partner. It mattered little to Quincy.

Quincy took a spoonful of the yellowish, thin soup, and thought that it needed a little salt and a lot of onion. When he raised his hand to catch Belle's attention, he saw her shuffling back to his table with a small plate.

"I nearly forgot your fortune cookie." She carelessly shoved the plate between his water and lemonade and immediately turned and headed for the kitchen.

Quincy stared at it a moment forgetting to ask for a small dish of diced onion. He hadn't had a fortune cookie since his short stint in the National Guard when he and a few rowdy boys in wrinkled uniforms took over a real Oriental restaurant in Mason City. He liked them; a crusty pastry, stiff and hard, but softening quickly in the mouth with a sweet vanilla flavor. And he always knew there would be a small printed piece of paper with a corny prediction or fortune that was sometimes witty. He broke open the cookie and smoothed the strip of paper.

*"Your life is in danger. Say nothing to anyone. You must leave the city immediately and never return. I repeat: say **nothing**!"*

Quincy stared uncomprehendingly at this fortune. He turned the paper over, but the other side was blank. Nothing else was written or printed, only this uncomfortable warning. He looked up for Belle, but she was nowhere in sight, and no noise came from the kitchen. He was the only customer in the whole diner, maybe the only person in the whole building.

Blank Slate Writers Group
For Whom the Belle Trolls

Quincy looked out the front windows, greasy with the day's cooking, *more likely a whole year's worth of cooking since he had never seen them cleaned.* Darkness was already clouding the empty streets and silhouetting the buildings on the edge of town. He got up and turned on the overhead lights, not wanting to call or wait for Belle or her father. There were no cars on the streets, nor were there any parked along them. One car remained in the lot for the local newspaper. He stood for awhile, considering the emptiness that confronted him, and then turned to finish his soup, which had grown cold.

Belle didn't return to bring Quincy his check, so he impatiently pulled several dollars from his wallet and placed them under the salt shaker, more than enough to cover his soup and Belle's unearned tip. Halfway to the door, he stopped, turned, and moved to grab the fortune that lay in cookie crumbs on the table. Once at the door, he uncharacteristically hurried for his car, the only one remaining in the newspaper lot.

Not knowing what to think, and not easily alarmed in any situation, Quincy fumbled for his keys, dropped them, and unlocked a car that was already unlocked. His only thought was to start the engine and leave as quickly as he could. Why was he so shaken, he wondered. A joke! It must have been a joke, even though he hardly knew Belle, and he was not a close friend with Sam, her father. But yet, he trembled, thinking only of getting home and turning on lights, lots of lights.

Quincy lived alone. His wife Vera had left him after only a few years of marriage claiming his interest—his *husbandly* interests—lay elsewhere, and she wasn't about to *waste her time* in Loup City. Vera was said to be in Mason City, remarried, and running for town council. Quincy resigned himself to her departure; in fact, he was rather relieved. Her ambition ran counter to his.

Quincy backed into the street and aimed for the closest way home. Within three blocks, he realized there

Night Light
Timothy Cole

were no lights in any houses or businesses, no people on the sidewalks, no cars in any direction. The town was empty, locked up, but this was, after all, a small Nebraska town in late evening. There were no businesses that stayed open past six, even on Friday night. The young element in town knew where the excitement was and left the town, wholesale, in clouds of Nebraska dust. The one bar in town, which only had a license for beer and wine, was owned by an elderly man whose wife required his care too often for him to justify staying open for the half dozen clients who could live on low proof alcohol.

No TV sets glowed in any window. The town was cable-less and dish-less, with most residents resigned to the three channels offered from the two cities close enough to deliver acceptable signals. Quincy swallowed what remained of his initial, irrational fear. The humming motor and soft drone of a newscaster on his radio spread a net of assumed safety around him. Cloaked in this new confidence and confined in the steel cage of his automobile against most dangers, he regained his composure. *How stupid! How silly!*—he beat himself with these words and the symbols they conveyed, submitting finally to a low turn into the one-block-long street where his home sat darkly next to a limitless field of rustling corn.

A movement in his rear-view mirror distracted him, and he slowed to a stop. Turning, he saw a lone gray figure walking across the street where he had turned. It was Belle. He was sure. It was her unmistakable shape and way of walking. He was not sure where she lived; he thought she lived with her father but he was unsure of where her father lived, also. In a small town there is much you know about everybody, but still there are secrets, secrets more tightly locked from discovery than you would expect. Should it be a secret that she lived—she and her father lived—only short blocks away from the diner? And him, too?

She was carrying something with her, maybe a sweater, bundled in her arms and walking as though she was

232

Blank Slate Writers Group
For Whom the Belle Trolls

involved in deep thought. She was taking slow, methodical steps, not plodding but resolute steps like pacing off a distance or stepping ritually down an aisle at a wedding. He wanted to turn the car around and ask where she was going, give her a ride or something. Find out where she really lived, that's what he really wanted, but the weirdness of it was too much for him to dwell on. It would scare her. She would cry out. People would come to their doors to find him in a trailing car speaking to a young girl walking home in the darkness of the night. Even now, with his car idling in the middle of a lonely street, he could be attracting attention from behind any one of the black windows along the block.

Belle lived close to him, he was certain, that much was evident, but in tiny Loup City everyone lived close to Quincy. All houses within the town limits were planted in an eight block area that was little more than two blocks deep off the main highway, north or south. If it weren't for the indignity of appearing carless, all people in the town could easily walk to where they needed to go. The few sidewalks were mostly used by little children with chalk and tricycles. Without giving away where he lived, Quincy pulled to the side of the street and turned off his lights and his motor.

He sat, thinking. Belle was being mysterious. He could not find her when it was time to leave and to pay his bill. She brought him the fortune cookie as an after-thought rather than a forgotten part of the meal. The puzzling fortune with the intimidating words could have been easily slipped into the cookie by Belle, herself. But what was the point? He barely knew her; he was an acquaintance of her father, and he knew her mother. He knew her mother from childhood, danced with her at the prom, was invited to her wedding, went to her funeral—had dated her, even exclusively for awhile. But Belle—he had no more conversation with her than to order a short stack or a cup of coffee; he was unsure of when she must have been

Night Light
Timothy Cole

born. Probably shortly after her mother, Brenda, married Sam—a marriage rumored to have been a *have-to.*

Brenda was really something in high school: popular, pretty, could have been a cheerleader *(but she claimed that wasn't her style).* Quincy knew what her style was. He had DIPPED HIS STICK into that soup of passion and emotion, too, along with a few other guys. She was quick, eager, and rewarding; she required no obligations. But he took her to the prom when they were Juniors, as a pay-back and thank-you. After that, His most memorable time with her was at the Senior picnic down at Baye's Lake. They had a *"tryst"*—that's what she called it—far from the others in a glade of apples that lasted long into the afternoon. She wanted a lasting reminder of their youth. That single occasion pulled both guilt and love out of Quincy's satisfied but still aching loins. He stumbled between responsibility and freedom for a day or two while he considered full and ongoing intimate involvement with Brenda, followed by a lifetime of babies and family evenings. But by the end of the school year it was Sam who took her into his arms, and then she was no longer "available." By the end of summer, Sam and Brenda were married in the small church in the center of town with nearly the whole school invited and attending. Brenda died a few years later, quietly and unremarkably, but from what, Quincy never knew.

Quincy never knew, because he entered the Armed Services the week after graduation. He served two years in the dusty grillwork of a time-stalled Army camp far away from the finer temptations of life, a saga of boredom and self-conscripted celibacy, and, as if that were not enough, he re-enlisted in order to sharpen some skills on obsolete motors and transmissions. Within time he was through and thoroughly finished with such low challenges. All Quincy wanted was to return home and stitch his life back together and to realize some nobler dream.

Blank Slate Writers Group
For Whom the Belle Trolls

Within days, Quincy adjusted to his new and more permanent life. Whatever happened in the Army was quickly packed away and out of memory. He had gained more experience than talent from his four years away, but he knew experience often counted more toward the stability of employment than talent, that employers prefer to teach their own talents to their new hirelings, with age and experience ranking high in their estimation. Quincy became a mechanic again, of sorts: he was the installer-apprentice of farm elevator machinery and systems, which was selling very well in the plains states.

Vera saw this. From the back porch of her family's farm house she watched as this muscular, tanned man climbed an elevator to replace the top bearing of a long screw that hoisted the bushels of her father's wheat into a forty-foot-high grain bin. The elevator could have been lowered, but Quincy chose to shinny up the long tube and enjoy the view and the cooler breeze. He was also aware of Vera watching intently from the house.

Vera turned and stepped inside. "Let me take that workman some water, Mother. He'll want some ice." Vera's mother nodded and picked out one of her sturdier glasses, one that bore only a little plainness, a special enough glass, but not one she could not bear to see broken. She knew that Vera could use some help in persuasion because of her long ears and nose. The neighbors called her "handsome" rather than "pretty." And without really knowing why, Quincy unbuttoned the front of his *company-embroidered* shirt before strutting over to this beaming girl bringing him a cool drink.

But that was several years ago, and Vera was now forgotten, their divorce shoving her into a closet of discontent, reduced to an item of gossip whenever her name was recalled. Fortunately, there had been no children. A pregnancy scare brought Quincy more dread than hope, unprepared as he was for fatherhood, and he was never sure if it had been a mistaken pregnancy or if

235

Night Light
Timothy Cole

Vera had secretly taken care of it herself. Nevertheless, Quincy had come home one day to find his evening's meal in the refrigerator with a note pinned to it.

* * *

Quincy stepped out of his car and quietly shut the door. He walked in the direction of the departing Belle. It was darker now and the word "gloaming" crossed his mind. *Gloaming*, the very word evoked grammar school poetry, some early song he had learned and sung heartily from his school desk. From a gray cloud of memorizations, of Robert Burns, and with nothing more than the context of the strange word's associations, the *gloaming* moment and its attitude are immediately recognized when you come upon it. And there she was, there was Belle, "in the gloaming," a solitary figure only distinguishable as a different shade of gray, abrupt in its contrast and movement against a still background, drifting to the place where she stayed, the place she called her home.

He followed her, feeling a bit "Sherlocky" and perverse at the same time. She turned down a dusty, graveled road that was used mostly by farmers coming into town for their business, a dark, treeless path of stale commerce that bore little traffic. Belle walked down the center, avoiding the weeds along the edge and the larger stones in the berm. Quincy had no advantage to hide himself. He was as conspicuous as the darkness would allow him, a stalking figure against the afterglow at the horizon. His purpose now outstripped his earlier fear of the cookie's fortune and the probable damage to his reputation if Belle should discover him behind her and call out.

But Belle neither turned nor paused. She kept her slow walk determinedly focused on reaching some destination. A blackened house stood out, along the road, about a half

Blank Slate Writers Group
For Whom the Belle Trolls

mile more from where she was. She kicked a stone into the weeds, maybe more to make noise and disturb the evening's quietness than to make some sort of game with herself. Quincy kept pace and maintained an even distance behind her. He kicked no stones.

As they neared the house, Quincy could see a porch light glowing in the darkness, a mailbox on a leaning post with its lid hanging open. A single tree stood in the yard that gave little protection from either sun or wind. Weeds scattered across the lawn tall enough to be seen in the growing darkness. Sam's house was farmless and without real purpose on this road outside the town, an afterthought for residency, convenient only for shelter, a blot on a field meant for grain, a wart on the pristine agricultural landscape of Custer County, Nebraska. Sam was a business owner who lived outside town, a man who preferred to be left alone, a man who valued his privacy as though it were his barrier against the town's invading curiosity. Even in high school, Quincy knew little about Sam; he played basketball with the other boys, occasionally showed up at school dances, drifted into town to have Cokes and burgers, had dated a few girls, sometimes stirring comments from those who knew of his quiet and reclusive ways.

Yet, Sam now ran a restaurant. He walked away from the family farm, letting it be sold to keep his parents living comfortably elsewhere. An only child, but unspoiled, he did not aspire to be a farmer. With his share of his inheritance he bought the building in Loup City and gave the town its only restaurant in fifteen years. He hired others to face the public while he kept himself busy and silent over the cook stove and serving counter.

Sam was a strange man, Quincy admitted. And Belle was stranger, still. She bore little resemblance to either Sam or Brenda, making one think that she could have been adopted. Quincy was not around when Belle was born; he had heard no honking horns, received no cigar, and saw no

Night Light
Timothy Cole

birth notice in the local paper. One day, Sam and Brenda were by themselves, and the next day they were three. Quincy was away fulfilling a dubious but patriotic obligation—and it would be nearly four years before he even heard about Belle.

Quincy found himself only a few steps behind Belle, and kept his shuffling feet in pace with hers to avoid giving himself away. Nervousness began to creep across his face, forcing sweat to bead on his forehead and soak his shirt. Of course, he would be discovered; he had gone too far to explain away an evening stroll, a chance meeting, a quick and courteous *hello* before a hasty departure. If he waited until they were at her driveway, she might scream and bring her father to the door to confront a man in the darkness following his daughter home on a lonely road. Quincy should talk to her now, gain her confidence, her trust.

Still, if he talked to her now, away from the safety of her house, it could all end in the same predictably bad way: her father at the door—maybe with a gun—unable to fathom who was talking out on the road, in his yard. A quiet man's voice and a girl's shrill, frightened one—words understood to say *don't scream, please stop, let me talk to you*—a hand upon an arm, a pulling away, another voice: LEAVE *me alone!, go away! who are you!* And then the sudden sound of running, two figures tearing across gravel, the breathless panting of a terrified girl stumbling through the weedy yard and tripping up porch steps, a desperate man reaching for her . . . And would a shot ring out?

Would Sam shoot?

What would Quincy do if he were Sam?

Why, he would shoot, of course, an instant solution to increasing aggravation. He would shoot. He would aim and shoot—shoot to kill!

So, instead, Quincy stopped in the road and allowed Belle to continue to the house. Instead of turning and plodding back to town, he stayed and watched Belle walk

Blank Slate Writers Group
For Whom the Belle Trolls

away. Watched, and watched, as Belle neared her driveway, neared the cockeyed mailbox, the lonely tree, and the weeds long gone to seed. Belle never knew that she was being followed—or maybe she pretended not to know. Quincy was unsure how long he would stay there to watch her, safely, now, to her door, unmolested and free to serve pancakes and chop suey for as long as she was able and wanted to. Queerly, he felt protective of her—loved her in a way, felt as though he had escorted her through an untrustworthy section of town.

But Belle did not turn into the driveway. She kept walking. She walked slowly past the long-ignored yard and was soon following the edge of the corn field, the long leaves chattering from growing in the night, flailing and clapping like foot-bound ogres. Belle continued walking, the dust gathering on her shoes and bare legs. Quincy stared. Finally, he followed. He passed the house with its porch light bright but dimmed by the overwhelming darkness under the roof. No other lights appeared in the house, and Quincy was suddenly fearful of Sam hiding behind the tree, crouched in the weeds, ready to grab his arm, slit his throat, or shoot him for stalking his daughter, his only family he had left in this world. Quincy quickened. He stared back and tried to see a name on the mailbox, and even in the blackness the faded white lettering told him this was not Sam's house, and then neither was it Belle's.

Quincy was unsure, but he remembered no more houses along this road for more than a mile. Did Sam live that far away? Did Belle still live with him? In another five hundred feet Belle would be at the crossroad, but that sandy old road only led to a swamp on one side and to huge fields on the other. There were no houses in either direction. She was heading straight.

When Quincy was sure they had walked over two miles out of town, he decided it was time to give in, to admit to Belle he had been following her, to question her

239

Night Light
Timothy Cole

about the fortune cookie, to solve the mystery of where she actually lived. He no longer had reservations about how she would take it. It was best that he be direct with her, forthright and to the point—and he should demand to speak with her father!

The thought of facing Sam after all these years brought a cold shudder to Quincy's frame, turning him rigid, his sweat cold. He stopped in his tracks and watched Belle disappearing into the darkness. How would he explain his actions tonight, or his reaction to a simple fortune cookie; how would he rationalize his following her more than two miles out of the city on a deserted farm road? What would he say to Sam, whose restaurant he ate at as often as twice a week but to whose face he had said little in all these years? Just how silly was he going to look? There had been a dearth of gossip in the town for months, and his little episode, about to get bigger, would be fodder for weeks to come. He would become the laughing stock, the butt of countless jokes—the Town Fool! Or a Pariah! A stalker of *young, innocent girls!* Sam would be the victim, and Belle, the naïve waif who served half the town its breakfast every morning, would be the guiltless prey!

Frozen by the fear of discovery or by the fear of lost reputation, Quincy found that he could neither speak nor move. The scene in front of him grew in proportion until he was dwarfed by everything around him—the road, the trees, Belle, even the gravel in the road. He was a significant nothing, completely vulnerable. There was an increasing roaring in his ears as he saw his life deconstructing.

Belle turned, steadily and resolutely. Her face was devoid of emotion and powerful as stone. Her eyes, even in the moonlit darkness, shined with their pale green color and focused entirely on Quincy.

"I put that fortune in that cookie. Do you know *why?*"

Blank Slate Writers Group
For Whom the Belle Trolls

She paused but did not wait for an answer, even if Quincy *could* answer.

"I knew you'd be in the restaurant someday when we'd be alone, but I didn't know when. Today, when you came in, I saw my chance, and I printed out the fortune, cut it, and slipped it into a fortune cookie. I've been waiting for this chance for over a year—*ever since I found out.*"

Quincy stood rooted to the middle of the road, Belle looming ever larger, her mouth able to devour him in one small bite.

"I *hate* you," she said, "I didn't think about you before then, but I began to hate you the moment I knew. *All these years.*! I should have *known*. You could have *told* me. You didn't have to leave me in all that suspense, all that uncertainty. Why? *Why? —Why?*"

Quincy stared. He realized now that she held—in the bundle that he'd seen her with while she walking—a small yellow-haired dog, its eyes shining red in the blackness of her sweater.

"Why didn't you tell me you were *my father?* Why did you ignore me all these years, avoiding me on the street, never coming to my games, forgetting my birthdays, my graduation?" She shook violently as she built up for a final shout. "*My mother's funeral?* You meant everything to her, and yet you left her without a word, without a cent, with only me as her only memory of you!"

Belle threw her arms out, her fingers wide, and she dropped her sweater and the dog, which ran out of fear into the weeds.

"I HATE YOU!" she bellowed, gleaming tears finally streaking her cheeks, her body quivering in anger.

She rushed at Quincy—who was unable to move even for his own safety—her arms rigid, her fingers clawed, her teeth bared and flashing…. The picture-memory of Brenda brought to life stabbing the air with the thought of Brenda's words on that picnic day twenty years ago: "*I*

241

Night Light
Timothy Cole

need to remember you; I want this last time to shine in my life for all eternity!"

...and Belle threw her arms around him and *sobbed* and *sobbed* and *sobbed*, her body convulsively falling into his arms and suddenly growing so limp that he had to hold her tightly.

Blank Slate Writers Group

Poem

Finding Inspiration
Christina Ortega Phillips

In an unexpected phone call,
an unworking clock on the wall,
being witness to a downfall;
somehow, a poem can be found there.

When life's load's too heavy to haul,
your lover no longer enthralls,
do not sit and let the tears fall;
if you look closely, a poem's there.

In any football ref's miscall,
events—normal or off-the-wall,
any problem that's big or small;
somehow, a poem can be found there.

When instead of rainbows, rainfall
is all there is to be seen, sprawl
out your findings in words and scrawl
all the poems you have just found there.

Blank Slate Writers Group

Short Story

Desert Escapade
Tom Saine

Evelyn and Bill Grant drove south out of Flagstaff, on US Hwy 89. They had come from having Thanksgiving dinner with Evelyn's parents, Janis and Harvey Evergreen. The day had been rather hot for this time of year, hitting nearly 95°; warm enough, Evelyn and her mother chose to serve Thanksgiving dinner on the picnic table under an umbrella.

As they drove, a thinnest sliver of moon rose above the mountain peaks; the temperature still hovered in the high 60's or low 70's at ten-thirty. They were headed home to their apartment in the rear of a used bookstore they owned in Sedona.

Evelyn had four glasses of Chardonnay with dinner, and afterwards—exceeding her usual limit of two—which had put her in a kittenish mood in the car. She ran her hand up and down Bill's thigh and nibbled on his ear as he drove.

"Bi-i-i ll," she cooed in his ear.

"Yeah," he said, turning his head to look at her.

Evelyn kissed him on the mouth. "Want to stop at our special spot tonight?"

"I thought it's that time of—um—ah."

"No, no. That's been over for more than a week. You don't remember making love night-before-last?"

"Oh, yeah!" he grinned at her, "You're right. We did, didn't we?"

Night Light
Tom Saine

She snaked her hand up to the top of his thigh and squeezed him. "It's a good time if we want to get pregnant. And we do want to get pregnant... Don't we?"

"Yes," he said as he brought his hand down from the steering-wheel and covered hers. He squeezed her hand firmly, "Yes we do."

"I know we haven't been trying for very long—but I feel excited—maybe it's the bassinet—tonight might be the night." She kissed his neck; glanced back at the bassinet her mother had insisted that she take with her— her bassinet—the same one her mother had used when she was born. She laid her head on his shoulder and began to knead the growing bulge in Bill's pants.

"You're certain? Have you checked your charts?"

"Yes, I'm sure." She pulled back and sat up in her seat murmuring, "and, besides, even if this isn't the night. . . " She slid back over to his side and returned her hand to his pants. She nibbled the lobe of his ear and purred, "I love practicing... Don't you?"

"Practice." He turned his head and smiled at her. "Yes, I love to *practice* with you. There's not a lot I like better than *practicing* with you," he laughed.

A few miles north of Sedona, Bill turned off the main highway onto Gasper canyon road, a badly maintained gravel road to Oak Creek. While not as popular as Grasshopper Point, a better maintained access a few miles further down the highway. This section of Oak Creek had the advantage—at night in particular—of being deserted. They would be alone here, no one would be the wiser if Evelyn still wanted to go skinny-dipping, and they could go undisturbed. They could practice—as Evelyn had put it—in the water or lie out on one of the flat sandstone rocks lining the bank. Or do whatever else she had in mind to do, and not be troubled by onlookers.

Bill struggled with the steering wheel, trying to avoid the many deep ruts in the dirt road. They'd traveled

Blank Slate Writers Group
Desert Escapade

halfway to the creek when the car lurched badly to the left and the steering wheel began to vibrate violently.

"Ah, shit." Bill slammed his hand on the steering wheel.

"What's wrong?" Evelyn said as she jerked back in her seat.

"A flat tire."

"How terribly romantic. Much better than running out of gas," Evelyn giggled as she slid even closer to him and kissed his neck.

Bill looked at her soberly. "Sure, if you think it's romantic," he brought the car to a stop and turned the ignition off, "then maybe you'd like to change the tire yourself."

"I've never changed a tire before, in my life, but I'm sure I could do it, if you show me what to do," she said as her hand returned to its earlier resting place. Bill's excitement had faded; but a few touches from Evelyn's deft fingers brought it back as strong as before. "But first, can't we, um, . . . practice for a while?" She kissed him hard on the mouth as her fingers began to work on his belt buckle.

"I'd love to practice," Bill said as he took hold of her hand, "but I should fix the tire first. There'll be plenty of time to practice afterwards or to do whatever else you want to do."

"Can we still go to the creek?"

"Sure, why not—I'll need to wash up—after I fix the tire," he said as he opened the car door and got out.

"OK. But—"

"No buts, Evelyn," he said, leaning back into the car. "I'll fix the tire first—then we can do whatever."

Bill opened the trunk and began loosening the tire and jack from under the trunk liner.

Evelyn got out of the car and ran around to the back asking, "What can I do?"

Night Light
Tom Saine

Bill opened a toolbox, stored at the side of the trunk, and pulled out a flashlight and handed it to her. "You can hold this while I work."

The sun had long ago set; the waning moon provided little light. The only real illumination came from the millions of stars overhead, the trunk light of the car, and the flashlight Evelyn held in her hand. Bill put the jack under the frame and began to loosen the lug nuts.

"Stop waving the light around—keep it on the tire."

"I'm sorry," Evelyn said with a quiver in her voice. "It feels a little creepy out here now."

"You weren't creeped out a minute ago with your hand down my pants."

"That was different."

The hoot of an owl came from the trees close by on their right. The hooting momentarily stopped the chirping of a few cicadas still in the area. Evelyn jumped at the sound and let out a high-pitched squeal, "Oh, shit! What's that?" She dropped the flashlight on the ground.

"It's only an owl hooting," Bill said as he picked up the flashlight and attached it to the fender with the magnet in its base. "If you're feeling jumpy, why don't you get back in the car and wait till I fix the tire."

Evelyn didn't answer. She hiked the hem up on her skirt, and, putting her foot on the bumper, she crawled up on the hood of the car. "I'll watch from up here," she said as she peered over the fender at the bewildered look on Bills face, which changed quickly to a grin.

"What's the matter? What's funny?"

"Nothing funny. I'm thinking of the last time you sat on the hood of the car."

"Yeah, last summer. We did have a great time that day—didn't we? You took pictures of me." She looked out the window. "Isn't this the same spot?"

He smiled a far off look in his eye. "You wore a lot less then."

Blank Slate Writers Group
Desert Escapade

"What do you mean less—as I remember it—I had nothing on at all—I was naked," she giggled as she sat up and began to pull the hem of her sweater up. "I can take my clothes off again if you want me to. Do you have the camera in the car?" She purred seductively.

Bill shined the flashlight at her. She had pulled the sweater above her breasts revealing she wasn't wearing a bra. "Yes, my camera bag is in the back seat. But it will have to wait till this's done. We can play all you want later." He re-attached the flashlight to the fender and brought his attention back to removing the lug nuts.

Evelyn lowered the sweater and pouted. "You don't know what you're missing," she teased as she clutched a breast in each hand and jiggled them at him.

"Oh, yes, I do. I know *exactly* what I'm missing," he said winking at her. "But I need to fix this tire first."

She stuck her head over the fender and smiled at him.

He didn't say more, but shook his head as he went back to removing the tire. He removed the old tire and took it back to the trunk and rolled the spare around to the front of the car. When he returned Evelyn had moved; she now leaned her back against the windshield, her legs outstretched across the hood. She looked up at the stars.

"You comfortable up there?" he said with a slight bit of sarcasm in his voice.

"Aren't the stars beautiful tonight?" she cooed, flashing him another seductive smile.

Bill glanced at the sky momentarily. "Yeah, great," he said as turned back to mounting the spare tire. "I'll be sure and check out the *Big Dipper* when I'm done with this."

"*Big Dipper*," She giggled, "I like the sound of that. Hurry up! I want you to show me your *Big Dipper.*"

Suddenly, an intensely bright blue-green light flooded the hood of the car. Bill heard a crackling sound, like the crumpling of a large amount of cellophane into a ball. Startled by the light Bill fell backwards landing on his butt in the bottom of a rut. A few seconds later, the light went

Night Light
Tom Saine

off as suddenly as it had come on—the crinkling stopped too. He rubbed his eyes and stood up. Evelyn no longer lay on the hood of the car. All her clothing remained, but Evelyn had vanished.

Bill looked around quickly—he saw nobody. He retrieved the flashlight from the fender and beamed it in all directions—still, nothing in sight. He went to the hood of the car and picked up one of Evelyn's now empty shoes. He could still feel the warmth of her foot in the shoe. He examined her skirt and her nearly transparent silk panties inside it. The panties were still warm.

A smudge on the windshield where Evelyn had rested her head caught Bill's attention. He touched the smudge, and looked at it closely under the flashlight beam. It looked like make-up—face-powder, along with eye shadow, mascara and lipstick. He looked more closely at the smudge on the glass; it all together resembled Evelyn's face. On the hood he found red spots, he thought might be her blood, but looking closer under the light he discovered it wasn't blood or paint, at all, but little flakes of nail polish.

Bill leaned against the front of the car, his mind having a hard time processing all this. It looked as if all the molecules of Evelyn's body had vanished, leaving only what she wore or had applied to her body behind on the hood of the car.

A noise in the distance made him look up. A figure stood in the middle of the road thirty yards ahead, silhouetted against a light source coming from behind, and outlined by trees. All details of the figure were obscured by a fog floating up from the creek. However, the basic contours of the figure resembled a woman's—a tall woman. She, or it, stood in a menacing—ready to fight—stance with a long straight object in its hand. He couldn't make out what it was. Was it a weapon?

Bill shined the flashlight at the figure and began to walk toward it. He called out, "Hey, who are you? What's

Blank Slate Writers Group
Desert Escapade

going on here? What do you want?" He had gotten three steps from the car when the bright blue/green light appeared over his head. He heard the same crackling cellophane sound he had heard when Evelyn vanished. A cold chill shook his body and he felt dizzy. He watched as the scene around him began to swirl and spin, then dimmed to gray, and then went black. He lost consciousness.

* * *

Bill awoke, to find himself immobilized, strapped down to a metal table. Bindings had been put around his wrists, ankles and across his chest, thighs and head. He was naked. He tried to speak, call out; but no sound would come from his mouth. He tried again—still nothing!

Subdued lighting filled the space surrounding him. The air smelt acidic with a tinge of cinnamon. A strange combination he thought. He could make out a multitude of flashing multicolored lights in the distance. A single bright spotlight pointed at his groin. A tube had been attached to his penis—the tube pulsated. The strap around his head restricted his head movements but he could see out of the corner of his eye. On his left he could make out another table holding Evelyn, also strapped down; also naked. He could see an apparatus with tubes and wires clamped across her chest. Her legs were strapped to a metal frame that raised them in the air. A probe, made of metal, was jammed up between her legs. The object had blinking lights and assorted tubes and wires attached to it, which ran to another apparatus on wheels which stood near the foot of the table where Evelyn lay.

On his right he could make out two figures standing by a view screen, which displayed strange hieroglyphic figures and pictures that looked like multicolored blobs moving about. On another screen he saw an overhead view of a car—his car—sitting in the middle of a dirt road.

Night Light
Tom Saine

Two figures moved around the car, one opened the passenger side door and looked inside. The creature pulled a Styrofoam coffee cup from the car interior. He, or it, removed the lid and smelled the contents, then replaced the lid and put the cup back inside the car. He closed the door and immediately vanished in a flash of light.

The two figures studying the view screen resembled humans, except for their heads, which had facial features more like those of a cat, rather than a human. The creatures wore no clothing, no head-gear, no belts and no shoes. They had short gray fur covering their head and body, except for their chest, belly and genital area, which remained bare—but the same gray color. In physical appearance they looked nearly human—two arms with fingers on their hands—two legs with toes on their feet. Their pointed ears sat up high on their heads, again like a cat's would be. The smaller of the two had female type breasts but no outward genitalia. The other one, larger in all respects, resembled a human male, with a flat chest and abdomen. In other aspects he was unlike any human male Bill had ever seen in a men's locker-room.

Both beings had tails, about two feet long, which emerged from the lower part of their spines above their buttocks. The tail moved about rhythmically, back and forth, again as an ordinary house cat's, or even a monkey's, might do.

The figure resembling a male spoke to the smaller creature. Bill couldn't understand what was said. It didn't sound like any language he had ever heard before. The man, if it was a man, walked toward the table where Bill lay. Bill closed his eyes—but by squinting—he could see the creature make changes to the apparatus attached to his body. More lights began to blink on the instrument and the pulsating tube began to pulse faster and faster. Within a few seconds Bill began to climax. The flood tide overwhelmed him with such intensity, the muscles in his whole body contracted spasmodically. His mouth flew

Blank Slate Writers Group
Desert Escapade

open; he could not breathe; he gasped for air; his eyes fluttered and the lights in the room dimmed to gray and then everything went black; he lost consciousness.

* * *

It was daylight—the sun was high in the sky—perhaps noon he thought. He looked around, scanned the nearby trees and bushes; except for a single bird perched on a tree branch, they were alone. He reached over to Evelyn and shook her shoulder. She began to wake up and pulled herself up to a seated position.

She looked at Bill with a perplexed expression; she rubbed her eyes and looked around again, "It's daylight—we're naked—what happened?"

Bill moved over next to her. "Do you remember about what happened last night?"

"You started to change the flat tire. I laid down on the hood of the car looking at the stars," she blinked her eyes several times, "and then you flashed the flashlight in my face—I don't remember anything after the flash of light."

"The light wasn't the flashlight—it came from the sky—when it went out, you had vanished."

"What do you mean I had vanished?"

Bill stood up and began to look around the grassy field where they lay. The car was still parked where it had been—still up on the jack—a dozen yards away. "You'd vanished, like in thin air, leaving only your clothes lying on the hood of the car."

"Only my clothes?"

Bill extended his hand, "Come with me and I'll show you—the car's still where it stopped last night."

As he pulled Evelyn to her feet she shrieked, "Oh, my God!" and pulled back from him. She pointed to his arm. "Look your tattoo! It's gone!"

The US Marines tattoo he had gotten in boot-camp many years ago was no longer on his right bicep—it was

Night Light
Tom Saine

gone—in its place, only smooth white skin. He looked at Evelyn. "I don't know, but it's definitely gone." He rubbed his arm where the tattoo had been. "It doesn't hurt. My arm feels OK."

"What do you think happened to us?"

He wrapped his arms around her and hugged her saying, "I remember waking up for a few moments. It's all a bit hazy, but I do remember seeing creatures—human-looking creatures—but at the same time not human. I'd been strapped to a steel table with a machine attached to me." His hand moved to his penis. "I had an orgasm—then it all went black. I must have passed out, and then I woke up a few minutes ago, lying here on the grass next to you. Both of us naked."

"You aren't hurt, are you? She pointed to his groin. "Turn around, let me look at you." Bill did as she asked, "I don't see anything else suspicious or unusual," she said. She pointed to his groin again, "You certain it's OK?"

He moved his hand around his whole groin area. "It feels normal. It doesn't hurt if that's what you mean. How about you? You'd also been hooked-up to a machine."

"You're not serious. No. Are you sure?" She felt her breast with her fingers and ran her right hand down between her legs, "I'm OK. I'm not hurt—no pain at all." She turned around as she'd asked him to do. "Look at me too."

"Nice ass," Bill chuckled.

Her expression instantly changed from confused to incredulous. "This is not the time for that." She punched his arm. "If what you say happened—really happened—it's serious, and also pretty damn weird. You sure this happened? You're not pulling my leg—are you? Because I don't remember anything at all after that light blinded me."

"Trust me," he leaned in, holding a cheek in each hand, he kissed her lightly on the mouth, "everything happened exactly like I said it did."

Blank Slate Writers Group
Desert Escapade

* * *

Bill found his clothes; they lay heaped in a rumpled clump over his shoes in the middle of the dirt road, ten feet from where they had awakened in the grass. He turned his white t-shirt inside out and found a blue stain resembling his tattoo where the shirt would have would have come into contact with his shoulder. The flashlight lay two feet away. Bill picked it up "Holy shit, look at this!"

"What's wrong?"

"The flashlight." He held it up for her to see. "It switched on, but the batteries are dead."

"Is that bad?"

"It's not good." He shook his head. "The batteries are brand new. They should have lasted two days, maybe more."

He picked up his clothing and shoes and walked with Evelyn to the car. He showed her the clothing still lying on the hood of the car. He also showed her the makeup smudge on the windshield and the fingernail polish particles on the hood.

She looked at her fingers; "I had polish on my nails last night. It's gone!" She looked at her feet, "There's none on my toes either."

Bill picked up one of her shoes and pulled the ankle sock out. He turned the sock inside out. He saw five flakes of pink fingernail polish stuck to the fabric. The flecks of polish matched the size of Evelyn's toes.

"What in the hell could have happened to us, Bill?"

"I don't know, what happened to us, but whatever happened, I would definitely declare it as strange. Something straight out of the *Twilight Zone*. I've been expecting Rod Sterling to tap me on the shoulder and tell me it all been a big joke."

Evelyn gasped; at the mention of the *Twilight Zone*, her previous bewilderment now turned to panic and terror as she cried out, "What the hell happened to us, Bill!"

Night Light
Tom Saine

"I don't know. I've been afraid to ask myself such a question." He said as he deposited his clothes on the hood of the car in a heap. "The blue-green light may have been a transporter beam—like they used in *Star Trek*. We may have been transported to a space ship."

"Are you nuts? That's crazy … Kirk and Spock aren't naked in the transporter—are they?"

"No they aren't." He smiled at her. "And, I must admit, it does sound crazy." He leaned against the grill of the car. Running his fingers through his hair, he said, "That part's strange all right. Unless …" he turned to Evelyn. "unless, unless they can set the machine to only take human flesh—nothing else; it would explain the nail-polish, and even the tattoo." He slapped his hand on his arm where the tattoo had been. "None of the material left behind is us. Those things were on us—the nail polish and the tattoo—but not actually a part of us."

Evelyn's eyes opened wide and she said in a low voice, as if she didn't want anyone to hear what she said, "Space ship?"

Evelyn's cell phone began to ring. She picked up her purse, which still lay on the front seat of the car where she had left it last night, and pulled it out and flipped it open, "Hello?"

"*Evelyn Jane Carpenter Grant, where on earth have you been?*" the familiar voice of her mother blasted from the speaker.

"Mother, what's gotten you so upset? Bill and I stopped at Oak Creek. We spent the night here."

"That's nonsense, Evelyn. I've been calling you for nearly three days. What have you been doing at Oak Creek for three days? Why didn't you answer the telephone?"

"Three days? What three days? We had dinner with you last night."

"No, Evelyn today is Monday, not Friday. What's the matter with you? Have you lost your mind?"

Blank Slate Writers Group
Desert Escapade

* * *

"I'm going to go Christmas shopping today," Evelyn said as she sat up on the side of their bed some weeks later. "Why don't you sleep in—I don't know how long I'll be, or when I'll be back."

"I need to open the store," Bill said as he too sat up on the edge of the bed. "We can't afford to miss out on even one Christmas shopper." He stood up and kissed her on the cheek as he headed to the bathroom. "You have a good time shopping. I'll take care of the shop,." he said as he entered the bathroom.

Evelyn returned to the little book shop in the early evening, nearly six. The tinkling of the bell above the door drew Bill's attention away from the movie he'd been watching on the TV behind the counter. Evelyn had two shopping bags full of packages in her hands as she came through the door. She also had a strange look on her face; a look of worry, fear and detachment.

"You OK?" Bill said as he muted the TV and put the remote on the counter top.

Evelyn walked through the shop, as if in a daze. She dropped the bags of packages she had been carrying in a heap on the floor. She sat down on the couch in the little seating area at the back of the shop.

Bill came out from behind the counter and followed her to the back of the store and sat down on the couch next to her. He pulled her into his arms. "What's wrong?"

"It... It... It can't be!" she wailed and buried her face into his chest in convulsive sobs.

"Tell me, what can't be?" Bill said as he held her tightly.

She pulled back. Looked at Bill, cried out louder, and flung herself at him again, burying her face deeply into his chest, "I, um, I went to the doctor today."

"What's the matter? What did the doctor say?"

Night Light
Tom Saine

She immediately burst into tears. "The doct... the doctor said..." she mumbled between sobs, but didn't finish.

Bill sat up, and holding Evelyn by the shoulders looked straight into her eyes, "What did the doctor say?"

"He... um, he ah..." her sobbing eased a bit and she finally spat it out "The doctor said I was pregnant."

"Holly, shit! That's great news!" Bill said. "Was he sure? A boy or a girl? When's it due? Have you called your mother yet? We should call my parents right away too."

As he stood up, Evelyn pulled him down onto the couch again. "No, you didn't hear me right," she cried out. She raised her voice, "I *was* pregnant. I'm not pregnant now. The doctor said I've already had a baby—more than three weeks ago."

In unison, they turned toward the bassinet in the corner where Bill had put it the day they had returned home after the strange events that had taken place at the Oak Creek.

Where was the child that should be there sleeping?

Blank Slate Writers Group

Poem

Fishing Expedition
Barbara Funke

Your grizzled cheek says, *Here I am, come back*
from days of fishing with the guys. Your smile
says, *It feels good to be here.* You unpack
by dumping gear then hold me for a while.
The water in the shower runs. You sing
a scale, emerge smooth-shaven, slick as fish
you caught and freed, regretful not to bring
me fish for dinner. But you share a wish
I'd join you, say I'd like it if I tried.
For each of us, I pour a glass of wine
that nets your stories, hours of humor, pride.
We toast your safe return. I reel my line,
my ear the hook, the bait this pool of peace
until you're off again: catch and release.

Blank Slate Writers Group

Short Story

Three Rail Christmas
Robert Thomas

The winter holiday season brings a time for family and celebration. For many of the boys in my father's generation, Christmas really meant colorful American Flyer or Lionel trains circling under the Christmas tree. For me, decades later, that season also brought out our special holiday trains, the ones with the third rail in the middle.

Back in December of 1940, when a baby was not known to be a girl or a boy before its arrival, my grandfather took the streetcar downtown in Chicago to go Christmas shopping for his unborn child. After a visit to Marshall Fields, he came home with a Lionel train set "for the baby." He already had a daughter and wanted to make sure that if there was another girl, well, he would already have his train set. My father arrived four days before Christmas, vindicating my grandfather's vision.

I never got to know my grandfather; he died twenty years before I was born. However, the same train was still among the ones circling our tree when I came along. He and my father built layouts together under the tree every year, as well as a permanent one in their basement, and they looked forward to additions to their collection that the Christmas season would always bring.

Christmas Time for me began around Veteran's Day. It was traditionally a three day weekend for parent-teacher conferences and was also right around my birthday. If there was no bad news from school, I could begin to petition my mother for the "land grants" I needed to begin

261

Night Light
Three Rail Christmas

construction of the annual under-the-tree railroad empire. With some begging, promises to clean, study, and other things I probably never really intended to fulfill, I could get permission to venture into the crawlspace and return with battered old cardboard boxes that held what I thought was our family treasure.

Each year's railroad would start the weekend before Thanksgiving with a simple oval of track. At the start of the Christmas break, that oval would grow into a pike that linked rooms, while it ran through the carpeted valleys formed by furniture mountains. As the weather got colder, I would ride those little trains in my imagination to all sorts of places.

I would spend hours building and changing track configurations, then routing speeding trains through switches to different destinations. Black steamers, with their oily smelling smoke and air whistles, pulled trains along with bright yellow diesels around impossibly tight curves. Certain cars would do different things—milk cans flew from a refrigerator car, wooden barrels vibrated up a ramp and dropped into a gondola that in turn tipped on command to dump them on to the carpet, a trolley reversed itself when it ran into the bumper at the end of the track, grade crossing gates came down while lights flashed, and unlike my toy trains, these trains could stop and still have lights, smoke, and whistle. That my other friends didn't have trains running on their floors didn't seem to occur to me, though now I definitely see it as their loss.

Every now and then, something wouldn't work right, and that meant a trip to my father's work bench. He had watched his father deal with the same problems, and usually after a few minutes of tweaking with a screwdriver, and maybe some oil, the item would be handed back to me ready to return to service.

On Christmas morning, piles of colorfully wrapped gifts would arise. Tomorrow they might be toys or games,

Blank Slate Writers Group
Robert Thomas

but today, stacked properly, they could form tunnels through the foothills of the mighty sofa range. Eventually the tree would come down, but the train might stay for another week or maybe more. Finally the track would come apart, and the locomotive and cars would go back into the weathered cardboard boxes to disappear back into the crawlspace for another year.

Then I went to college a plane ride away, and the time to get the train up was less. More elderly holiday guests limited the routes I could take. Finally a new puppy that liked to chew put an end to the holiday railroads at the house where I lived as a child. Then ten years in the Merchant Marine made holidays, much less the trains I remembered, a memory.

When I finally did have a Christmas at home again, two young nephews made it a new experience. The older nephew was raised on "I love Toy Trains" and "Thomas the Tank Engine" videos, and loves nothing more than to see the CSX Trains racing through our little Indiana town. There was no question the 1940 Lionel train would make another appearance at Grandma and Grandpa's, now blowing its old air whistle alongside more modern plastic trains with digital sound systems.

As my parents sort through items from their recent move, more trains from the past appear out of boxes from the old house, and my nephew loves each new discovery. I get to watch him enjoy the same trains my grandfather, my father, and I had as a child. He has to run everything, but the older trains are his favorite, because they can be pushed around the track just like his Wooden Thomas trains. When he sees a locomotive for the first time he always asks if it is a "pusher engine" or not. He likes to lie on his side and watch the valve motion on the old die cast steam locomotives. Back and forth, he rolls the colorful little trains, until the movements get smaller, and finally stops when he falls asleep on the floor with his hand on his great-grandfather's locomotive.

Night Light
Three Rail Christmas

Christmas morning, at my house for the first time ever, a passenger train negotiated its route along the floor between mountains of presents and furniture. Though there is a large model railroad under construction in my basement, the three-rail Lionel trains remain the special ones. I hope they create the same fond memories of family for my nephews as they did for me.

Blank Slate Writers Group

Poem

Hostage Situation
Barbara Funke

Don't move.
Hot, damp breath invades our space.
Weakling leaves of a book cringe.
Hair hangs limp, gripped by ugly waves futile to resist.
My hands are tied, gestures fluid but foolish.
In 97% humidity, motion feels surreal,
heavy trudge through loose Jello.
A 90-degree pool forces lying wilted, supine,
no lapping, cool escape not in the cards (also flaccid).

Fantasy water lifts languorously in one tropical mask,
a turquoise rectangle in the great quilt of oceans.
But that's too romantic, a Stockholm illusion.

Water is cramped in two-thirds of Earth's surface,
and malcontent molecules have made a break for it,
first hanging around in creepy suspense,
now holding us hostage for weeks. It's criminal!
Just pay the ransom and get me out of here.
Dispositions are reckless.
My patience
is shot.

Blank Slate Writers Group

Poem

Static & Silence
John Schaub

Three hours and something
outside of nowhere,
a moon, solid as silence,
slips behind trees, whose leafless branches,
tangles of dark cracks,
shatter the moon's solidity
like static shatters silence.
A radio turns on,
the tuner travels
through its range
and back again
searching for a voice,
a compression wave companion,
carried through night,

but only technological silence
pours from speakers, static
couched in narrow bandwidths
buried among silent frequencies,
as obscure electromagnetic waves
stumble across a wire antenna
under empty moonlight.

Blank Slate Writers Group

Short Story

The Waiting Room
Christina Ortega Phillips

Harold tried not to wince as the anesthesiologist inserted the needle into his left hand. His wife let out a nervous chuckle.

"My Harold," she said, stroking his hair, "always so scared of needles."

"I'm not scared," he said, scowling.

"Sure you're not, honey." She leaned over the rail of the bed and gave him a kiss on his forehead.

"OK," the anesthesiologist said, pushing his chair back from the bedside and rising. "Now I'm going to give you a little something to help you relax. The nurse will be in in a few minutes to wheel you down to the operating room and we'll put you to sleep once there."

"OK," Harold mumbled, staring at the needle in his hand.

"Any questions?"

"How long until I can see him after the surgery?" Her hand had moved to hold Harold's right hand and her grip was increasing as the time for him to go under was nearing.

"Probably no more than twenty minutes, but that's just an estimate," the man answered. "We will take him into another room after the surgery to give him time to wake up. Once he's awake, we will bring him back here."

Harold's wife nodded. "Thank you."

Night Light
Christina Ortega Phillips

"It's going to be OK," Harold told her once the young man left. Despite his nerves, he forced a smile. He hated seeing her worry like this.

"I know," she said, but she didn't sound very convincing.

He wished he could say something to make her feel better, but he was beginning to feel fuzzy because of what the man had given him. The nurse came then and as she pushed his bed to the operating room, he was drifting off to sleep.

* * *

In the waiting room, the swishing sound of the corduroy fabric was beginning to grate on Celeste's nerves. The man next to her was either very nervous or had a serious twitching problem because his leg had not stopped moving the entire time Celeste had been sitting in the waiting room. Celeste bit her lip, trying to not say something to him.

Maybe it's a very focused form of Parkinson's, she told herself. It's a disease he can't control and I would be a jerk to say something to him.

Swish, swish, swish.

Celeste closed her eyes and rubbed her temples. The man with the noisy pants was obviously very nervous for someone there at the hospital. So am I, Celeste thought irritably. I hate hospitals, but I'm not disturbing everyone. Celeste opened her eyes. Hospitals were full of fear and hope, life and death, and everything in-between...

Swish, swish, swish.

She tried to distract herself by looking around the room at its occupants:

There were the two parents: the man with his arm protectively around the wife who finally said she could not just sit there and wait and was going to go get them coffee.

Blank Slate Writers Group
The Waiting Room

There was the elderly woman who was on the phone with someone saying that they had just taken Harold into the operating room. Her other hand was clutching her purse so tightly, her knuckles were white. Poor woman, Celeste thought. She's terrified.

There was the woman around Celeste's age whose nose had not been taken out of a book the whole time Celeste had been in the room. Celeste saw that she was reading *A Great and Terrible Beauty* and continued staring at her, hoping to catch her eye so they could talk about the book.

And then there was the twitchy man who looked to be in his late forties.

Celeste sighed, and then pulled out her Kindle hoping to distract herself from the swishing sound. She didn't get very far, though, since not long after she had opened whatever book she was working on, she heard a frustrated grunt, making her look up.

The elderly woman was glaring at her phone and trying to punch buttons. No one else seemed to notice so Celeste put down her Kindle.

"Ma'am," Celeste said, moving to sit next to her, "do you need any help with that?"

"Oh, yes, please," the woman said, sounding relieved. "This phone's buttons are so darn small. I'm trying to call my son, his dad's in surgery and I am just so nervous and-" she stopped suddenly and smiled. "You didn't ask for all that, though, did you?"

Celeste smiled back at her kindly. "It's OK. I can help you call your son. And I can listen, too, if you need me to." She gently took the phone from the woman's hands. "What's your son's number?"

* * *

Harold heard his name being called. He opened his eyes, bracing himself for the pain he assumed he would

Night Light
Christina Ortega Phillips

feel, but there was none. He tried to look around: there was no oxygen tent on his mouth like the nurses had told him there would be.

And no one was near his bed.

So who had called his name, waking him up?

Harold sat up slowly, again bracing himself for pain and again feeling none. He saw a nurse sitting at the foot of the bed behind the curtain to his right.

"Excuse me," he called out, but the nurse did not react.

"Excuse me," he said again, just a tad louder. Again there was no reaction.

Frustrated and painfree, Harold decided to get up on his own. He was obviously fine as there was no oxygen on him nor was he in any pain. Heck, the IV had even been taken out from his hand. He wanted to hurry back to his wife, to let her know that he was OK. He figured he would just try and walk himself there since no one seemed to be paying him any attention.

"Miss," he called out, sitting on the edge of the bed. The nurse got up and walked away in the opposite direction.

Fuck it, Harold thought. *I can walk on my own.*

There was another nurse at a nurses' station not far from his bed. He was filling out some paperwork.

"Excuse me," Harold said.

He kept writing.

"I just woke up from surgery. I'd like to be taken back to see my wife now."

The nurse finished writing and got up and walked over to another patient, giving no indication that he had even heard Harold.

Harold gritted his teeth and turned to walk away. He walked slowly at first, looking for signs to tell him where to go, but he was not sure which ones to follow. Nothing was clearly labeled "pre-operation room you were just in."

272

Blank Slate Writers Group
The Waiting Room

Harold ended up in a hallway he hoped would lead him to the waiting room or at least to someone who would acknowledge him. At the farthest end of the hallway, he saw a nurse wheeling a patient in a hospital bed and they were heading in his direction. Good, he thought, maybe they can help me.

"Excuse me," Harold called out. "Do you think you can help me?"

The nurse just kept wheeling and didn't reply.

Harold frowned and called out louder, but the nurse just kept heading his way and Harold had to flatten himself against a wall so as not to get hit by the bed.

"Hey! What's your problem!?" Harold yelled out after them. He continued to walk in the direction that they had come from.

After walking for a minute more, he saw a woman sitting by herself. She was hugging her knees to her chest and her dark hair was draped over her arms, as if hiding her face from anyone who would pass her by. Harold briefly wondered if he should leave her alone, but his desire to see his wife beat his consideration for the weeping woman.

As he neared her, she lifted her head and turned, looking in his direction. She made a puzzled face, but quickly made her face blank and looked away. Harold shrugged, knowing it must have looked odd, a middle-aged man in nothing but a hospital gown and footies wandering the hallway alone; he didn't blame her for the odd look…but she had seen him. She reacted to my appearance, he realized. When others had ignored him, she had seen him. He was even more determined to disturb her and talk to her now.

Celeste shifted uncomfortably as he rushed over to her. She had seen him and worse, he knew that she had seen him. She wanted to curl up in a ball and mourn. She did not want to help him. But she had always had a hard time saying no, especially to them.

273

Night Light
Christina Ortega Phillips

He hurried his steps until he was next to her and squatted by her left arm.

"Excuse me, miss," he said. "Can you tell me where I am? I'm trying to get to the waiting room."

The woman shifted uncomfortably and turned her head to look down the opposite end of the hall. Maybe, she thought, I can just act like I didn't see him and he will leave me alone.

"Miss," he said urgently.

She still did not answer.

"You saw me," he said, his voice rising. "I saw you. You looked at me. You saw me."

The woman shook her head. "Not now," she muttered, still trying to avoid looking at him again.

"Excuse me," he insisted.

She let out an irritated noise. "I'm sorry," she said, finally turning to look at him, "but I just can't. Not right now. I'm very sorry." Her voice cracked. "I just can't. At least, not right now. Maybe later."

She wanted to kick herself. Later? Like she was going to willingly hang around the hospital until she felt better? Felt like helping him?

Harold was confused. "Can't what? Can't help me?" He tried but couldn't keep the increasing anger out of his voice. "I'm just trying to find my way to the waiting room to see my wife and everyone is ignoring me. And you— you're the first one to see me, to acknowledge me and you can't do something so simple as to point me in the right direction?" By the time he was done, his voice practically filled the hallway, but he didn't care. If this woman wouldn't help him, maybe his yelling would attract someone else's attention, someone else who would help him.

Celeste looked at him. Fresh tears stung her eyes as she was hit with a new wave of sadness, this time for him, not herself.

Blank Slate Writers Group
The Waiting Room

"Crap. You don't know," she muttered before she could stop herself.

"Know what?"

She shook her head, realizing he had heard her last statement. This was a first for her. Normally by the time they found her they already knew. Well I sure as hell am not going to tell him, she thought.

"Where you are," she said quickly. "And you know what? I don't either. I was in the waiting room and I got some bad news and started walking and I'm not really sure where I am either so I can't help you. Sorry." She went to grab her purse, but he did, too. He didn't want the only person who had acknowledged him to go, but his hand went right through her bag and he fell forward. Something was obviously wrong and he thought he was beginning to figure out what it was, but he had to hear someone say it to be sure and this lady seemed to be able to help him.

"Please," he said, not getting up yet from the floor. He just looked up at her and let her see the frustration on his face.

Celeste's resolve broke. Maybe it was a combination of the desperation in his voice, or the sad sight of him there on the floor. Or maybe she would have rather helped him than deal with her own mess. She sighed and leaned her head back against the wall. She looked at him, an ocean of sadness in her eyes. "OK," she said finally. "I'll help."

He got up slowly to sit up next to her. He was slowly figuring something out but needed to hear someone say it to be sure.

"Am I—am I dead?"

"Yes," she said, sadly.

He nodded and looked down, avoiding her eyes.

That was easy, Celeste thought.

"But you can see me?"

"Yes."

"How is that possible?"

275

Night Light
Christina Ortega Phillips

"It's just this thing I can do," she said and let the bitterness fill her voice.

He looked at her questioningly, but he did not want to ask her about specifics. If he was dead, then she would be the only one able to get a final message to his wife.

* * *

As Celeste and Harold walked back to the waiting room, she found herself walking slowly. Even though she had told Harold she would help him, she was not eager to return to the room where her life had been forever changed. As she stood in the doorway she was relieved to see that it was emptier. The relief was quickly replaced with jealousy and anger. Obviously the others, including the annoying man with the noisy pants, had gotten good news unlike her. She shook her head, trying to shake away the negative emotions. You have to help Harold now, she chided herself. She could take of herself later. Herself could wait. It always did.

Celeste sat near Harold's wife. She shifted uncomfortably, not knowing how to start.

"Tell her that I love her," Harold said, sitting on Celeste's other side.

Celeste nodded slightly and kept thinking about how to start talking to the recent widow.

"I saw the doctor talk to you," his wife said, interrupting Celeste's thoughts.

"Oh. Yeah, he did…" Celeste bit her lip. She couldn't talk about herself right now.

"It didn't look like good news."

"You just lost someone?" Harold asked. "I am so sorry, I didn't realize…"

Celeste shook her head, fighting off the tears that were stinging her eyes.

"I'm not trying to pry. I just—I just want to tell you I'm sorry. I want to offer my condolences."

Blank Slate Writers Group
The Waiting Room

"I appreciate that. Thanks, but he's in a better place now…" She cleared her throat softly. She wiped away the tears before they could distract her from helping Harold.

"Her name is Mabel," Harold said, leaning more into Celeste's space.

"Mabel, I wanted to tell you …"

Mabel looked at her, puzzled. She clearly didn't remember telling Celeste her name.

"Well, go on!" Harold said.

"What is it, dear?" Mabel asked. "Do you need to use my phone? Is there someone you'd like to call?"

"You're very sweet, but no."

"Come on! She needs to know!" Harold said, getting more impatient.

"Shh," Celeste snapped before she could stop herself.

"Dear?"

"Sorry," Celeste smiled apologetically. "Those insurance papers you were talking to your son about?"

Mabel's face hardened.

"I didn't mean to eavesdrop," Celeste said quickly. "I just—"

"Go on, tell her," Harold instructed.

"I just thought that maybe you should look in his bottom desk drawer," Celeste rushed out. That said, she got up and retreated to a corner of the waiting room. She pulled out her phone, pretending like she had a phone call to make.

"What was that?" Harold demanded, sitting next to her.

"I told her what you wanted me to," Celeste said quietly, pretending to be on the phone.

"You—you told her to find the papers," Harold said angrily. "What about everything else I said? About love? About going on with her life?"

"I told you before I couldn't help you right now," Celeste said. She got up and hurried out of the room.

Harold found her in the hallway, crying softly.

Night Light
Christina Ortega Phillips

"I'm sorry," he said. "But you're the only one who can help me. I needed you to tell her things and you chickened out."

"She'll find the damn papers, won't she?" Celeste snapped. She took in a deep breath. "I'm sorry. You're right. I said I would help you. I'll go back in there and—"

"It's my doctor," Harold interrupted her.

"What?"

"That's my doctor. He's headed this way," Harold said, pointing down the hall. "Oh, my, she doesn't know yet."

Celeste felt relieved that she had spoken to Mabel the way she had. Mabel would have thought she were even crazier if she had gone to her with Harold's full message before she even knew Harold was dead.

Celeste followed Harold back into the waiting room. Harold went and sat by Mabel. He tried to touch her, but couldn't so his hand just hovered over her shoulder.

Celeste went back to the corner of the waiting room. She wanted to give Mabel some kind of privacy, but wanted to be near in case she took the news too badly.

"I am so sorry," she could hear the doctor saying.

"No," Mabel said, her eyes filling with tears. "Not Harold, no."

The doctor kept talking, but Mabel just stood there, shaking her head and clutching her bag to her chest. When he left, Mabel slumped down into her chair and began sobbing.

Celeste watched as Harold tried to talk to his widow and comfort her, but she couldn't hear him and was clearly too upset to feel him. Celeste's eyes filled with tears. She didn't know which was worse: a loved one crossing over immediately or a loved one staying behind and not being able to communicate with his or her family.

"Help her," Harold told Celeste, suddenly in front of her.

Blank Slate Writers Group
The Waiting Room

"I can't," she said. "She needs to grieve." She looked down, not wanting to see the desperation in Harold's face.

"She does or you do?" Harold snapped, losing patience with Celeste. "Tell her I'm still here."

"But you're not. Knowing you're here, like this, it might hurt her more."

"You need to try," Harold pleaded.

"How did you know?" Mabel asked sharply. She was standing in front of Celeste, looking angry and sad.

"Ma'am?"

"The insurance papers you told me about," Mabel said impatiently. "How did you know to tell me about them? Are they really in a drawer? Who are you?"

"I'm no one," Celeste said, sighing.

"Please," Harold begged. "Tell her I'm here."

Celeste sighed again. "Mabel," she said, preparing for the old woman to hit her or yell, "Harold's spirit is still here."

There was no slap or anything. Celeste slowly looked up to see if Mabel was still standing near her.

Mabel sat down next to Celeste. "I—I don't believe you," she said, but her voice let Celeste know that she wanted to believe her.

"Tell her that I love her," Harold said, moving to sit by Mabel's feet. He stared up at his widow and smiled sadly. "Tell her I wouldn't have left her if I had had the choice."

"He said he loves you," Celeste repeated. "And that if it were up to him, he'd still be here with you."

Mabel began to sob again. "Stop it. You're lying."

"She doesn't believe me," Celeste told Harold. "I told you."

"You need to tell her something only I know." Harold's brow furrowed, trying to pull out a special memory, sacred to the couple. "Hawaii," he said, finally.

"Hawaii?" Celeste asked.

279

Night Light
Christina Ortega Phillips

Mabel heard, and turned to look at her. "What about it?" She regretted reacting to the state's name, knowing she just gave the maybe crazy lady an opening to continue playing with her.

"We went there on our honeymoon," Harold continued quickly.

"He said you went there after your wedding and you were—*intimate*—on the beach and you got an infection from the sand."

Mabel closed her eyes and looked away, telling herself that Celeste could be playing with her. That could have happened to anyone.

Harold groaned, seeing that Mabel wasn't fully convinced.

"She has a tattoo of my name on her upper thigh," he said, and after Celeste repeated the information continued to list secrets. "We were going to retire together and move to Arizona to be near our grandkids. Every Sunday morning we do the crossword puzzle together..." He kept going on and on, each new piece of information making Mabel more inclined to listen. "And she thinks that I don't have life insurance."

"That's how you knew about the papers," Mabel whispered.

"Yes," Celeste said. "He found me in the hallway and told me to tell you that he took out a life insurance policy on himself just before he found out about the surgery. He put the papers in his desk and wanted me to tell you where to find them."

"Thank you," Mabel said. "He's here now?"

Celeste nodded. "He's sitting on the floor in front of you."

"Harold?"

At the sound of his name, he leaned forward and placed his hand near her cheek.

"Harold," she said, smiling. "I can feel you." A single tear rolled down her cheek, sliding through his hand.

Blank Slate Writers Group
The Waiting Room

"Tell her to go to Arizona. Tell her to live the life we planned and to take my ashes with her."

Celeste repeated his instructions.

Mabel shook her head. "I don't want to be in a world without you," she sobbed.

Harold frowned. "I don't either…"

Celeste saw it then: a soft light coming from the opposite corner of the room. It wasn't very big or bright, but she knew what it meant. "Harold," she said softly. She nodded her head towards the corner.

He looked and must have seen something different than what Celeste did. "Is that for me?"

"Yes."

"What? What is it?"

"He needs to go now."

"Harold, I will never stop loving you."

"He knows," Celeste said. "He said he will be there for you when it is your time."

Harold got up and walked into the light.

"He's gone now," Celeste told Mabel.

Mabel nodded. "Thank you." She reached over and grabbed Celeste's hand as if trying to hold on to her last connection to Harold.

The two women sat there like that, not wanting to leave the waiting room and not yet ready to start their lives without their loved ones.

Blank Slate Writers Group

Short Story

Hard Boiled

Joyce Hicks

Divine was hurrying to get ready in her spotless, Pullman kitchen—granite countertops, sub-zero fridge, silver grey cabinets. After pouring herself a coffee from her French press and precisely six ounces of *pog* (pineapple, orange, guava), she turned to the oven from which she extracted a soft and yummy-looking, creamy leather handbag.

She opened the door of the far right upper cabinets. Inside, shoes were arranged on four shelves. Stiletto pumps were grouped together on the most easily reached level, lowly clogs banished to the upper shelves. For Divine, shoes substituted for significant others.

She snatched a pair of red sling-backs, addressing them at eye-level. "Today, you get to go out."

"No, no complaining now!" She chided the right shoe as she slipped it on. "We're not going to step in spit and bird crap. Don't worry, we'll take cabs all day." The insole of the pump met her blue lacquered toes like a warm puppy tongue.

Turning the kitchen into a walk-in closet was the latest trend for the up-and-coming professional in media where wardrobe was everything. Why cram cashmere sweaters into under-bed boxes or smoosh them into airtight plastic like a salmon steak when gliding shelves were going to waste in the kitchen appliances and cupboards? A rattan basket of delivery menus was all she needed in the way of groceries.

Night Light
Joyce Hicks

Divine's sub-zero fridge stored ice, pricey wine, an ice pack, yogurt (past dated), half-and-half, and juice. And, this morning, it held something special she had never before purchased.

Yesterday, on the nail salon television, she had watched Martha Stewart smile beatifically while showing three ways to fix eggs—hard boiled (declared "purr-fect" and creamy), scrambled (with "lovely curds"), and lastly a masterful frittata, peaked and lightly browned. It could be filled with "anything you have on hand," Martha declared. Well, the frittata was a fine recipe for the kind of people who obsessed over leftover broccoli flowerets, but not for Divine.

What had inspired Divine to pay attention wasn't learning to cook eggs at home but Martha's self-satisfied smile as she tasted each dish. Her expression was the face of a woman who *knows*. Divine admired her greatly, since Divine knew knowledge, or the appearance of it, was one of the ways to have superiority over others. If cooking eggs well was a route to acquiring this expression, she would do it.

So on the way home last night Divine had bought a dozen eggs. "Martha makes cooking look so easy and fun," she had confided to the cashier, grandly placing the carton on the check-out counter.

At her building, she had let the doorman carry her package to the elevator. Getting the carton to her fridge with no mishaps, she pondered which was the correct storage area for this product. Fortunately as Martha had described, a sweet egg icon guided her to the proper compartment.

This morning before going to work she would begin her education by conquering the hardboiled egg.

Divine discovered that she did have a saucepan. Step one was filling it with water and placing an egg in it. She opened the fridge and lifted the plastic carton of eggs to the counter. Using fingertips so as not to wreck a nail, she

Blank Slate Writers Group
Hard Boiled

was able to unlatch the lid. The eggs looked very clean and neat in their little cubicles. Should she take one from the middle or the end of a row instead, so as not to ruin the symmetry?

Fingertips in action again, Divine plunged in, grabbing an egg from the center. "Oh, cold! And slimy!"

She hadn't noticed the telltale crack. The egg slipped from her fingers, and like Humpty Dumpty made a splat when it hit the floor. Divine jumped her red sling-backs out of the way just in time.

She regarded the egg on her tile floor, the yoke intact, a cheerful tiny sun swimming in the clear goo of egg white, which wasn't *white* at all. The egg definitely had a Martha smile of superiority.

"You mean thing! You knew it was my first time." She spoke in a tone reserved for delivery people, interns, and former lovers.

There were ways to deal with this impudence. Divine reached for her phone.

When she heard, "Luxor Realty, good morning," she said, "Tell Milosh to list my condo immediately. *As is.*" She grabbed her handbag, laid her keys on the counter, and marched out.

.

Blank Slate Writers Group

Short Story

Seth Donald Saves the Day
Stefan Barkow

Seth stepped up to the plastic folding table. The film wasn't wrapped yet but his part was done, just like all the rest of the extras in line around him. It was time to get paid.

"Seth Donald," he said to the balding man who shuffled through the stack of envelopes. There seemed to be a problem.

"Donald your first or last name?" the man asked. Seth felt his hands begin to sweat. *Don't make a scene,* he told himself, *this happens all the time; just tell him your name!*

"That's my first—no, I mean, uh—that's my last name. It's: Donald, Seth."

The pause wasn't enough to convey a silent comma to the bored assistant. The man let out an exasperated "Whatever" and handed over the envelopes. "Find your own," he told Seth. Seth heard the others behind him grumble.

He found his name in the little plastic window of the envelope, signed on the indicated line, and made for the parking lot of the movie studio as quickly as possible. He jammed the envelope into his pocket with his keys. Glancing at the sky, he saw that it looked like it might rain soon, so he zipped up his old brown jacket. Not that the jacket would help. The thing was so frayed and thin, all but one of the pockets had holes in them. Time to go to the bank so he could pay back his mom for the rent.

Night Light
Stefan Barkow

He found his scooter lying on its side. He wasn't mad that it had fallen over—he hated the damn thing. When his parents bought it for him back when he was in high school it had been red. But two years of sitting in the sun while Seth was away failing at college had faded the paint job to a delicate pink. He picked it up, jumped on, and pulled into the street, heading downtown.

Since the left turn signal had fallen off months ago, he stuck his arm out to indicate that he was turning into the bank's parking lot. Left turns scared him. He couldn't help but imagine a car speeding past, knocking his outstretched arm clean off at the shoulder. Then it would bounce into a semi going the other way and Seth would watch his own arm pass from wheel to wheel in a gruesome recreation of the gears scene in Chaplin's *Modern Times*.

A gruff voice interrupted Seth's thoughts. "Hey buddy, you going in or what?"

Lost in thought, Seth had parked his scooter and for some time had been standing at the door of the bank staring back at the street, his hand resting on the handle.

"Oh! I'm sorry," Seth stuttered. He pulled the door open. "Here, go ahead."

"After you, pal," the guy said. He was wearing a long black coat and sported three days' worth of beard. His eyes were hidden behind big silver sunglasses. The man gestured with the corner of his coat, and it was then that Seth noticed the outline of a gun barrel pressed to the inside of the pocket.

Seth stepped into the bank lobby with the grace of a wooden marionette. It was an old bank he went to, the same one he'd opened his first savings account with when he was six. Seth was too intimidated by all the new banks to go somewhere with an interest rate that actually kept up with inflation. But on the plus side, all the clerks knew him by sight. That's not to say that they liked him, just that they knew him.

Blank Slate Writers Group
Seth Donald Saves the Day

The bank itself—Second Savings and Trust—wasn't eighty-percent glass like all the new places. Second Savings was built like a bunker: narrow windows high up on concrete walls let only thin ribbons of natural light through to illuminate droll carpets long ago beaten into the floor by road salt and hard-soled formal shoes.

Seth heard his blood rushing in his ears as he looked around the place. He saw Mrs. Nimsy, the 80-year old who used to give him hard candy and pat him on the head before she got Alzheimer's. By the loan department was Sergeant Chekov, who served on both sides during World War II. The big steel vault door, shining brightly under the florescent lights, was open at the far end of the lobby. That's where Seth spotted a group of school children on a tour of the financial institution. Their teacher was with them.

She was beautiful. Her name was Ellen and she had graduated from high school with Seth. After college she'd returned to her hometown to teach elementary. They hadn't talked in years, but Seth felt the strong urge to tell her that her Facebook pictures didn't do her justice.

The sound of the man behind him stepping into the bank snapped Seth out of his voyeuristic reverie.

Seth Donald knew what he had to do.

His palms practically raining from nerves, Seth turned and pushed the man in the trench coat backwards. The man cursed and stumbled as Seth used all of his 115 pounds to push the door closed again. He threw the deadbolt, letting out a little gasp of relief as the steel clicked into place.

But they weren't safe from the thief yet; he might break the door in, and then what would they do? Seth braced the door with his back and jammed his hand into his coat pocket, digging past the envelope for the keychain bottle of mace he kept there.

Night Light
Stefan Barkow

Mrs. Nimsy was looking at him, one thin eyebrow raised, shoving all the other wrinkles out of the way to create entirely new ones.

Behind Seth, the door shook in its frame. Seth pushed himself harder against it, blocking the robber's entrance.

Seth couldn't breathe. In all his movie experience, he'd never had a spoken line. They offered him one once, but he had been so nervous that his ears had turned red and his tongue had swelled up.

Seth looked around. Everybody but Mrs. Nimsy was still going about their business. They didn't know what was going on, didn't know how much danger they were in. This was his moment, his debut. He had to warn them. Seth Donald dug down deep within himself and found his voice:

"It's a hold-up!"

Faces turned towards him. Understanding flashed across Mrs. Nimsy's face.

"He's got a gun!" she yelled.

Cripes, yes he does! And I've got my back to a glass door! thought Seth. He side-stepped to the right, keeping his back against the rough concrete wall. "She's right!" he said out loud. "Everyone get down! I don't want anyone to get hurt!"

A woman screamed. One of the kids began to cry. An aging gentleman wearing dark blue slacks peered out from a bullet-proof vest with a security badge stitched to it. The vest was much too big for him. He had a nose like a beak and as a whole he looked like a turtle hiding in its shell.

"Son, I'm just going to get all these folks over here, alright? They don't give me a gun," the turtle man said, waving at the far left wall of the bank. There was nothing over there but a silk plant and a few chairs.

"Good idea, everyone do what—sorry, what was your name?" Seth asked, a little distracted. He'd finally found the tiny bottle of mace, but in his excitement he'd ripped a bigger hole in his pocket. The black cylinder had jammed

Blank Slate Writers Group
Seth Donald Saves the Day

partway out of the hole and loose threads had ensnared the plastic trigger mechanism inside the pocket, so now Seth couldn't get his hand free.

"My name's John, son." The security guard said. "And I'm not going to try anything, I'm just going to take care of these people, alright?"

He's old, Seth thought, *He's giving me the lead, saying that it's all up to me.*

Adrenaline had replaced nerves now. Seth's hands were dry and steady, his body tense, the few muscles he'd developed were wound like springs. He had to do something. He was ready. It was like all his life he'd been pretending to be happy, but now that he knew what it was to be in the middle of the action, he couldn't get enough. What next? There wasn't a script to follow. All Seth knew was that he had to do something heroic; something to move the plot forward.

Seth risked a peek through the glass door.

Across the wide granite steps leading up to the door, there was nobody in sight.

He's gone! thought Seth, *I did it! I scared him off! But wait, that van with the tinted windows looks kind of suspicious...*

"OK everyone," he said out loud, surprising himself at how steady his voice sounded. "It looks pretty clear out there. There's a van across the street, so I don't want anyone to leave yet, got it?"

The school kids, watching him wide-eyed and open-mouthed, nodded meekly from beneath the chairs and coffee tables over by the wall. Ellen had both hands clamped over her mouth. Seth could see her nostrils twitching as she took short, sharp breaths.

Maybe that had come off too frightening. He peeked out the door again. Still no sign of the man, and now that he gave it a good look, the van had a bright orange boot on the driver's side wheel. Time to let them all know that they can relax. Maybe a joke?

Night Light
Stefan Barkow

"It's OK, everyone," Seth said, forcing a smile and still trying to pull his hand out of his pocket. "I just came by to cash a check."

A few pity chuckles from the crowd, but they still looked scared. Well, it had been the best he could come up with on the spot. He'd never been good at *improv*.

A tall man addressed Seth from behind the teller's counter. "Seth, come on over, I'll help you here. No need to stretch this out." It was the bank manager, Mr. Tersnik. He seemed oddly calm, given the circumstances.

"Don't you need to call the police or something?" Seth asked.

Mr. Tersnik's eyes darted behind the counter, then back to Seth. "No, I don't think that's necessary today. Come on, we'll just get on with business, alright, Seth?"

Seth felt very small. He'd thought he'd seen some admiration in the eyes around him, but Mr. Tersnik made it sound like stopping a robbery happened every day. Like he wanted to forget about it and get everyone out of here. Seth's collar felt tight around his neck, and his armpits itched. Maybe he'd been wrong. Maybe he wasn't that much of a hero after all.

Seth began to feel ashamed that he'd made such a big deal out of the whole situation now. He walked toward the teller window, his shoes clicking loudly and unevenly on the tile between the old carpets.

"Hi, Mr. Tersnik."

"Hello, Seth," said the manager. "What do you need?"

Mr. Tersnik seemed very tense and a little sad today. *Maybe he's just putting on a brave face for the other customers*, thought Seth. *I'd better play along*.

Seth still couldn't get his right hand untangled from the threads in his jacket pocket, so he had to reach across with his left hand to retrieve his check. "Sorry, can't really take my other hand out of my pocket right now," he said, realizing how stupid it sounded even as the words left his mouth. Mr. Tersnik just nodded.

Blank Slate Writers Group
Seth Donald Saves the Day

When Seth laid the check on the counter, the printing was streaked across the paper. Some of the mace must've discharged in his pocket, smearing the ink. Mr. Tersnik leaned in to try to decipher the skinny sheet.

Seth felt his face burning. "I'm really sorry; I didn't know that would happen. Is it still good? Can you read it OK?"

Mr. Tersnik left the check where it was and pressed a key at his terminal. There was a cheerful ding and Seth saw the cash drawer slide open. "Well enough," said Mr. Tersnik coldly.

Then Mr. Tersnik set a thick stack of twenties on the counter. The bills themselves were a bit wrinkled, but they were bound by a clean, crisp paper with "$1,000" printed across it.

Seth couldn't believe what he was seeing; that was ten times what he usually made for a shoot. "There must be some mistake!"

Mr. Tersnik hesitated, then set another stack of twenties on the counter beside the first.

Seth grabbed both the stacks and shoved them into his other pocket. The blood was rushing in his ears again, but this time it wasn't because he was nervous or anxious or anything like that. "Wow, thanks Mr. Tersnik. Didn't I always tell you I'd make it someday?"

"Yes, Seth, you did. I guess I just didn't think—"

Seth turned his back on the bank manager. That's right, no one had thought Seth Donald would ever be anything, but today had proved them wrong. Hero and professional actor. He couldn't wait to go home and tell his mom what had happened.

"He didn't even wear a mask," Mr. Tersnik murmured behind him.

All the other patrons were still watching him from the floor of the bank, but at long last Seth didn't mind being the center of attention. *This is why the stars do it,* he was thinking, *this feeling, this love and adoration. After this, things are*

293

Night Light
Stefan Barkow

going to be different. I think I found my confidence. I can do a speaking part, no problem. I'm going to have a talk with the director, maybe he can find a few more parts for me. If nothing else, the press on this has got to be worth something.

Seth saw Ellen, still on her knees, some of her students huddled protectively behind her like little ducklings. Seth couldn't help it. He was drunk on the adrenaline and the sudden wealth. He pulled his money out of his pocket and waved it towards her. "Hey Ellen, wanna get a drink sometime? It's on me!" he said. She just stared at him. Seth shrugged. Ellen had never been interested in him anyway, but there were plenty of girls—prettier girls—down at the studio who'd give him another chance now.

The street was still empty except for that van. Seth twisted the deadbolt, and it *thunked* back into the door. Outside, the world was wide and the opportunities endless. Seth Donald was a new man.

I feel…good, he thought. *It's not just the cash, either. I did something today. I stopped a robbery. Those people in there, those old men, Mrs. Nimsy, Ellen, they're just jealous. Tonight, I'm going out. I'm going to call up some of the other extras, and we're going to paint the town red.*

As Seth Donald stepped off the last granite step, he heard a quiet beep from his pocket. Curious, he held one of the stacks of cash up by his ear to listen—

—And that's when the dye pack exploded, right in his face.

Blank Slate Writers Group

Poem

Mi Familia
Bob Moulesong

She drains her glass.
Another morning at the bar. Another morning blur.
She feels it's her destiny. Like her mother before her. And
    her grandmother.
She lifts her empty glass in silent salute.
To fragments of days gone by.
To shattered dreams and broken promises.
To family.
She orders another.

Blank Slate Writers Group

Short Story

The Passengers in Cabin 6742
Robert Thomas

The *Eyewana Prince* is a fairly new ship with all the amenities the cruising public demands. The newest piece of the Eyewana Corporation's puzzle of premium priced theme parks and hotels aimed at separating families with children from their money. Special attention was paid to areas in the hull for children's activities, and she is topped off with a figurehead of Gerry Gerbil, the company's loveable animated film star mascot. The cruise experience always begins with the mandatory dock side boat drill, followed by the departure party. The ship's mighty seven tone whistle plays the notes of Eyewana's classic tune, "When you rub a genie's lamp," as she departs for three days of passenger bliss.

Aboard Eyewana's cruise ships parents can drop off their children with the crew for day long parentless activities for kids. Trading their children for pagers in case of emergency they head for day long childless activities for adults. A ship is vertical by nature, everyone spends time waiting for the too few elevators to speed them on their way, and it was there that everyone saw them.

A large multi generational family they stood out already, but it was the son everyone noticed. He was strapped into his gurney, bundled in blankets, his I.V. swung from its hook in a motion that eerily mimicked that of his eyes, rolling randomly with no sign of purpose.

The doors opened to an elevator that was half full, and then finally one that was empty. The adults rolled him in,

Night Light
Robert Thomas

and then the rest of his family filed in around, tightly packing the little space. The doors closed, taking them out of sight but not out of mind.

"Did you see that poor boy," mother said? "Isn't nice that they could come on this trip together? I think it's nice that the company can make allowances for them, he must require special care."

"I don't know," said father, "It seems a waste to me. This trip is so expensive and he can't enjoy any of it. How can they justify that?"

"Maybe they aren't paying," Mother replied, "he doesn't look long for the world, maybe he is here as part of Eyewana's 'Wishes Come True' for terminal children. It is nice that they can take a trip together."

"But what if he had to go in a lifeboat?" Father retorted, "or if there was a fire? He would have to be carried down the stairs. People could be trapped by his equipment, that air bottle could explode, it isn't right to risk us all for an experience he can't appreciate." Then he changed the topic "I'm hungry," he declared

"It will be awhile till our dinner seating," mother surrendered.

I think I will order the BLT from room service, do you want anything?" father asked as he picked up the phone. "What's our room number?"

299

— About the Authors —

Stefan Barkow

Stefan graduated from Purdue University with degrees in economics and English literature and a minor in Medieval and Renaissance studies. He writes from Chesterton, Indiana, and is currently working on a book of Medieval fairy tale adaptations.

Mel Braun

Melissa Braun has been writing from her rural home in Valparaiso, IN. for thirty-some years. She has published non-fiction articles in *Youth* magazine, poetry and photos in *The Writer's Eye* and *Umbrella* online magazines. She is a multiple winner of the Amy Foundation's Roaring Lamb award for Letters to the Editor in secular papers representing her religious views and scripture.

Timothy Cole

Timothy Cole is a lifelong resident of Northwest Indiana. A Purdue graduate, Tim gathered his degree from an association of math, physics, and modern languages, unable to decide what he wanted to be when he grew up. He taught English and beginning algebra in a secondary school for a few years when he decided to try engineering. A local steel company hired him to process statistical data related to production. He began with antique, noisy, mechanical calculators and finished his career writing statistical programs on personal computers as well as main-frame systems.

He harbored a desire to write, so when the boss wasn't looking, Tim was polishing his fiction and enhancing his vocabulary. A poetry war with a close friend drove him to avoid most rhyme and meter, except in challenging circumstances. Fearing rejection, Tim never submitted anything for publication, leaving all for his children and subsequent heirs to find and analyze for anything hereditary that might keep them from honest employment or political aspirations.

Now retired on the 175 year-old property his family settled, Timothy lives with his wife of forty-plus years, two horses, some requisite dogs and cats, and a few philandering chickens. He is always eager to express political views to those looking for revenge or entertainment and sits by the side of the road with a well-practiced scowl to discourage speeders or drivers of fancy cars.

Blank Slate Writers Group
About the Authors

Rich Elliott

Rich Elliott's writing reflects his wide variety of interests in the fields of sports, history, fiction, and technology.

Elliott is the author of *The Competitive Edge: Mental Preparation for Distance Running*, a book that explores the psychological aspects of training and racing. His background as a national-class distance runner, high school English teacher, and distance coach gave him a unique perspective on his topic. Track and Field News magazine called the book "a modern classic."

For many years Elliott worked in educational publishing as a textbook editor and technology producer. He edited and wrote content for middle school and high school programs, including literature anthologies and history textbooks, several which became industry best-sellers. With the growth of technology ancillaries, he became a multimedia producer, working on award-winning video programs, software, and online products.

Elliott came out with a new book in 2010: "*Runners on Running: The Best Nonfiction of Distance Running*, a collection of the greatest nonfiction pieces from the world of running." This book won the Cordner Nelson Book Award, given by the Track and Field Writers of America. He is currently doing freelance writing for *Running Times Magazine*.

Elliott and his wife Aileen live in Valparaiso, Indiana.

Barbara J. Funke

Barbara Funke taught English and theater arts and coached competitive speaking for 36 years before retiring from Duneland Schools in Chesterton, Indiana, to St. George, Utah. A member of Indiana State Federation of Poetry Clubs, Blank Slate Writers Group, The League of Utah Writers, and Utah State Poetry Society, she is Director of Redrock Writers, which held both its 18th successful Creative Writing Seminar and its 12th successful national poetry contest in 2014. Her winning poems have appeared in *Chaparral Poetry Forum* chapbooks, *Sandcutters* chapbook, and *Panorama* and National Federation of State Poetry Societies' *Encore* anthologies. Her husband Bob is a generous cheerleader for her poetic activities and endeavors.

- "Fishing Expedition": *Encore: Prize Poems of the National Federation of State Poetry Societies,* 2011
- "Hostage Situation": *Chaparral Poetry Forum* chapbook of winning poems, 2011, and
  Panorama anthology of the Utah State Poetry Society, 2012
- "Last Night": *Sandcutters* chapbook of winning poems from the Arizona State Poetry Society, 2010 and
  Panorama anthology of the Utah State Poetry Society, 2011
- "Nightwalk": *Chaparral Poetry Forum* chapbook of winning poems, 2008, and
  Panorama anthology of the Utah State Poetry Society, 2009
- "Ode to the Eraser": *Encore: Prize Poems of the National Federation of State Poetry Societies,* 2011

Blank Slate Writers Group
About the Authors

- Open, Sesame: *Encore: Prize Poems of the National Federation of State Poetry Societies*, 2013

Gail Galvan

Gail Galvan grew up in Gary, Indiana, a subdivision called Glen Park. A loving family, dog-pal Frisky, cool kids in the neighborhood, allergies, asthma, and Lake Robinson (a nearby man-made lake) were all part of her life. True love hit one summer when she began to pay attention in English Literature in eleventh grade at Lew Wallace High School—that's when her literary creativity burst into her life.

After receiving her B.A. in Health and Wellness Education, she returned to Valparaiso, Indiana, with her cat Geno. Currently, she is a member of Write-On Hoosiers, the Chicago Writers Association, and The Northwest Indiana Poetry Society. Two of her books have won awards: *Sneezing Seasons: The Inside Story about Allergies and Immunology* (Five Star Publications Royal Dragonfly Book Contest, 2013—First place in the Health category) and *New Jack Rabbit City: Starring the Chicago Hares* (Dan Poynter's Global Ebook Awards contest, 2014—Silver Medal in the Juvenile Fiction category).

About the Authors

Joyce Hicks

After a university career in the Midwest, Joyce Hicks has joined the many of the Boomer generation who write, do improv, blog, found non-profits, and give to others. Her debut novel *Escape from Assisted Living* sprang from her interest in the minutiae of family life, particularly at gateways to new stages. Joyce is an ardent observer in public spaces of the serious, mundane, or hilarious interchanges of strangers. Quilting, knitting, weaving and gardening are other pursuits. Her stories have appeared in *Literary Mama*, *Uncharted Frontier*, *Touch: The Journal of Healing*, *Passager*, *Boomer Café*, and *Midnight Oil*.

Marilyn Kosmatka

Marilyn Kosmatka is a writer of fiction: co-author of the novel *Time Spike*, with Eric Flint (ISBN 13: 978-1-4165-5538-4), author of numerous short stories, and an occasional poem. She enjoys reading, writing and arithmetic. Her passions are many, but the one she spends the most hours on is early literacy. At this time she is living in Northwest Indiana and working on her next novel.

She was born in Paducah, Kentucky. Her mother wrote songs and sang them to her three little girls as she cleaned and cooked. Her father was a migrant construction worker and moved his family three to four times a year. Her happiest childhood memories are those of Chicago: two room apartments, El Trains, the bookmobile, playing on rooftops, playing in open fire hydrants, going to the museums and the zoo and Riverview Park, and of course, visiting Maxwell Street.

Bob Moulesong

Moulesong is a life-long Region Rat. He attended Indiana University Northwest, where he was recognized for his writing at the annual Arts & Sciences Honors Tea. He has written professionally for over 15 years and has published over 2,500 articles and stories in newspapers, magazines, and e-zines. He retired from journalism in 2013 to focus on writing fiction. His current work is published online at Short Fiction Break *http://shortfictionbreak.com*. His publishing plans include a short story collection titled *Lunacy* (spring, 2015) and a series of children's works titled *The Adventures of Rugs* (summer, 2015). He resides with his wife and soul mate, Lynda, in Griffith, Indiana.

He retains professional memberships in:

- Write On Hoosiers
- Magic Hour Writers
- Highland Writers Group
- Indiana Writers & Poets Organization
- Chicago Writers Association

Night Light
About the Authors

Christina Ortega Phillips

Christina Ortega Phillips teaches English to international students at Valparaiso University. In addition to teaching, she has a background in journalism, writing on topics as fun as pop culture and as weighty as diversity, marriage, and PTSD. An avid gamer, she loves everything "geek," co-founding and co-creating the site *www.geekcurious.com*. She is a regular contributor to *Being Latino*. For the past four years she has also successfully completed NaNoWriMo.

To keep up with Christina and her writing projects, go to *www.mywritingdom.blogspot.com*.

Mike Ripley

Mike Ripley is a lifelong Hoosier, a husband of nearly forty years, and a father of five. He's a writer who enjoys fictional tales of relationships, suspense, and the occasional ghost. In *Night Light*, the fourth anthology he's been included in, the story "Spotlight News' explores the relationship between our lives and the things we're told to be important input for our day. I hope you enjoy this and all the stories from every writer in *Night Light*. Please check out *www.michaelripley.com*.

Blank Slate Writers Group
About the Authors

Tom Saine

Tom Saine is a retired mechanical engineer with a long history in the American space program. During the early part of his career, while working at HRM in Burbank, CA, he was privileged to be on the team of engineers who designed the gimbal actuators for the F-1 engine of the Saturn V moon rocket. Later at Parker-Hannifin in El Segundo, CA, he was also privileged to be on the team that designed the "Oxygen Control Assembly" of the Lunar Excursion Module (LEM) for the Apollo moon landing missions. Tom has also worked for such well-known companies as Lockheed Aircraft, Bell Aircraft, Hewlett-Packard, Polaroid, and IBM.

Tom was born in Indiana and went to school in Southern California. He has also lived and worked in Atlanta, GA; Boston, MA; Raleigh, NC; Cedar Rapids, IO; and Buffalo, NY. After he retired, he moved back to his native Indiana where he now lives with his fiancée Faith Duncan and his cats Rusty and Smoky.

As a writer Tom didn't really get started until he acquired his first computer in 1990. Even then he didn't really begin writing seriously until he retired in 2001. While a late bloomer, Tom has written a dozen novels since then and has several new titles in the outline and planning stages. *The Conrad Kidnapping* (ISBN-13: 978-1470166427) is the first in a series of Mark Steele Mystery stories and is due for release in the spring of 2014. The second Mark Steele Mystery *Pepper Creek Murder* (ISBN-13: 978-1492814610) is due for released in the late summer of 2014.

Night Light
About the Authors

John Schaub

John Schaub constantly looks for ways to bring physics and poetry together. These pieces are part of a larger collection in progress, one that he hopes will *explain* a lot of physics, and, taken all together, will tell the complete story of the relationship. He currently lives in Olympia, WA, with his wife and son.

Carla Lee Suson

Carla Lee Suson started writing late in life after working in molecular and cellular biology. She took up the pen while raising her three kids and a passel of dogs in the Coastal Bend area of Texas. During that time, she spent ten years developing short stories, articles, and standardized test materials. Her topics included travel articles, parenting advice, children's stories, and science work. In addition, she also collaborated with local experts in editing their books in art, art history, climatology, and water rights. After moving to Northwest Indiana, she obtained a Master's degree in Professional Writing and published her first book, *Independence Day Plague*. When not sculpting tales of ghosts, murder, and mayhem, she dives into one of her many hobbies such as woodworking, leather craft, and quilting.

Blank Slate Writers Group
About the Authors

Robert Thomas

Robert "Robb" Thomas was born on 12 November 1971, an underweight baby he has since devoted his life to becoming a huge pain in the ass. The Merchant Marine, entered at 17, has provided him with a variety of experiences, half of which—no matter how hard he tries—he can't remember and half he can't forget. In his 19 years of service as a mate and pilot on the Great Lakes, he sailed aboard the last American straight decker, the largest vessel ever to sail the Lakes, and is presently First Officer of the first thousand foot vessel built for Lakes service. He also possesses a Bachelor's Degree in Transportation Management with a minor in International Business from SUNY Maritime College. Photo used in *Stepping Stones* story courtesy: National Archives photo no. LC-B8184-B115

Peggy Westergard

Peggy Westergard grew up in the town of Lee in Western Massachusetts, model for the fictitious town of Laurel Mountain where her Berkshire County stories are set. In this series she portrays life in small-town New England during the late 1940s in hopes of bringing back memories to those who recall those times and of painting a picture, creating an atmosphere, for those who don't.

After leaving New England at age 19, she spent 51 years in the glorious climate of San Diego and was active in several writing groups there. Her short story, "Morning at the

Night Light
About the Authors

Earth Window Café" was published in Volume I of *A Year in Ink* (a San Diego Writers' Ink anthology) and her monologue, *Boof*, was performed on stage at the 10th Avenue Theater and the Old Town Theater, both in San Diego. She currently resides in Lawrence, Kansas.

Olga Marie Zulich

Olga Zulich was born and raised in Mishawaka, Indiana, a medium sized town known for its large Italian and Belgian populations, its rubber plant (now defunct), and its proximity to Notre Dame University. As the daughter of an Italian immigrant (dad) and a first generation American (mom), she was taught that school was the way to succeed in America and loved it so much that she earned bachelors and masters degrees from Ball State University in Muncie, Indiana.

After graduating and marrying, she moved with her husband Mike to Corcoran, California, where they both taught school in a town as different from Indiana as could be imagined. After three years she returned to Hoosierland, worked as a bookkeeper and raised two children.

Poems written for co-workers' birthdays and retirements and the encouragement of Joyce Hicks led Olga to join Blank Slate Writers Group. Blank Slate provided the impetus for more poetry and short stories, some based on people and situations from her life. Now retired, she looks forward to improving her writing skills.